Greatest Short Stories

VOLUME III

AMERICAN

P. F. COLLIER & SON CORPORATION

NEW YORK

PUBLISHERS

CONTENTS

CONTENTS

THE PHONOGRAPH AND THE GRAFT

BY O. HENRY

THE PHONOGRAPH AND THE GRAFT

BY O. HENRY

I LOOKED in at the engine-room of the Bloomfield-Cater Mfg. Co. (Ltd.), for the engineer was Kirksy, and there was a golden half-hour between the time he shut down steam and washed up that I coveted. For Kirksy was an improvisatore, and he told stories from the inside outward, finely leaving his spoken words and his theme to adjust themselves as best they might.

I found Kirksy resting, with his pipe lighted, smut-faced and blue overalled.

"'Tis a fair afternoon," I said, "but bids to be colder."

"Did I ever tell you," began Kirksy honorably, "about the time Henry Horsecollar and me took a phonograph to South America?" and I felt ashamed of my subterfuge, and dropped into the wooden chair he kicked toward me.

"Henry was a quarter-breed, quarter-back Cherokee, educated East in the idioms of football and West in contraband whiskey, and a gentleman, same as you or me. He was easy and romping in his ways; a man about six foot, with a kind of rubber-tire movement. Yes, he was a little man about five foot five, or five foot eleven. He was what you would call a medium tall man of average smallness. Henry had quit college once, and the Muscogee jail three times—once for introducing, and twice for selling, whiskey in the Territories. Henry Horsecollar never let any cigar stores come up and stand behind him. He didn't belong to that tribe of Indians.

"Henry and me met at Texarkana, and figured out this phonograph scheme. He had $360 which came to him out of a land allotment in the reservation. I had run down from Little Rock on account of a distressful scene I had witnessed on the street there. A man stood on a box and passed around some gold watches, screw case, stem-winders, Elgin movement, very elegant. Twenty bucks they cost you over the counter. At three dollars the crowd fought for the tickers. The man happened to find a valise full of them handy, and he passed them out like putting hot biscuits on a plate. The backs were hard to unscrew, but the crowd put its ear to the case, and they ticked mollifying and agreeable. Three of those watches were genuine tickers; but the rest, they were only kickers. Hey? Why, empty cases with one of them horny black bugs that fly around electric lights in 'em. Them bugs kick off minutes and seconds industrious and beautiful. The man I was speaking of cleaned

8

up $288, and went away, because he knew that when it came time to wind watches in Little Rock an entomologist would be needed, and he wasn't one.

"So, as I say, Henry had $360 and I had $288. The phonograph idea was Henry's, but I took to it freely, being fond of machinery of all kinds.

"'The Latin races,' says Henry, explaining easy in his idioms he learned at college, 'are peculiarly adapted to be victims of the phonograph. They possess the artistic temperament. They yearn for music and color and gayety. They give up wampum to the hand-organ man or the four-legged chicken when they're months behind with the grocery and the breadfruit tree.'

"'Then,' says I, 'we'll export canned music to the Latins; but I'm mindful of Mr. Julius Cæsar's account of 'em where he says, "*Omnia Gallia in tres partes divisa est*," which is the same as to say, "We will need all of our gall in devising means to tree them parties."' I hated to make a show of education, but I was disinclined to be overdone in syntax by a mere Indian, to whom we owe nothing except the land on which the United States is situated.

"We bought a fine phonograph in Texarkana —one of the best make—and half a trunkful of records. We packed up, and took the T. and P. for New Orleans. From that celebrated centre of molasses and disfranchised coon songs we took a steamer for—yes, I think it was South

9

America or Mexico—I am full of inability to divulge the location of it—'tis on the rural delivery route, 'tis colored yellow on the map, and branded with the literature of cigar boxes.

"We landed on a smiling coast at a town they denounced by the name, as near as I can recollect, of Sore-toe-kangaroo. 'Twas a palatable enough place to look at. The houses were clean and white, sticking about among the scenery like hard-boiled eggs served with lettuce. There was a block of skyscraper mountains in the suburbs, and they kept pretty quiet, like they were laying one finger on their lips and watching the town. And the sea was remarking 'Sh-sh-sh!' on the beach; and now and then a ripe cocoanut would fall kerblip in the sand, and that was all there was doing. Yes, I judge that town was considerably on the quiet. I judge that after Gabriel quits blowing his horn, and the car starts, with Philadelphia swinging to the last strap, and Pine Gulley, Arkansas, hanging on to the hind rail, Sore-toe-kangaroo will wake up and ask if anybody spoke.

"The captain went ashore with us, and offered to conduct what he seemed to like to call the obsequies. He introduced Henry and me to the United States Consul, and a roan man, the head of the Department of Mercenary and Licentious Dispositions, the way it read upon his sign.

"'I touch here again a week from to-day,' says the captain.

PHONOGRAPH AND THE GRAFT

"By that time,' we told him, 'we'll be amassing wealth in the interior towns with our galvanized prima donna and correct imitations of Sousa's band excavating a march from a tin mine.'

"'Ye'll not,' says the captain. 'Ye'll be hypnotized. Any gentleman in the audience who kindly steps upon the stage and looks this country in the eye will be converted to the hypothesis that he's but a fly in the Elgin creamery. Ye'll be standing knee deep in the surf waiting for me, and your machine for making Hamburger steak out of the hitherto respected art of music will be playing "There's no place like home." '

"Henry skinned a twenty off his roll, and received from the Bureau of Mercenary Dispositions a paper bearing a red seal and a dialect story, and no change.

"Then we got the consul full of red wine, and struck him for a horoscope. He was a thin, youngish kind of man, I should say past fifty, sort of French-Irish in his affections, and puffed up with disconsolation. Yes, he was a flattened kind of a man, in whom drink lay stagnant, inclined to corpulence and misery. Yes, I think he was a kind of Dutchman, being very sad and genial in his ways.

"'The marvelous invention,' he says, 'entitled the phonograph, has never before invaded these shores. The people have never heard it. They would not believe it if they should. Simple-

11

hearted children of nature, progress has never condemned them to accept the work of a can-opener as an overture, and rag-time might incite them to a bloody revolution. But you can try the experiment. The best chance you have is that the populace may not wake up when you play. There's two ways,' says the consul, 'they may take it. They may become inebriated with attention, like an Atlanta colonel listening to "Marching through Georgia," or they will get excited and transpose the key of the music with an axe and transpose the key of the music with an axe and yourselves into a dungeon. In the latter case,' says the consul, 'I'll do my duty by cabling to the State Department, and I'll wrap the Stars and Stripes around you when you come to be shot, and threaten them with the vengeance of the greatest gold export and financial reserve nation on earth. The flag is full of bullet holes now,' says the consul, 'made in that way. Twice before,' says the consul, 'I have cabled our Gov-ernment for a couple of gunboats to protect American citizens. The first time the Depart-ment sent me a pair of gum boots. The other time was when a man named Pease was going to be executed here. They referred that appeal to the Secretary of Agriculture. Let us now dis-turb the señor behind the bar for a subsequenc of the red wine.'

"Thus soliloquized the consul of Sore-toe-kan-garoo to me and Henry Horsecollar.

"But, notwithstanding, we hired a room that

PHONOGRAPH AND THE GRAFT

afternoon in the Calle de los Angeles, the main street that runs along the shore, and put our trunks there. 'Twas a good-sized room, dark and cheerful, but small. 'Twas on a various street, diversified by houses and conservatory plants. The peasantry of the city passed to and fro on the fine pasturage between the sidewalks. 'Twas, for the world, like an opera chorus when the Royal Kafoozlum is about to enter.

"We were rubbing the dust off the machine and getting fixed to start business the next day when a big, fine-looking white man in white clothes stopped at the door and looked in. We extended the invitations, and he walked inside and sized us up. He was chewing a long cigar, and wrinkling his eyes, meditative, like a girl trying to decide which dress to wear to the party.

"'New York?' he says to me finally.

"'Originally, and from time to time,' I says, 'Hasn't it rubbed off yet?'

"'It's simple,' says he, 'when you know how. It's the fit of the vest. They don't cut vests right anywhere else. Coats, maybe, but not vests.'

"The white man looks at Henry Horsecollar and hesitates.

"'Injun,' says Henry; 'tame Injun.'

"'Mellinger,' says the man—'Homer P. Mellinger. Boys, you're confiscated. You're babes in the wood without a chaperon or referee, and it's my duty to start you going. I'll knock out the props and launch you proper in the pellucid waters of Sore-toe-kangaroo. You'll have to be christened, and if you'll come with me I'll break a bottle of wine across your bows, according to Hoyle.'

"Well, for two days Homer P. Mellinger did the honors. That man cut ice in Sore-toe-kangaroo. He was it. He was the Royal Kafoozlum. If me and Henry was babes in the wood, he was a Robin Redbreast from the topmost bough. Him and me and Henry Horsecollar locked arms and toted that phonograph around and had wassail and diversions. Everywhere we found doors open we went in and set the machine going, and Mellinger called upon the people to observe the artful music and his lifelong friends, the two Señors Americanos. The opera chorus was agitated with esteem, and followed us from house to house. There was *vino tinto* and *vino blanco* to drink with every tune. The aborigines had acquirements of a pleasant thing in the way of drinks that gums itself to the recollection. They chop off the end of a green cocoanut, and pour in on the liquor of it French brandy and gin. We had them and other things.

"Mine and Henry's money was counterfeit. Everything was on Homer P. Mellinger. That man could find rolls of bills in his clothes where Hermann the Wizard couldn't have conjured out an omelette. He could have founded universities and had enough left to buy the colored vote

14

of his country. Henry and me wondered what his graft was. One evening he told us.

"'Boys,' says he, 'I've deceived you. Instead of a painted butterfly, I'm the hardest worked man in this country. Ten years ago I landed on its shores, and two years ago on the point of its jaw. Yes, I reckon I can get the decision over this ginger-cake commonwealth at the end of any round I choose. I'll confide in you because you are my countrymen and guests, even if you have committed an assault upon my adopted shores with the worst system of noises ever set to music.

"'My job is private secretary to the President of this Republic, and my duties are running it. I'm not headlined in the bills, but I'm the mustard in the salad dressing. There isn't a law goes before Congress, there isn't a concession granted, there isn't an import duty levied, but what H. P. Mellinger he cooks and seasons it. In the front office I fill the President's inkstand and search visiting statesmen for dynamite; in the back room I dictate the policy of the government. You'd never guess how I got the pull. It's the only graft of its kind in the world. I'll put you wise. You remember the topliner in the old copy-books—"Honesty is the best policy." That's it. I'm the only honest man in this republic. The government knows it; the people know it; the boodlers know it; the foreign investors know it. I make the government keep its faith. If a man is promised a job he gets it.

If outside capital buys a concession they get the goods. I run a monopoly of square dealing here. There's no competition. If Colonel Diogenes were to flash his lantern in this precinct he'd have my address inside of two minutes. There isn't big money in it, but it's a sure thing, and lets a man sleep of nights.'

"Thus Homer P. Mellinger made oration to me and Henry Horsecollar in Sore-toe-kan-garoo. And, later, he divested himself of this remark:

"'Boys, I'm to hold a *soirée* this evening with a gang of leading citizens, and I want your assistance. You bring the musical corn sheller and give the affair the outside appearance of a function. There's important business on hand, but it mustn't show. I can talk to you people. I've been pained for years on account of not having anybody to blow off and brag to. I get home-sick sometimes, and I'd swap the entire perquisites of office for just one hour to have a stein and a caviare sandwich somewhere on Thirty-fourth Street, and stand and watch the street cars go by, and smell the peanut roaster at old Giuseppe's fruit stand.'

"'Yes,' said I, 'there's fine caviare at Billy Renfrow's café, corner of Thirty-fourth and——'"

"'God knows it,' interrupts Mellinger, 'and if you'd told me you knew Billy Renfrow I'd have invented tons of ways of making you happy. Billy was my side kicker in New York. That

PHONOGRAPH AND THE GRAFT

is a man who never knew what crooked was. Here I am working Honesty for a graft, but that man loses money on it. *Carrambos!* I get sick at times of this country. Everything's rotten. From the Executive down to the coffee pickers, they're plotting to down each other and skin their friends. If a mule driver takes off his hat to an official, that man figures it out that he's a popular idol, and sets his pegs to stir up a revolution and upset the administration. It's one of my little chores as private secretary to smell out these revolutions and affix the kibosh before they break out and scratch the paint off the government property. That's why I'm down here now in this mildewed coast town. The Governor of the district and his crew are plotting to uprise. I've got every one of their names, and they're invited to listen to the phonograph tonight, compliments of H. P. M. That's the way I'll get them in a bunch, and things are on the programme to happen to them.'

"We three were sitting at table in the cantina of the Purified Saints. Mellinger poured out wine, and was looking some worried; I was thinking.

" 'They're a sharp crowd,' he says, kind of fretful. 'They're capitalized by a foreign syndicate after rubber, and they're loaded to the muzzle for bribing. I'm sick,' goes on Mellinger, 'of comic opera. I want to smell East River and wear suspenders again. At times I feel like

17

throwing up my job, but I'm d—n fool enough to be sort of proud of it. "There's Mellinger," they say here, "Por Dios! you can't touch him with a million." I'd like to take that record back and show it to Billy Renfrow some day; and that tightens my grip whenever I see a fat thing that I could corral just by winking one eye—and losing my graft. By ——! they can't monkey with me. They know it. What money I get I make honest and spend it. Some day I'll make a pile and go back and eat caviare with Billy. To-night I'll show you how to handle a bunch of corruptionists. I'll show them what Mellinger, private secretary, means when you spell it with the cotton and tissue paper off.'

"Mellinger appears shaky, and breaks his glass against the neck of the bottle.

"'I says to myself, 'White man, if I'm not mistaken there's been a bait laid out where the tail of your eye could see it.'

"'That night, according to arrangements, me and Henry took the phonograph to a room in a 'dobe house in a dirty side street, where the grass was knee high. 'Twas a long room, lighted with smoky oil lamps. There was plenty of chairs and a table at the back end. We set the phonograph on the table. Mellinger was there, walking up and down disturbed in his predicaments. He chewed cigars and spat 'em out, and he bit the thumb nail of his left hand.

"'By and by the invitations to the musicale

PHONOGRAPH AND THE GRAFT

came sliding in by pairs and threes and spade flushes. Their color was of a diversity, running from a three-days' smoked meerschaum to a patent-leather polish. They were as polite as wax, being devastated with enjoyments to give Señor Mellinger the good evenings. I understood their Spanish talk—I ran a pumping engine two years in a Mexican silver mine, and had it pat—but I never let on.

"Maybe fifty of 'em had come, and was seated, when in slid the king bee, the Governor of the district. Mellinger met him at the door and escorted him to the grand stand. When I saw that Latin man I knew that Mellinger, private secretary, had all the dances on his card taken. That was a big, squashy man the color of a rubber overshoe, and he had an eye like a head waiter's.

"Mellinger explained, fluent, in the Castilian idioms, that his soul was disconcerted with joy at introducing to his respected friends America's greatest invention, the wonder of the age. Henry got the cue and run on an elegant brass-band record and the festivities became initiated. The Governor man had a bit of English under his hat, and when the music was choked off he says:

"'Ver-r-ree fine. Gr-r-r-racias, the American gentleemen, the so esplendeed moosic as to playee.'

"The table was a long one, and Henry and me sat at the end of it next the wall. The Governor

19

sat at the other end. Homer P. Mellinger stood at the side of it. I was just wondering how Mellinger was going to handle his crowd, when the home talent suddenly opened the services.

"That Governor man was suitable for uprisings and policies. I judge he was a ready kind of man, who took his own time. Yes, he was full of attentions and immediateness. He leaned his hands on the table and imposed his face toward the secretary man.

"'Do the American Señors understand Spanish?' he asks in his native accents.

"'They do not,' says Mellinger.

"'Then, listen,' goes on the Latin man, prompt. 'The musics are of sufficient prettiness, but not of necessity. Let us speak of business. I well know why we are here, since I observe my compatriots. You had a whisper yesterday, Señor Mellinger, of our proposals. To-night we will speak out. We know that you stand in the President's favor, and we know your influence. The government will be changed. We know the worth of your services. We esteem your friendship and aid so much that'—Mellinger raises his hand, but the Governor man bottles him up.

"'Do not speak until I have done.'

"The Governor man then draws a package wrapped in paper from his pocket, and lays it on the table by Mellinger's hand.

"'In that you will find one hundred thousand dollars in money of your country. You can do nothing against us, but you can be worth that for us. Go back to the capital and obey our instructions. Take that money now. We trust you. You will find with it a paper giving in detail the work you will be expected to do for us. Do not have the unwiseness to refuse.'

"The Governor man paused, with his eyes fixed on Mellinger, full of expressions and observances. I looked at Mellinger, and was glad Billy Renfrow couldn't see him then. The sweat was popping out on his forehead, and he stood dumb, tapping the little package with the ends of his fingers. The Colorado maduro gang was after his graft. He had only to change his politics, and stuff six figures in his inside pocket.

"Henry whispers to me and wants the pause in the programme interpreted. I whisper back: 'H. P. is up against a bribe, senator's size, and the coons have got him going,' I saw Mellinger's hand moving closer to the package. 'He's weakening,' I whispered to Henry. 'We'll remind him,' says Henry, 'of the peanut roaster on Thirty-fourth Street, New York.'

"Henry stooped and got a record from the basketful we'd brought, slid it in the phonograph, and started her off. It was a cornet solo, very neat and beautiful, and the name of it was 'Home, Sweet Home.' Not one of them fifty odd men in the room moved while it was playing, and the Governor man kept his eyes steady on Mellinger. I saw Mellinger's head go up little by little, and his hand came creeping away from the package. Not until the last note sounded did anybody stir. And then Homer P. Mellinger takes up the bundle of boodle and slams it in the Governor man's face.

"'That's my answer,' says Mellinger, private secretary, 'and there'll be another in the morning. I have proofs of conspiracy against every man of you. The show is over, gentlemen.'

"'There's one more act,' puts in the Governor man. 'You are a servant, I believe, employed by the President to copy letters and answer raps at the door. I am Governor here. Señors, I call upon you in the name of the cause to seize this man.'

"That brindled gang of conspirators shoved back their chairs and advanced in force. I could see where Mellinger had made a mistake in massing his enemy so as to make a grand-stand play. I think he made another one, too; but we can pass that, Mellinger's idea of a graft and mine being different, according to estimations and points of view.

"There was only one window and door in that room, and they were in the front end. Here was fifty odd Latin men coming in a bunch to obstruct the legislation of Mellinger. You may say there were three of us, for me and Henry, simultaneous, declared New York City and the Cherokee Nation in sympathy with the weaker party.

22

PHONOGRAPH AND THE GRAFT

"Then it was that Henry Horsecollar rose to a point of disorder and intervened, showing, admirable, the advantages of education as applied to the American Indian's natural intellect and native refinement. He stood up and smoothed back his hair on each side with his hands as you have seen little girls do when they play.

"'Get behind me, both of you,' says Henry.

"'What is it to be?' I asked.

"'I'm going to buck centre,' says Henry, in his football idioms. 'There isn't a tackle in the lot of them. Keep close behind me and rush the game.'

"That cultured Red Man exhaled an arrangement of sounds with his mouth that caused the Latin aggregation to pause, with thoughtfulness and hesitations. The matter of his proclamation seemed to be a co-operation of the Cherokee college yell with the Carlisle war-whoop. He went at the chocolate team like the flip of a little boy's nigger shooter. His right elbow laid out the Governor man on the gridiron, and he made a lane the length of the crowd that a woman could have carried a step-ladder through without striking anything. All me and Mellinger had to do was to follow.

"In five minutes we were out of that street and at the military headquarters, where Mellinger had things his own way.

"The next day Mellinger takes me and Henry to one side and begins to shed tens and twenties.

23

"'I want to buy that phonograph,' he says. 'I liked that last tune it played. Now, you boys better go back home, for they'll give you trouble here before I get the screws put on 'em. If you happen to ever see Billy Renfrow again, tell him I'm coming back to New York as soon as I can make a stake—honest.'

"'This is more money,' says I, 'than the machine is worth.'

"'"'Tis government expense money,' says Mellinger, 'and the government's getting the tune grinder cheap.'

"Henry and I knew that pretty well, but we never let Homer P. Mellinger know that we had seen how near he came to losing his graft.

"We laid low until the day the steamer came back. When we saw the captain's boat on the beach me and Henry went down and stood in the edge of the water. The captain grinned when he saw us.

"'I told you you'd be waiting,' he says. 'Where's the Hamburger machine?'

"'It stays behind,' I says, 'to play "Home, Sweet Home."'

"'I told you so,' says the captain again. 'Climb in the boat.'

"And that," said Kirksy, "is the way me and Henry Horsecollar introduced the phonograph in that Latin country along about the vicinity of South America."

BROTHER RABBIT'S CRADLE

BY JOEL CHANDLER HARRIS

BROTHER RABBIT'S CRADLE

BY JOEL CHANDLER HARRIS

"I WISH you'd tell me what you tote a hankcher fer," remarked Uncle Remus, after he had reflected over the matter a little while.

"Why, to keep my mouth clean," answered the little boy. Uncle Remus looked at the lad, and shook his head doubtfully. "Uh-uh!" he exclaimed. "You can't fool folks when dey git ez ol' ez what I is. I been watchin' you now mo' days dan I kin count, an' I ain't never see yo' mouf dirty 'nuff fer ter be wiped wid a hankcher. It's allers clean—too clean fer ter suit me. Dar's yo' pa, now; when he wuz a little chap like you, his mouf useter git dirty in de mornin', an' stay dirty plum twel night. Dey wa'n't sca'cely a day dat he didn't look like he been playin' wid de pigs in de stable lot. Ef he yever is tote a hankcher, he ain't never show it ter me."

"He carries one now," remarked the little boy with something like a triumphant look on his face.

"Tooby sho'," said Uncle Remus; "tooby sho' he do. He start ter totin' one when he tuck an' tuck a notion fer ter go a-courtin'. It had his name in one cornder, an' he useter sprinkle it wid stuff out'n a pepper-sauce bottle. It sho'

By permission of McClure, Phillips & Co.

27

wuz rank, dat stuff wuz; it smell so sweet it make you fergit whar you live at. I take notice dat you ain't got none on yone."

"No; mother says that cologne or any kind of perfumery on your handkerchief makes you common."

Uncle Remus leaned his head back, closed his eyes, and permitted a heartrending groan to issue from his lips. The little boy showed enough anxiety to ask him what the matter was. "Nothin' much, honey; I wuz des tryin' fer ter count how many diff'unt kinder people dey is in dis big worl', an' 'fo' I got mo' dan half done wid my countin', a pain struck me in my mizry, an' I had ter break off."

"I know what you mean," said the child. "You think mother is queer; grandmother thinks so too."

"How come you to be so wise, honey?" Uncle Remus inquired, opening his eyes wide with astonishment.

"I know by the way you talk, and by the way grandmother looks sometimes," answered the little boy.

Uncle Remus said nothing for some time. When he did speak, it was to lead the little boy to believe that he had been all the time engaged in thinking about something else. "Talkin' er dirty folks," he said, "you oughter seed yo' pa when he wuz a little bit er chap. Dey wuz long days when you couldn't tell ef he wuz black er white, he wuz dat dirty. He'd come out'n de big house in de mornin' ez clean ez a new pin, an' 'fo' ten er-clock you couldn't tell what kinder clof his cloze wuz made out'n. Many's de day when I've seed ol' Miss—dat's yo' great-gran'-mammy—comb 'nuff trash out'n his head fer ter fill a basket."

The little boy laughed at the picture that Uncle Remus drew of his father. "He's very clean, now," said the lad loyally.

"Maybe he is an' maybe he ain't," remarked Uncle Remus, suggesting a doubt. "Dat's neeier here ner dar. Is he any better off clean dan what he wuz when you couldn't put yo' han's on 'im widout havin' ter go an' wash um? Yo' gran'mammy useter call 'im a pig, an' clean ez he may be now, I take notice dat he makes mo' complaint er headache an' de heartburn dan what he done when he wuz runnin' roun' here half-naked an' full er mud. I hear tell dat some nights he can't git no sleep, but when he wuz lit-tle like you—no, suh, I'll not say dat, bekaze he wuz bigger dan what you is fum de time he kin toddle roun' widout nobody he'pin' him; but when he wuz ol' ez you an' twice ez big, dey ain't narry night dat he can't sleep—an' not only all night, but half de day ef dey'd 'a' let 'im. Ef dey'd let you run roun' here like he done, an' git dirty, you'd git big an' strong 'fo' you know it. Dey ain't nothin' mo' wholesomer dan a peck er two er clean dirt on a little chap like you."

There is no telling what comment the child would have made on this sincere tribute to clean dirt, for his attention was suddenly attracted to something that was gradually taking shape in the hands of Uncle Remus. At first it seemed to be hardly worthy of notice, for it had been only a thin piece of board. But now the one piece had become four pieces, two long and two short, and under the deft manipulations of Uncle Remus it soon assumed a boxlike shape.

The old man had reached the point in his work where silence was necessary to enable him to do it full justice. As he fitted the thin boards together, a whistling sound issued from his lips, as though he were letting off steam; but the singular noise was due to the fact that he was completely absorbed in his work. He continued to fit and trim, and trim and fit, until finally the little boy could no longer restrain his curiosity. "Uncle Remus, what are you making?" he asked plaintively.

"Larroes fer ter kech meddlers," was the prompt and blunt reply.

"Well, what are larroes to catch meddlers?" the child insisted.

"Nothin' much an' sump'n mo'. Dicky, Dicky, killt a chicky, an' fried it quicky, in de oven, like a sloven. Den ter his daddy's Sunday hat, he tuck 'n' hitched de ol' black cat. Now what you reckon make him do dat? Ef you can't tell me word fer word an' spellin' fer spellin' we'll go out an' come in an' take a walk."

He rose, grunting as he did so, thus paying an unintentional tribute to the efficacy of age as the partner of rheumatic aches and stiff joints. "You hear me gruntin'," he remarked—"well, dat's bekaze I ain't de chicky fried by Dicky, which he e't 'nuff fer ter make 'im sicky." As he went out the child took his hand, and went trotting along by his side, thus affording an interesting study for those who concern themselves with the extremes of life. Hand in hand the two went out into the fields, and thence into the great woods, where Uncle Remus, after searching about for some time, carefully deposited his oblong box, remarking: "Ef I don't make no mistakes, dis ain't so mighty fur fum de place whar de creeturs has der playgroun', an' dey ain't no tellin' but what one un um'll creep in dar when deyer playin' hidin', an' ef he do, he'll sho be our meat."

"Oh, it's a trap!" exclaimed the little boy, his face lighting up with enthusiasm.

"An' dey wa'n't nobody here fer ter tell you," Uncle Remus declared, astonishment in his tone. "Well, ef dat don't bang my time, I ain't no free nigger. Now, ef dat had 'a' been yo' pa at de same age, I'd 'a' had ter tell 'im forty-lev'm times, an' den he wouldn't 'a' b'lieved me twel he see sump'n in dar tryin' fer ter git out. Den he'd say it wuz a trap, but not befo'. I ain't blamin' 'im,'" Uncle Remus went on, "kaze 'tain't eve'y chap dat kin tell a trap time he see it, an' mo' dan dat, traps don' allers sketch what dey er sot fer."

He paused, looked all around, and up in the sky, where fleecy clouds were floating lazily along, and in the tops of the trees, where the foliage was swaying gently in the breeze. Then he looked at the little boy. "Ef I ain't gone an' got los'," he said, "we ain't so mighty fur fum de place whar Mr. Man, once 'pon a time—not yo' time ner yit my time, but some time—tuck'n' sot a trap for Brer Rabbit. In dem days, dey hadn't l'arnt how ter be kyarpenters, an' dish yer trap what I'm tellin' you 'bout wuz a great big contraption. Big ez Brer Rabbit wuz, it wuz lots too big fer him.

"Now, whiles Mr. Man wuz fixin' up dis trap, Mr. Rabbit wa'n't so mighty fur off. He hear de saw—er-rash! er-rash!—an' he hear de hammer—bang, bang, bang!—an' he ax hisse'f what all dis racket wuz 'bout. He see Mr. Man come out'n his yard totin' sump'n, an' he got furder off; he see Mr. Man comin' todes de bushes, an' he tuck ter de woods; he see 'im comin' todes de woods, an' he tuck ter de bushes. Mr. Man tote de trap so fur an' no furder. He put it down, he did, an' Brer Rabbit watch 'im; he put in de bait, an' Brer Rabbit watch 'im; he fix de trigger, an' still Brer Rabbit watch 'im. Mr. Man look at de trap an' it satchify him. He look at it an' laugh, an' when he do dat, Brer Rabbit wunk one eye, an' wiggle his mustache, an' chaw his cud.

"An' dat ain't all he do, needer. He sot out in de bushes, he did, an' study how ter git some game in de trap. He study so hard, an' he got so errytated, dat he thumped his behime foot on de groun' twel it soun' like a cow dancin' out dar in de bushes, but 'twan't no cow, ner yit no calf— 'twuz des Brer Rabbit studyin'. Atter so long a time, he put out down de road todes dat part er de country whar mos' er de creeturs live at. Eve'y time he hear a fuss, he'd dodge in de bushes, kaze he wanter see who comin'. He keep on an' he keep on, an' bimeby he hear ol' Brer Wolf trottin' down de road.

"It so happen dat Brer Wolf wuz de ve'y one what Brer Rabbit wanter see. Dey wuz perlit ter one an'er, but dey wan't no frien'ly feelin', 'twix um. Well, here come ol' Brer Wolf, hongrier dan a chicken-hawk on a frosty mornin', an' ez he come up he see Brer Rabbit set by de side er de road lookin' like he done lose all his family an' his friends terboot.

"Dey pass de time er day, an' den Brer Wolf kinder grin an' say, 'Laws-a-massy, Brer Rabbit! what ail you? You look like you done had a spell er fever an' ague; what de trouble?' 'Trouble, Brer Wolf? You ain't never see no trouble twel you git whar I'm at. Maybe you wouldn't min' it like I does, kaze I ain't usen ter it. But

33

I boun' you done seed me light-minded fer de
las' time. I'm done—I'm plum wo' out,' sez
Brer Rabbit, sezee. Dis make Brer Wolf open
his eyes wide. He say, 'Dis de fus' time I ever
is here you talk dat-a-way, Brer Rabbit; take yo'
time an 'tell me 'bout it. I ain't had my brekkus
yit, but dat don't make no diffunce, long ez
youer in trouble. I'll he'p you out ef I kin, an'
mo' dan dat, I'll put some heart in de work.'
When he say dis, he grin an' show his tushes, an'
Brer Rabbit kinder edge 'way fum 'im. He say,
'Tell me de trouble, Brer Rabbit, an' I'll do my
level bes' fer ter he'p you out.'

"Wid dat, Brer Rabbit 'low dat Mr. Man
done been had 'im hired fer ter take keer er his
truck patch, an' keep out de minks, de mush-rats
an' de weasels. He say dat he done so well
settin' up night atter night, when he des might
ez well been in bed, dat Mr. Man prommus 'im
sump'n extry 'sides de mess er greens what he
gun 'im eve'y day. Atter so long a time, he say,
Mr. Man 'low dat he gwineter make 'im a present uv a cradle so he kin rock de little Rabs ter
sleep when dey cry. So said, so done, he say.
Mr. Man make de cradle an' tell Brer Rabbit he
kin take it home wid 'im.

"He start out wid it, he say, but it got so heavy
he hatter set it down in de woods, an' dat's de
reason why Brer Wolf seed 'im settin' down by
de side er de road, lookin' like he in deep trouble.
Brer Wolf sot down, he did, an' study, an' bine-

BROTHER RABBIT'S CRADLE

by he say he'd like mighty well fer ter have a cradle fer his chillun, long ez cradles wuz de style. Brer Rabbit say dey been de style fer de longest, an' ez fer Brer Wolf wantin' one, he say he kin have de one what Mr. Man make fer him, kaze it's lots too big fer his chillun. 'You know how folks is,' sez Brer Rabbit, sezee. 'Dey try ter do what dey dunner how ter do, an' dar's de fence wid mo' holes in it dan what dey is in a saine, an' kaze dey have great big chillun dey got de idee dat eve'y cradle what dey make mus' fit der own chillun. An' dat's how come I can't tote de cradle what Mr. Man make fer me mo' dan ten steps at a time.'

"Brer Wolf ax Brer Rabbit what he gwineter do fer a cradle, an' Brer Rabbit 'low he kin manage fer ter git 'long wid de ol' one twel he kin 'suade Mr. Man ter make 'im an'er one, an' he don't speck dat'll be so mighty hard ter do. Brer Wolf can't he'p but b'lieve dey's some trick in it, an' he say he ain't see de ol' cradle when las' he wuz at Brer Rabbit house. Wid dat, Brer Rabbit bust out laughin'. He say, 'Dat's been so long back, Brer Wolf, dat I done fergit all 'bout it; 'sides dat, ef dey wuz a cradle dar, I boun' you my ol' 'oman got better sense dan ter set de cradle in der parler, whar comp'ny comes'; an' he laugh so loud an' long dat he make Brer Wolf right shame er himse'f.

"He 'low, ol' Brer Wolf did, 'Come on, Brer

35

Rabbit, an' show me whar de cradle is. Ef it's too big fer yo' chillun, it'll des 'bout fit mine.' An' so off dey ent ter whar Mr. Man done sot his trap. 'Twa'n't so mighty long 'fo' dey got whar dey wuz gwine, an' Brer Rabbit say, 'Brer Wolf, dar yo' cradle, an' may it do you mo' good dan it's yever done me!' Brer Wolf walk all roun' de trap an' look at it like 'twuz live. Brer Rabbit thump one er his behime foots on de groun' an' Brer Wolf jump like some un done shot a gun right at 'im. Dis make Brer Rabbit laugh twel he can't laugh no mo'. Brer Wolf, he say he kinder nervous 'bout dat time er de year, an' de leas' little bit er noise'll make 'im jump. He ax how he gwineter git any purchis on de cradle, an' Brer Rabbit say he'll hatter git inside an' walk wid it on his back, kaze dat de way he done done.

"Brer Wolf ax what all dem contraptions on de inside is, an' Brer Rabbit 'spon' dat dey er de rockers, an' dey ain't no needs fer ter be skeer'd un um, kaze dey ain't nothin' but plain wood. Brer Wolf say he ain't 'zactly skeer'd, but he done got ter de p'int whar he know dat you better look 'fo' you jump. Brer Rabbit 'low dat ef dey's any jumpin' fer ter be done, he de one ter do it, an' he talk like he done fergit what dey come fer. Brer Wolf, he fool an' fumble roun', but bimeby he walk in de cradle, sprung de trigger, an' dar he wuz! Brer Rabbit, he holler out, 'Come on, Brer Wolf; des hump yo' se'f, an'

BROTHER RABBIT'S CRADLE

I'll be wid you.' But try ez he will an' grunt ez he may, Brer Wolf can't budge dat trap. Bimeby Brer Rabbit git tired er waitin', an' he say dat ef Brer Wolf ain't gwineter come on he's gwine home. He 'low dat a frien' what say he gwineter he'p you, an' den go in a cradle an' drap off ter sleep, dat's all he wanter know 'bout um; an' wid dat he made fer de bushes, an' he wa'n't a minnit too soon, kaze here come Mr. Man ter see ef his trap had been sprung. He look, an', sho 'nuff, it 'uz sprung, an' dey wuz sump'n in dar, kaze he hear it rustlin' an' kickin' ter git out.

"Mr. Man look thoo de crack, an' he see Brer Wolf, which he wuz so skeer'd twel his eye look right green. Mr. Man say, 'Aha! I got you, is I? Brer Wolf say, 'Who?' Mr. Man laugh twel he can't sca'cely talk, an' still Brer Wolf say, 'Who? Who you think you got?' Mr. Man 'low, 'I don't think I knows. Youer ol' Brer Rabbit, dat's who you is.' Brer Wolf say, 'Turn me outer here, an' I'll show you who I is.' Mr. Man laugh fit ter kill. He 'low, 'You neenter change yo' voice; I'd know you ef I met you in de dark. Youer Brer Rabbit, dat's who you is.' Brer Wolf say, 'I ain't not; dat's what I'm not!'

"Mr. Man look thoo de crack ag'in, an' he see de short years. He 'low, 'You done cut off yo' long years, but still I knows you. Oh, yes! an' you done sharpen yo' mouf an' put smut on it— but you can't fool me.' Brer Wolf say, 'Nobody ain't tryin' fer ter fool you. Look at my fine

37

long bushy tail.' Mr. Man 'low, 'You done tied an' er tail on behime you, but you can't fool me. Oh, no, Brer Rabbit! You can't fool me,' Brer Wolf say, 'Look at de ha'r on my back; do dat look like Brer Rabbit?' Mr. Man 'low, 'You done wallered in red san', but you can't fool me.'

"Brer Wolf say, 'Look at my long black legs; do dey look like Brer Rabbit?' Mr. Man 'low, 'You kin put an' er j'int in yo legs, an' you kin smut um, but you can't fool me,' Brer Wolf say, 'Look at my tushes; does dey look like Brer Rabbit?' Mr. Man 'low, 'You done got new toofies, but you can't fool me.' Brer Wolf say, 'Look at my little eyes; does dey look like Brer Rabbit?' Mr. Man 'low, 'You kin squinch yo' eye-balls, but you can't fool me, Brer Rabbit.' Brer Wolf squall out, 'I ain't not Brer Rabbit, an' yo' better turn me out er dis place so I kin take hide an' ha'r off'n Brer Rabbit.' Mr. Man say, 'Ef bofe hide an' ha'r wuz off, I'd know you, kaze 'tain't in you fer fool me.' An' it hurt Brer Wolf feelin's so bad fer Mr. Man, dat he bust out inter a big boo-boo, an' dat's 'bout all I know.''

"Did the man really truly think Brother Wolf was Brother Rabbit?" asked the little boy.

"When you pin me down dat-a-way," responded Uncle Remus, "I'm bleeze ter tell you dat I ain't too certain an' sho' 'bout dat. De tale come down fum my great-gran'daddy's great-gran'daddy; it come on down ter my daddy, an' des ez he gun it ter me, I done gun it ter you.''

AFTER THE BATTLE

BY JOSEPH A. ALTSHELER

AFTER THE BATTLE

BY JOSEPH A. ALTSHELER

THE falling dusk quenched the fury of the battle. The cannon glimmered but feebly on the dim horizon like the sputter of a dying fire. The shouts of combatants were unheard, and Dave Joyce concluded that the fighting was over for that day at least. In his soul he was glad of it.

"Pardner," he said to the wounded man, "the battle has passed on an' left us here like a canoe stuck on a sand bank. I think the fightin' is over, but if it ain't we're out of it anyhow, an' I don't know any law why we shouldn't make ourselves as comf'table as things will allow."

"If there's anythin' done," said the wounded man, "you'll have to do it, for I can't walk, an' I can't move, except when there's a bush for me to grab hold of and pull myself along by."

"That's mighty bad," said Joyce, sympathetically. "Where did you say that bullet took you?"

"I got it in my right leg here," the other replied, "an' I think it broke the bone. Leastways the leg ain't any more use to me than if it

41

was dead, though it hurts like tarnation sometimes. I guess it'll be weeks before I walk again."

"Maybe I could do somethin' for you," said Joyce, "if there was a little more light. I guess I'll take a look, anyhow. I haven't been two years in the army not to know anythin' about bullet wounds."

He bent down and with his pocket-knife cut away a patch of the faded blue cloth from the wounded man's leg.

"I guess I'd better not fool with that," he said, looking critically at the wound. "The bullet's gone all the way through, but the blood's clotted up so thick over the places that the bleedin' has stopped. You won't die if you don't move too much an' start that wound to bleedin' again."

"That's consolin'," said the wounded man; "but, since I can't move, I don't know what's to become of me but to lay here on the field an' die anyway."

"Don't you fret," said Joyce, cheerfully. I'll take care of you. You're Fed. and I'm Confed., but you're hurt an' I ain't, an' if the case was the other way I'd expect you to do as much for me. Besides, I've lost my regiment in the shuffle, and the chances are if I tried to find it again to-night I'd run right into the middle of the Yankee army, and that would mean Camp Chase for your humble servant, which is a bunk he ain't

AFTER THE BATTLE

covetin' very bad just now. So I guess it'll be
the safe as well as the right thing for me to do
to stick by you. Jerusalem! listen to that! Just
hear them crickets chirpin', will you!"

There was a blaze of light in the west, followed by a crash which seemed to roll around
the horizon and set all the trees of the forest to
trembling. When the echoes were lost beyond
the hills the silence became heavy and porten-
tous. The night was hot and sticky, and the
powdery vapor that still hung over the field
crept into Joyce's throat and made him cough
for breath.

"Thunderation!" he said at length, still looking in the direction in which the light had blazed
up. "I guess at least a dozen of the big cannon
must have been fired at once then. Can't some
fellows get enough fightin' in the daytime, without pluggin' away in the night-time too? Now
I come of fightin' stock myself—I'm from Kentucky—but twelve hours out of the twenty-four
always 'peared to me to be enough for that sort
of thing. Besides, it's so infernal hot to-night,
too."

"It was hotter than this for me a while ago,"
said the wounded man.

"So it was, so it was," said Joyce, apologetically, "an' I mustn't forget you, either. Let 'em
fight over there if they want to, an' if they're big
enough fools to spile a night that way when they
might be restin'. What you need just now is

43

water. I think there's a spring runnin' out of the side of that hill there. If you'll listen you'll hear it tricklin' away, so cool and refreshin' like. I guess it was tricklin' that same way, just as calm an' peaceful as Sunday mornin', while the battle was goin' on round here. Don't you feel as if a little water would help you mightily, pardner?"

"'Twould so," said the wounded man. "I'm burnin' up inside, an' if you'd get me a big drink of it I'd think you were mighty nigh good enough to be one of the twelve apostles."

"It's easy enough for me to do it," said Joyce. "I'll be back in a minute."

He took off his big slouch hat and walked toward the source of the trickling sound. From beneath an overhanging rock in the side of the hill near by a tiny stream of water flowed. After a fall of five feet it plunged into a little basin which it had hallowed out for itself in the rock, and formed a deep and cool little pool. Around the edge of the pool the tender green grass grew. The overflow from it wandered away in a little rill through the woods.

"Thunder, but ain't this purty?" exclaimed Joyce, forgetting that the wounded man was out of hearing. "It's just like our springhouse back in old Kentuck. I've put out butter-crocks an' milk-buckets a hundred times to cool in our pool when I was a boy. Wish I had some of them things now!"

AFTER THE BATTLE

The stirring of peaceful memories caused Joyce to linger a little, in forgetfulness of the wounded man. It was cool in the shadow of the hill, and the gay little stream tinkled merrily in his ears. He would have liked to remain there, but he pulled himself together with an impatient jerk, filled the crown of his hat with the limpid water, and started back to the relief of the wounded man.

He followed the channel of the stream for a little way, and as he turned to step across it he noticed the increasing depth of its waters.

"It's dammed up," he muttered. "I wonder what's done that."

Then he started back shuddering and spilled half the water from his hat, for he had almost stepped on the body of a man that had fallen across the channel of the poor little rivulet, checking the flow of its waters and deepening the stream.

The body lay face downward, and Joyce could not see the wound that had caused death. But as he stooped down he saw again the broad red flash in the west, and heard the heavy crash of the cannon.

"Will them cannon always be hungry?" he muttered. "But I guess I must give this poor little stream which 'ain't done no harm to any-body the right of way again."

He stooped and pulled the body to one side. With a thankful rush and gurgle the waters of the recent pool sped on in their natural channel, and Joyce returned to the fountain-head to fill his hat again.

He found the wounded man waiting with patience.

"I was gone longer than I ought to have been. Did you think I had left you, pardner?" asked Joyce.

"No," said the man. "I didn't believe you'd play that kind of a trick on me."

"An' so I haven't," said Joyce, "an' for your faith in me I've brought you a hatful of the nicest an' freshest an' coolest water you ever put your lips to in all your born days. Raise your head up, there, an' drink."

The wounded man drank and drank, and then when the hat was emptied he laid his head back in the grass and sighed as if he were in heaven.

"I must say that you 'pear to like water, pardner," said Joyce.

"Like it?" said the wounded man. "Wait till you've been wounded, an' then you'll know what it is to want water. Why, till you brought it I felt as if my inside was full of hot coals an' I'd burn all up if I didn't get something mighty quick to put the fire out."

"Then I reckon I've stopped a whole conflagration," said Joyce, "an' with mighty little trouble to myself, too. But I don't wonder that you get thirsty on a night like this. Thundera- tion, but ain't it clammy!"

AFTER THE BATTLE

He sat down on a fallen tree and d coat-sleeve across his brow. Then he l the sleeve: it was wet with sweat. There wind. The night had brought no coolness. The thick and heavy atmosphere hung close to the earth and coiled around and embraced everything. Through it came the faint gunpowdery vapor that crept into the throats and nostrils of the two men.

"I wish I was at home sleepin' on the hall floor," said Joyce. "I'll bet it would be cool there."

The wounded man made no answer, but turned his face up to the sky and drew in great mouthfuls of the warm air.

"Them tarnation fools over yonder 'pear to have their dander up yet," said Joyce, pointing to the west, where the alternate flashing and rumbling showed that the battle still lingered. "I thought the battle was over long ago, but I guess it ain't. I've knowed some all-fired fools in my time, but the fellows that would keep on fightin' on a hot night like this must be the all-firedest."

Then the two lay quite still for a while, watching the uneasy rising and falling of the night battle. Had they not known so much of war, they might have persuaded themselves that the flashes they saw were flashes of heat-lightning and the rumbling but the rumbling of summer thunder. But they knew better. They knew

47

it was men and not the elements that fought.

"It's mighty curious," said Joyce, "how the sand's all gone out of me for the time. To-day I felt as if I could whip the whole Yankee army all by myself. To-night I don't want to fight anythin'. I'm as peaceful in temper as a little lamb friskin' about in our old field at home. I hope that there fightin' won't come our way; at least not to-night. How are you feelin', pardner?"

"Pretty well for a wounded man," replied the other; "but I'd like to have some more water."

"Then I'm the man to get it for you," said Joyce, springing up. "An' I'm goin' to see if I can't get somethin' to eat, too, for my innards are cryin' cupboard mighty loud. There's dead men layin' aroun' here, an' there may be somethin' in their haversacks. I hate to rob the dead, but if they've got grub we need it more'n they do."

He returned with another hatful of water, which the wounded man drank eagerly, gratefully. Then he went back and searched in the grass and bushes for the fallen. Presently he came in great glee, and triumphantly held up two haversacks.

"Luck, pardner!" he exclaimed. "Great luck! Bully luck! One of these I got off a dead Fed. and t'other off a dead Confed., and both must have been boss foragers, for in one haversack

AFTER THE BATTLE

there's a roast chicken an' in t'other there's half a b'iled ham, an' in both there's plenty of bread. I haven't had such luck before in six months. You're a Yank, pardner, and a Northerner, an' maybe you don't know much about the vanities of roast chicken an' cold b'iled ham. But it's time you did know. I've come from the field at home when I'd been plowin' all day, an' my appetite was as sharp as a razor an' as big as our barn. I'd put up old Pete, our black mule that I'd been plowin' with, an' feed him; then I'd go to the house an' kinder loosen my waist-ban', an' mother would say to me, 'Come in the kitchen, Dave; your supper's ready for you.' Say, pardner, you ought to see me then. There'd be a pitcher of cold buttermilk from the spring-house, and one dish of roast chicken, an' another of cold ham, an' all for me, too. An' say, pardner, I can taste that ham now. When you eat one piece you want another, an' then another, an' you keep on till there ain't any left on the dish, an' then you lean back in your chair an' wish that when you come to die you'd feel as happy as you do then. Pardner, I wish them times was back again."

"I wish so too," said the wounded man.

"We can't have 'em back, at least not now," said Joyce, cheerily, "but we can make believe, an' it'll be mighty good make-believe, too, for we've got the ham an' the chicken, an' we can get cold water to take the place of cold milk. I

49

guess you can use your arms all right; so you can spread this ham an' chicken out on the grass, an' I'll see if I can't find a canteen to keep the water in. Say pardner, we'll have a banquet, you an' me, that's what we'll have."

The stalwart young fellow, full of boyish delight at the idea that the thought of home had suggested to him, swung off in search of the canteen. He found not one alone, but two. Then he returned clanking them together to indicate his success. As he came up he called out, in his hearty voice:

"Pardner, is the supper-table ready? Have you got the knives an' forks? You needn't min' about the napkins. I guess we can get along without 'em just this once."

"All ready," said the wounded man; "an' I guess I can keep you company at this ham an' chicken an' bread, for I'm gettin' a mighty sharp edge on my appetite too."

"So much the better," said Joyce. "There's plenty for both, an' it wouldn't be good manners for me to eat by myself."

He sat down on the grass in front of the improvised repast, and placed one canteen beside the wounded man and the other beside himself.

"Now, pardner," he said, "we'll drink to each other's health, an' then we'll charge the ham an' chicken with more vim than either of us ever charged a breastwork."

They drank from the canteens; and then they

made onslaught upon the provisions. Joyce ate for a while in deep and silent content, forgetting the heat and the battle which still lowered in the west. But presently, when his appetite was dulled, he remembered the cannonade.

"There they go again!" he said. "Boom! Boom! Boom! Won't them fellows ever get enough? I thought I was hungry, but the cannon over there 'pear to be hungrier. I suppose there ain't men enough in all this country to stop up their iron throats. But bang away! They don't bother us, do they, pardner? They can't spile this supper, for all their boomin' an' flashin'."

The wounded man bowed assent and took another piece of the ham.

Joyce leaned back on the grass, held up a chicken leg in his hand, and looked contemplatively at it.

"Ain't it funny, pardner," he said, "that you, a Tommy Yank, an' me, a Johnny Reb, are sittin' here, eatin' grub together, as friendly as two brothers, when we ought to be killin' each other? I don't know what Jeff Davis an' old Abe Lincoln will say about it when they hear of the way you an' me are doin'."

The wounded man laughed.

"You can say that I was your prisoner," he said, "when they summon you before the court-martial. An' so I am, if you choose to make me. I can't resist."

"I'm thinkin' more about gettin' back safe to our army than makin' prisoners," said Joyce, as he flung the chicken bone, now bare, into the bushes.

"That may be hard to do," said the wounded man; "for neither you nor me can tell which way the armies will go. Listen to that boomin'! Wasn't it louder than before? That fightin' must be movin' round nearer to us."

"Let it move," said Joyce. "I tell you I've had enough of fightin' for one day. That battle can take care of itself. I won't let it bother me. I don't want to shoot anybody."

"Is that the way you feel when you go into battle?" asked the wounded man.

"I can't say exactly," replied Joyce. "Of course when I go out in a charge with my regiment I want to beat the other fellows, but I don't hate 'em, no, not a bit. I've got nothin' against the Yanks. I've knowed some of 'em that was mighty good fellows. There ain't any of 'em that I want to kill. No, I'll take that back; there is one, just one, a bloody villain that I'd like to draw a bead on an' send a bullet through his skullin' body."

"Who is that?" asked the wounded man; "an' why do you make an exception of him?"

Joyce remained silent for a moment or two and drew a long blade of grass restlessly through his fingers.

"It's not a pleasant story," he said at last, "an'

AFTER THE BATTLE

it hurts me now to tell it, but I made you ask the question, an' I guess I might as well tell you, 'cause I feel friendly toward you, pardner, bein' as we are together in distress, like two Robinson Crusoes, so to speak."

The wounded man settled himself in the grass like one who is going to listen comfortably to a story.

"It's just a yarn of the Kentuck hills," said Joyce, "an' a bad enough one, too. We're a good sort of people up there, but we're hot-blooded, an' when we get into trouble, as we sometimes do, kinfolks stan' together. I guess you're from Maine, or York State, or somewhere away up North, an' you can't understand us. But it's just as I say. Sometimes two men up in our hills fight, an' one kills the other. Then the dead man's brothers, an' sons if he's got any old enough, an' cousins, an' so on, take up their guns an' go huntin' for the man that killed him. An' the livin' man's brothers an' sons an' cousins an' so on take up their guns an come out to help him. An' there you've got your feud, an' there's no tellin' how many years it'll run on, an' how many people will get killed in it.—Thunderation, but wasn't them cannon loud that time! The battle is movin' round toward us sure!"

Joyce listened a moment, but heard nothing more except the echoes.

"Our family got into one of them feuds," he said. "It was the Joyces and the Ryders. I'm

Dave Joyce, the son of Henry Joyce. I don't remember how the feud started; about nothin' much, I guess; but it was a red-hot one, I can tell you, pardner. It was fought fair for a long time, but at last Bill Ryder shot father from ambush and killed him. Father hadn't had much to do with the feud, either; he didn't like that sort of thing—didn't think it was right. I said right then that if I ever found the chance when I got big enough I'd kill Bill Ryder."

"Did you get the chance?" asked the wounded man.

"No," replied Joyce. "Country got too hot for Ryder, and he went away. He came back after a while, an' I was big enough to go gunnin' for him then, but the war broke out, an' off he went into the Union army before I could get a chance to draw a bead on him. I ain't heard of him since. Maybe he's been killed in battle an' his bones are bleachin' somewhere in the woods."

"Most likely," said the wounded man.

"There's no tellin'," said Joyce. "Still, some day when we're comin' up against the Yanks face to face I may see him before me, an' then I'll hold my gun steady an' shoot straight at him, instead of whoopin' like mad an' firin' lickety-split into the crowd, aimin' at nothin', as I generally do."

"It's a sad story, very sad for you," said the wounded man.

AFTER THE BATTLE

"Yes," said Joyce. "You don't have such things as feuds up North, do you?"

"No," replied the other, "an' we're well off without 'em. Hark, there's the cannon again!"

"Yes, an' they keep creepin' round toward us with their infernal racket," said Joyce. "Cannon love to chaw up people an' then brag about it. But if them fellows are bent on fightin' all night I guess we'll have to give 'em room for it. What do you say to movin'? I've eat all I want, an' I guess you have too, an' we can take what's left with us."

"I don't know," said the wounded man. "My leg's painin' me a good deal, an' the grass is soft an' long here where I'm layin'. It makes a good bed, an' maybe I'd better stay where I am."

"I think not," said Joyce, decidedly. "That night fight's still swingin' down on us, an' if we stay too long them cannon'll feed on us too. We'd better move, pardner. Let me take a look at your wound. It's gettin' lighter, an' I can see better now. The moon's up, an' she's shinin' for all she's worth through them trees. Besides, them cannon-flashes help. Raise up your head, pardner, an' we'll take a look at your wound together."

"I don't think you can do any good," said the wounded man. "It would be better not to disturb it."

"But we must be movin', pardner," said Joyce, a little impatiently. "See, the fight's warmin'

55

up, an' it's still creepin' down on us. Seems to me I can almost hear the tramp of the men an' the rollin' of the cannon-wheels. Jerusalem! what a blaze that was! I say, it's time for us to be goin'. If we stay here we're likely to be ground to death under the cannon-wheels, if we ain't shot first. Just let me get a grip under your shoulders, pardner, an' I'll take you out of this."

The cannon flamed up again, and the deep thunder filled all the night.

"Listen how them old iron throats are growlin' an' mutterin'," said Joyce; "an' they're sayin' it's time for us to be travelin'."

"I believe," said the wounded man, "that I would rather stay where I am an' take my chances. If I move I'm afraid I'll break open my wound. Besides, I think you're mistaken. It seems to me that the fight's passin' round to the right of us."

"Passin' to the right of us nothin'," said Joyce. "It's coming straight this way, with no more respect for our feelin's than if you an' me was a couple of field-mice."

The wounded man made no answer.

"Do you think, pardner," asked Joyce, slight offence showing in his voice, "that the Yanks may come this way an' pick you up an' then you won't be a prisoner? Is that your game?"

As his companion made no answer, Joyce continued:

AFTER THE BATTLE

"You don't think, pardner, that I want to hold you a prisoner, do you? an' you a wounded man, too, that I picked up on the battle-field and that I've eat and drank with? Why, that ain't my style."

He waited for an answer and as none came he was seized with a sudden alarm.

"You ain't dead, pardner?" he cried. "Jerusalem! what if he's died while I've been standin' here talkin' an' wastin' time?"

He bent over to take a look at the other's face, but the wounded man, with a sudden and convulsive movement, writhed away from him and struck at him with his open hand.

"Keep away!" he cried. "Don't touch me! Don't come near me! I won't have it! I won't have it!"

"Thunderation, pardner!" exclaimed Joyce; "what do you mean? I ain't goin' to harm you. I want to help you." Then he added, pityingly, "I guess he's got the fever an' gone out of his head. So I'll take him along whether he wants to go or not."

He bent over again, seized the wounded man by the shoulders, and forcibly raised him up. At the same moment the cannonade burst out afresh and with increased violence. A blaze of light played over the face of the wounded man, revealing and magnifying every feature, every line.

Joyce uttered no exclamation, but he dropped

the man as if he had been a coiling serpent in his hands, and looked at him, an expression of hate and loathing creeping over his face.

"So," he said, at last, "this is the way I have found you?"

The wounded man lay as he had fallen, with his face to the earth.

"No wonder," said Joyce, "you wanted to keep your face hid in the grass! No wonder you hide it there now!"

"Oh, Dave! Dave!" exclaimed the man, springing to his knees with sudden energy, "don't kill me! Don't kill me, Dave!"

"Why shouldn't I kill you?" asked Joyce, scornfully. "What reason can you give why I shouldn't do it?"

"There ain't any. There ain't any. Oh, I know there ain't any," cried the wounded man. "But don't do it, Dave! For Christ's sake don't do it!"

"You murderer! You sneakin' ambushin' murderer!" said Joyce. "It's right for you to beg for your life an' then not get it! Hear them cannon! Hear how they growl, an' see the flash from their throats! They'd like to feed on you, but they won't. That sort of death is too good for the likes of you. The death for you is to be shot like a ravin' cur."

He drew the loaded pistol from his belt and cocked it with deliberate motion.

"Dave! Dave!" the man cried, dragging him-

AFTER THE BATTLE

self to Joyce's feet, "you won't do that! You can't! It would be murder, Dave, to shoot me here, me a wounded man that can't help myself!"

"You done it, an' worse," said Joyce. "Of all the men unburnt in hell I think the one who deserves to be there most is the man who hid in ambush and shot another in the back that had never harmed him."

"I know it, Dave, I know it!" cried the wounded man, grasping Joyce's feet with both hands. "It was an awful thing to do, an' I've been sorry a thousand times that I done it, but all the sorrow in the world an' everythin' else that's in the world can't undo it now."

"That's so," said Joyce, "but it don't make any reason why the murderer ought to be kept on livin'."

"It don't, Dave; you're right, I know; but I don't want to die!" cried the man. "I'm a coward, Dave, and I don't want to die by myself here in the woods an' in the dark!"

"You'll soon have light enough," said Joyce, "an' I won't shoot you."

He let down the hammer of his pistol and replaced the weapon in his belt.

"Oh, Dave! Dave!" exclaimed the man, kissing Joyce's foot. "I'm so glad you'll let me have my life. I know I ain't fit to live, but I want to live anyhow."

"I said I wouldn't shoot you," said Joyce, "but

I never said I'd spare your life. See that blaze in the trees up there."

A few hundred yards away the forest had burst into flame. Sparks fell upon a tree and blazed up. Long red spirals coiled themselves around the trunk and boughs until the tree became a mass of fire, and then other tongues of flame leaped forward and seized other trees. There was a steady crackling and roaring, and the wind that had sprung up drove smoke and ashes and fiery particles before it.

"That," said Joyce, "is the wood on fire. Them cannon that's been makin' so much fuss done it. I've seen it often in battle when the cannon have been growlin'. The fire grows an' it grows, an it burns up everythin' in its way. The army is still busy fightin', an' the wounded, them that's hurt too bad to help theirselves, have to lay there on the ground an' watch the fire comin', an' sure to get 'em. By an' by it sweeps down on 'em, an' they shriek an' shriek, but that don't do you no good, for before long the fire goes on, an' there they are, dead an' burnt to a coal. I tell you it's an awful death!"

The wounded man was silent now. He had drawn himself up a little, and was watching the fire as it leaped from tree to tree and devoured them one after another.

"That fire is comin' for us, an' the wind is bringin' it along fast," said Joyce, composedly, "but it's easy enough for me to get out of its way. All I've got to do is to go up the hill, an' the clearin's run for a long way beyond. I can stay up there an' watch the fire pass, an' you'll be down here right in its track."

"Dave!" cried the man, "you ain't goin' to let me burn to death right before your eyes?"

"That's what I mean to do," said Joyce. "I don't like to shoot a wounded man that can't help himself, an' I won't do it, but I ain't got no call to save you from another death."

"I'd rather be shot than burned to death," cried the man, in a frenzy.

"It's just the death for you," said Joyce.

Then the wounded man again dragged himself to the feet of Joyce.

"Don't do it, Dave!" he cried. "Don't leave me here to burn to death! Oh, I tell you, Dave, I ain't fit to die!"

"Take your hands off my feet," said Joyce. "I don't want 'em to touch me. There's too much blood on 'em."

"Don't leave me to the fire!" continued the man. "You've been kind to me to-night. Help me a little more, Dave, an' you'll be glad you done it when you come to die yourself!"

"I must be goin'," said Joyce, repulsing the man's detaining hands. "It's gettin' hot here now, an' that fire will soon be near enough to scorch my face. Good-by."

"For the sake of your own soul, Dave Joyce," cried the man, beating the ground with his

61

hands, "don't leave me to be burned to a coal! Think, Dave, how we eat an' drank together to-night, like two brothers, an' how you waited on me an' brought the water an' the grub. You'll remember them things, Dave, when you come to die yourself!"

The fire increased in strength and violence. The flames ran up the trees, and whirled far above them in red coils that met and twined with each other, and then whirled triumphantly on in search of fresh fuel. A giant oak, burned through at the base and swept of all its young boughs and foliage, fell with a rending crash, a charred and shattered trunk. The flames roared, and the burning trees maintained an incessant crackling like a fire of musketry. The smoke through which the sparks of fire were sown in millions grew stifling.

"God, what a sight!" cried Joyce.

"Dave, you won't leave me to that?" cried Ryder.

Joyce drew down his hat over his eyes to shield them from the smoke. Then he stooped, lifted the wounded man upon his powerful shoulders, and went on over the hill.

"MANY WATERS"

BY MARGARET DELAND

"MANY WATERS"

BY MARGARET DELAND

I

"WELL?"

"True bill; I'm awfully sorry."

Thomas Fleming took his cigar out of his mouth, and contemplated the lighted end. He did not speak. The other man, his lawyer, who had brought him the unwelcome news, began to make the best of it.

"Of course, it's an annoyance; but—"

"Well, yes. It's an annoyance," Fleming said, dryly.

Bates chuckled. "It strikes me, Tom, considering the difference between this and the *real thing*, that 'annoyance' is just the right word to use!"

Fleming leaned over and knocked off the ashes from his cigar into his waste basket. He was silent.

"As for Hammond, he won't have a leg to stand on. I don't know what Ellis & Grew meant by letting him take the case before the Grand Jury. He won't have a leg to stand on!"

"Give me a light, will you, Bates? This cigar has gone out again."

"What has Hammond got, anyhow?" Bates continued, pulling a box of wax matches out of his waistcoat pocket; "what's he got to support his opinion that you pinched $3,000 from the Hammond estate? His memory of something somebody said twelve years ago, and an old check. Well, we won't do a thing to 'em!"

Fleming got up and began to pull down his desk top with a slow clatter. "Hammond's a fool," he said; "and you'll punch a hole in his evidence in five minutes. But it's—well, as you say, it's 'annoying.'"

The lawyer rose briskly and reached for his hat. "What we want now is to get the case up near the head of the list as soon as we can. Get it over! Get it over! Then, if you want revenge, we can turn round and hit back with 'malicious prosecution'!" He laughed, good-naturedly, and shrugged himself into his overcoat.

His client stood absently locking and unlocking his desk. "I suppose it will be in the evening papers?" he said.

"Oh, I guess so," the younger man said, easily; "the findings of the Grand Jury were reported at eleven this morning. Plenty of time for the first editions."

"Then I'll take an early train home," Thomas Fleming said, quickly; "my wife——" he paused.

"MANY WATERS"

"Doesn't Mrs. Fleming know about it?" the lawyer said, with a surprised look.

"No," the other man said, gloomily; "I didn't want her to worry over it, so I didn't say anything. But, of course, now she's got to know."

"Yes," Bates said, sympathetically; "but after all, Fleming, it's a small matter, except for the nuisance of it. You tell her I say it's a sure thing."

Fleming let his key-ring drop, jingling, into his pocket. Except for the occasional faint clangor of cars far down in the streets, the room, high up in the big office building, was quiet; but its quiet was the muffled, inarticulate, never-ending roar of living, rising from below. Fleming sighed, and, turning his back to his lawyer, stared absently out of the window. Before him, in the afternoon dusk, lay the struggling, panting city. Far off to the south he could see the water, and ferryboats crawling like beetles back and forth. Below, the deep canyons of the streets were blurred with creeping yellow fog; but higher up, above the crowding roofs and chimneys and occasional spires, the air was clearer; it was full of tumultuous movement—sudden jets of white steam ballooning from hundreds of escape pipes; shuffling, shifting coils of black smoke; here and there the straining quiver of flags, whipping out from their masts. Fleming, his hands in his pockets, stood staring and listening—with unseeing eyes, unhearing ears. The lawyer behind him, at the office door, hesitated.

"Fleming, really, it isn't going to amount to anything. Of course, I know how you feel about Mrs. Fleming, but—"

The man at the window turned round. "Rather than have her disturbed, I'd compromise on it. I'd pay him. I'd—"

The lawyer raised his eyebrows. "This time, I think, Hammond is honest. I guess he really believes he has a case; but Ellis & Grew are sharks, and you'd be encouraging blackmail to compromise. Anyway, you couldn't do it. Grew volunteered the information that their man 'couldn't be bought off'; he meant to put it through, Grew said. I told him they'd got the wrong pig by the ear. I told him that Thomas Fleming wasn't the kind of man who purchases peace at the cost of principle. They're shysters, and I gave 'em plain talk. Now, don't let Mrs. Fleming take it to heart. Tell her I say it will be a triumph!"

He went off, laughing; and a minute later Fleming heard his step in the corridor, and then the clang of the elevator door. He took up his black cloth bag and poked about in it among some papers; then unlocked his desk and found what he had been looking for—a box of candy for his wife. He slipped it into his bag, and a minute or two later he was down in the muddy dusk of the street. As he moved along with the

68

steady surge of the homeward-bound crowd, he looked doubtfully into the flower stores; he wished he had bought violets for Amy instead of candy; he had taken her candy last Saturday. He debated whether he had not better get the violets too, but decided against them, because Amy was stern with him when he was extravagant for her sake. She never saw extravagance in any purchase he made on his own account! He smiled to himself at the thought of her sweet severity.

"Amy keeps me in order," he used to say, whimsically; "she insists that I shall be *her* best; it appears that my own best isn't good enough for her!" This she would always deny, indignantly, and indeed justly; for Thomas Fleming stood on his own legs, morally, in his community. But in the ten years of their married life no doubt her ideals, in small matters, had created his. With his indolent good-nature, he had found it easier to agree with Amy's delicate austerities of thought than to dispute them. Her hair-splitting in matters of conscience always amused him, and sometimes touched him, but he accepted her standards of duty with real tenderness—which, for all practical purposes, was as good as conviction. Gradually, too, she pushed him, gently, before he knew it, into civic affairs; not in any very large way; perhaps hardly more than in a readiness to do his part as a citizen; but such readiness was sincere, and had given him a reputation for public-spiritedness in which Amy took a quiet pride. He had never had time, though he had had opportunity, to hold office, because his business demanded his entire energy; and, in fact, he had to be energetic, for he had hardly any capital, his income being almost entirely dependent upon his earnings; so he was not at all a rich man—except, indeed, as he was rich in the honor and respect of the community, and the love of a woman like Amy.

But then, if they were not rich in this world's goods, neither were they poor. There had been happy, anxious years, when they were first married, when they had ridiculously little to live on; but in those days Amy had steered their house-keeping bark between all rocks of hardship, as well as past breakers of extravagance. Even now, when things were easier each year, Amy was still prudent and economical, at least where she herself was concerned.

So Fleming, smiling, forbore to add a bunch of violets to his box of candy. After all, it was his thought that would bring the delicate and happy color up into her face, not the gift itself. They were very happy, these two; perhaps because they were only two. There had been a baby, but it had only lived long enough to draw them very close together, and not, as sometimes happens, to push them apart again; and there were many friends. But they were alone in their household and in the real heart of life.

Naturally, all the thwarted maternity of the woman was added to the wife's love; and the paternal instinct of the man (which is, for the most part, only amusement, and the sense of protecting and giving joy) was centred in his wife.

So it was no wonder that that night, going home on the train, he winced at the thought of telling her that that "fool Hammond," who "would not have a leg to stand on," had prosecuted him criminally for misappropriation of funds as trustee of old Mrs. Hammond's estate. The trusts had been closed at her death a month or two before, and the estate handed over to her son—this same Hammond who "thought he remembered" hearing old Smith say, twelve years before, that he, Smith, had paid the Hammond estate $17,400 for a parcel of land; whereas Fleming's trustee account put the sum received at $14,400.

Amy's husband set his teeth as he sat there in the train, planning how he should tell her. Her incredulous anger he foresaw; and her anxiety—the anxiety of the woman unversed in legal matters. He damned Hammond in his heart; and pulled out his evening paper. There it was, in all the shamelessness of the flaring headline: "A Leading Citizen Indicted!" and so on. The big black letters were like a blow in the face. Fleming felt that every commuter on the train was looking over the top of his newspaper at him. He found himself glancing furtively across the aisle to see what page of the paper another passenger was reading; he thanked God that none of the men he knew well were on the five o'clock, so he would not have to listen to friendly assurances of astonishment at Hammond's impudence.

His skin was prickly over his whole body; his ears were hot. And he had to tell Amy! He sank his head down between his shoulders and pulled his hat over his eyes, in pretence of a nap; then, suddenly, sat bolt upright. The fact was, Thomas Fleming had no experience in disgrace, and did not know how to conduct himself. When the door banged open at his station, he swung off on to the rainy platform, and plodded slowly up the lane in the darkness to his own house. It seemed to him as though his very feet hung back!

As the gate closed behind him, he saw an instant crack of light at the front door; and when his foot touched the lowest step of the porch, the door opened wide, and Amy stood there—it was rarely Jane who let him in or even his own latchkey!

"Go right into the house! You'll take cold," he commanded.

But she drew him inside with eager welcome. "Why, how *did* you manage to get the five o'clock? I heard the gate shut, and could hardly believe my ears! Oh, your coat is damp; has it begun to rain? Hurry! take it off. Then come into the library and get warm." She possessed

72

herself of one of his hands, so that he had to dive into his bag as best he could with the other, to fish out her box of candy. She took it, smiling, with gay pretence of scolding, and then checked herself. "You look tired, Tom. When you've had your dinner (we have a good dinner to-night; I wish you had brought some man home with you!) you'll feel better."

He dropped down into his chair by the fire in silence, frowning slightly, and drawing impatiently away from her. Thomas Fleming did not always like to be fussed over; there were times when, perhaps, he endured it with a mildly obvious patience. Every tender woman knows this patience of a good and bored man. Amy Fleming knew it, and smiled to herself, quite unoffended. Something had bothered him? Well, he should not be talked to! But she looked at him once or twice. In her soft gray dress, with her gray eyes, and the sweet color in her cheeks, she brooded over him like a dove. At dinner his silence continued. Amy, being wise beyond her sex, fell into a silence of her own—the blessed, comprehending silence of love. When they came back from the dining-room to the library fireside, she let him smoke uninterruptedly, while she sewed. Sometimes her eyes rested on him, quietly content with his mere presence. But she asked no question. Suddenly, with a half-embarrassed cough, he said:

"Ah, Amy——"

73

"Yes? Tell me; I knew you hadn't had a good day."

When he had told her, she sat dumb before him. Her face was white, and her eyes terror-stricken. But that was only for the first moment. Almost instantly there was the relief of anger. She stood up, her delicate face red, her voiced strained.

"To accuse you! *You!*"

It was just what Bates had said. The first thought everywhere would be of the absurdity of such a charge against Thomas Fleming.

"It's blackmail," Amy said, trembling very much.

"Of course we shall have no difficulty in throwing them down," he said. "They bring their case, really, on Smith's old check to me for $17,400."

"I don't understand?" Amy said. It had always been a joke between them that Amy did not know anything about business, so she tried to smile when she asked him to explain.

"Oh," he said, impatiently, "it's simple enough. L. H. Smith owed me $3,000—a personal matter. I once sold him some stock; he gave me his note; had to renew two or three times; thing sort of hung fire. You wouldn't understand it, Amy. But when he bought this Hammond property for $14,400, he made out the check for $17,400;—

he'd had a windfall, so he could pay me what he owed me, see? I got my money. Understand?"

"Perfectly," she said; "what a rascal Hammond is!"

"Oh, well, I suppose this time he really thinks he has a case; though on general principles I believe he's equal to blackmail! But he has succeeded in getting from the Smith heirs that old check for the total amount, and I suppose he thinks he has me. He'll find himself mistaken. But it's a nasty business," he ended, moodily; "there will always be people who will think——"

"What do we care what such people think?" she said, passionately.

Her husband was silent. Amy's knees were shaking under her. "Oh, I could kill that man, I could kill him!"

Well as he knew her, he looked at her with astonishment—this mild creature to speak with such deadly, vindictive passion! She came and knelt down beside him; he felt her heart pounding in her side.

"Oh," she said, brokenly, "I know——"

"You know what?"

She spoke very softly. "I know how they felt; those women, 'looking on, afar off.'"

"Looking on?" he said, vaguely. And Amy, her face still hidden on his breast, said in a whisper:

"It must have been easier for—for Him, on the cross, than for them to see Him there."

He moved abruptly in his chair; then, with a faint impatience, said she mustn't talk that way. "It's foolish!" he said, irritably. She kissed him, silently; and went back to her seat by the fire.

"I'll get out of it all right," Fleming said; "Bates says so. It's annoying"—he found himself falling back on Bate's word—"but there's nothing to it. You mustn't worry. Bates says Hammond is crazy to undertake it; Smith being dead, and—" Then he stopped.

"I don't worry; in the sense of being afraid that—" she could not even put into words the fear that she did not have. "But to have your name mixed up with anything dishonorable—even though it will come out clear and shining as heaven!"

He made no answer. The fatigue of the day was showing in his face—a heavy, handsome face, with a somewhat hard mouth. His wife, looking at him, said, quietly:

"Don't let's talk about it, dearest, any more to-night. It's only on the surface; it isn't a real trouble."

He nodded, gratefully; and they did not speak of it again.

But that night Amy Fleming, lying motionless in her bed, stared into the darkness until the glimmering oblong of the window told her that dawn had come.

"MANY WATERS"

II

"Trouble shows us our friends," Amy said, smiling. And indeed it did, in the Flemings' case. When the news of the indictment of Thomas Fleming fell upon his community, there was a moment of stunned astonishment; then of protest and disbelief.

"Hammond is up against it," men said to each other; "Fleming? What nonsense!"

The first day or two, while it was still a nine days' wonder, public confidence was almost an ovation. The small house behind the trim hedges was crowded with Amy's women friends, coming and going, and quoting (after the fashion of women friends) what their respective husbands said:

"*Of course* Mr. Hammond has no case, Amy, darling! My Tom—or Dick or Harry—says so."

Amy did not need such assurances. She knew her husband! So she held her head proudly, and with certainty. Not certainty of the outcome of the trial—because, secretly, she had the un-reasoning terror of most women of sheltered lives for the very word *law*; it meant power; wicked power, even! The opportunity of evil to get the better of goodness. But her pride and certainty were for Thomas Fleming's honor, and goodness, and courage. She was a little cold when these tender women friends tried to reassure her, quoting the opinion of their menfolk; she did not want, by eager agreement, to imply that she needed reassurance. She said, with gentle dignity, that she was sorry Mr. Hammond was so—foolish. Tom had been trustee of the Hammond estate for nearly twenty years, and he had given time and service——"service," she said, the color rising faintly in her face, "that money could not have paid for." And to have the Hammonds turn upon him now!——"Though, of course, it is only Mr. Hammond," Amy corrected herself, carefully just; "the rest of the family are nice people. And his wife—I am sorry for his wife." Amy thought a great deal about this wife. "She must know what he is, poor soul!" she said to herself. And knowing, she could not respect him. And without respect, love must have crumbled away. She said something like this to her most intimate friend, almost in a whisper, because expression was not easy to Amy. "When Mrs. Hammond realizes that he is a blackmailer, what *will* she do!"

"Poor thing!" said the other woman; "but, Amy, I suppose she is fond of him? He has been a good husband, they say."

"A good husband? How do you mean? Kind? A good provider?" Amy said, with a droop of her lip.

"Well, my dear, at least the man has been faithful to her; among all the horrid things that

have been said about him, nobody has said—
that."

"They had better have said 'that'!" Amy
said. "Oh, Helen, faithful to her with his body;
but what about his mind? Don't you suppose a
good woman could forgive the poor, sinful body?
But the mind, the sinful mind! It is so much
worse."

Her friend looked doubtful. "I suppose it is,"
she said; "but I think most wives could forgive
the sinful mind more easily than—other things.
And she is fond of him," she repeated.

"Fond of him! when she can't respect him?
Oh, no, no!"

"Perhaps she doesn't know how bad he is," the
other said, thoughtfully.

"What!" said Amy, "when she has lived with
him for fifteen years? Of course she knows him.
And I truly pity her," she ended simply.

So in spite of her deep resentment at Hammond, Amy felt something like tenderness for
Hammond's wife—losing both respect and love,
poor soul!

As the weeks passed before the day set for the
trial, Amy grew perceptibly thinner and whiter.
For beneath all her certainties, the fear of the
Law remained. She brooded over instances of
goodness suspected, of innocent men condemned,
of the blunders and mistakes of Justice. It was
not until three or four days before the trial that
Bates realized what even Thomas Fleming had

not understood, that she was consumed with *fear*. Fear of prison walls, of unmerited disgrace, of her house left unto her desolate. When the lawyer penetrated the tense cheerfulness with which she held herself in Tom's presence, and saw the fright below, he roared with laughter; which, though ill-mannered, was the best thing he could have done.

"You think I'm a fool?" she said, with a quivering smile.

"My dear lady, it would not be polite for me to use such a word; but certainly you—well, you are mistaken."

"Oh, *say* I am a fool," she pleaded; "I would like to think I was a fool! But, Mr. Bates, the Law can be made to do such dreadful things. Innocent people have been put into jail; oh, you know they have," she said, her face trembling; "and at night I lie awake and think—" He saw her hands grip each other to keep steady.

"Now let me explain it to you," he said kindly; "and then you won't be frightened; why, you'll be so sure you'll send out invitations for a dinner party on the 19th, so we can celebrate! And mind you have plenty of champagne."

Then, very explicitly, he laid before her the grounds of his confidence. Hammond, to start with, was a fool. "He always has been a cheap fellow; a sort of smart Aleck, you know; but this time he's just a fool." He had fallen into the hands of a shyster firm, who were milking him—"If you'll forgive the slang."

"Oh, go on, go on!" she entreated.

Hammond, being a fool, and having this vague idea about the price paid by Smith for the land, and having secured the old check to prove (as he thinks) that such a price was paid, falls into the hands of these sharks. "They know there is nothing to it, but they think they can pull out a plum somehow," said Mr. Bates. Then, carefully, he told her the story point by point. Briefly, it was, that while there was no question that $17,400 had been paid to Thomas Fleming, Hammond could not disprove Fleming's defence that only $14,400 of it was to go to the Trust; and that the remaining $3,000 was in payment of Smith's debt to him. "See?" said Bates, kindly. As he spoke, the drawn look in her face lessened, and she drew one or two long breaths; and then, suddenly, she put her hands over her eyes, and he knew she wept. This sobered the rather voluble man. He protested, with friendly vociferation, that she must promise him not to give the matter another thought. And she, still trembling a little, looked up, smiling, and promised.

And, such being her temperament, she kept her promise. Perhaps it was the rebound from having gone down to the depths of fear; but certainly there was almost bravado in the reaction. She made up her mind to have the dinner party!

Tom would come home, cleared, crowned with the vindication of his own integrity; and he would find love, and friendship, and respect ready to exult with him. Tom, however, objected to her project.

"It's all right," he said; "it's perfectly safe, as far as the verdict goes; but——" he stopped and frowned. It was evident that the plan did not please him. But for the once Amy did not consult his pleasure. She had her own views; and she did actually invite a party of old friends to dine with them on the evening when it was expected that the verdict would be given.

III

Amy, in her dove-colored dress, entered the court-room with her husband. During the trial, very quietly, and with a beautiful serenity, she kept her place at his side. If the proceedings troubled her, there was no indication of it. She looked a little tired, and once or twice a little amused. Sometimes she smiled at Thomas Fleming, and sometimes exchanged a word or two with Mr. Bates. But for the most part she was silent; and her repose was a spot of refreshment and beauty in the dingy court-room. Bates looked at her occasionally, with rather jovial encouragement; but she displayed no need of encouragement, and returned his smile cheerfully. Once he leaned over and said:

"You make me think of a poem I read somewhere; now, what was the name of it? I can only
remember two lines:

"'In the fell clutch of circumstance,
I have not winched or cried aloud!'

That's as far as I can go; but that's what you
make me think of."

She turned, smiling, and finished the verse.
"It's Henley's 'I am the captain of my soul,'"
she said. "I have it somewhere: I copied it once,
because I cared so much for it. I'll read it to you
to-night, after dinner."

"Do!" Bates said heartily, and turned away
to listen to Fleming, who was on the stand.
Fleming's evidence was as straightforward as
the man himself. Yes, Smith (now deceased)
had paid him in March, 1887, the sum of $17,400.
Of this, $3,000 was on a personal account; $14,-
400 was for a parcel of land belonging to the
Hammond estate. The check was made to his
order; he deposited it in his own bank account
and immediately drew against it a check for $14,-
400 to the order of the Trust. Then followed
a very clear and definite statement of that money
Smith owed him; a debt which he was unable to
corroborate by his books, for the simple reason
that his books had been burned in the great fire
of that year. Over and over, back and forth,
round and round, the prosecution went, gaining
not an inch.

83

Indeed, the end was obvious from the beginning. To assert that Thomas Fleming was an honest man was, so Bates told the jury, to utter a commonplace. He was so cheerful and kindly, in his reference to the unfortunate Mr. Hammond, that the jury grinned. The verdict, Bates declared, was a foregone conclusion. And so, in fact, it was, being rendered fifteen minutes after the jury had been charged.

"And now," said the good Bates, shaking hands with his client, "let's go and get something to eat! Come, Mrs. Fleming, you'll go with us? You look like an army with banners!"

But Amy, with proud eyes, said no; she must go home. "You will come out with Tom this evening?" she said. "Dinner is at half-past seven; you can dress at our house; and, of course, you must stay all night." Bates promised, and Fleming silently squeezed his wife's hand. Amy's heart was beating so that her words were a little breathless, but her eyes spoke to him.

She did not want to go to lunch with the two men; she had it in mind to go into a church which was near the court-house, and there, alone, in the silence and sacred dusk, return thanks upon her knees. And deep human experience gives the soul a chance to see God; and when Amy came out afterward into the roar of the street, her face shone like the face of one who has touched the garment hem of the Eternal, and bears back the Tables of Law....

The joyous and beautiful day passed; the afternoon was gay with congratulations; but the succession of friendly calls was fatiguing and at half-past five she said, courageously, "Now, dear friends, I'll have to leave you! It's delightful to hear all these nice things about Tom, but I must go and lie down, or I shall go to sleep at dinner."

So there was more handshaking and gayety, and then, at last, she had the house to herself. She reflected that it would be well to have a little nap, so that she might be bright and rested for the jubilant evening;—oh, that poem Mr. Bates wanted to see! She had forgotten all about it; she must find it before she went upstairs. But she must first look into the dining-room to be sure about the candles and flowers and wine-glasses; three kinds of wine to-night! Generally Tom had just his glass of sherry; but to-night—! The economical Amy would have broached the tun of malmsey if she had been able to secure it. The dinner, she knew, would be good. She had picked out the partridges herself, knowing well, under her calm exterior, that her market man, looking at her with sidewise, curious eyes, was thinking to himself, "My! and her husband to be tried for a State's prison offence!" The partridges were superb; and the salmon—Amy's eyes sparkled with joy at the thought of such extravagance—salmon in February! the salmon was perfect; and the salad, the ices, the coffee—well, they would be worthy of the occasion!

The dining-room was satisfactory, with its ten friendly chairs drawn up about the sparkling table. And her best dress was upstairs spread out on the bed, with her slippers and gloves; her flowers—Tom would bring her her flowers! She thought to herself that she would wear them, and then put them away with her wedding bouquet, that had been lying, dry and fragrant, for all these years, with her wedding dress and veil. Sighing with the joy of it all, she climbed wearily half-way upstairs; then remembered Mr. Bates's poem again, and went back to the library, with an uneasy look at the hall clock. She would not get much of a nap! And the chances of the nap lessened still more, because she could not at once find her Commonplace Book, in which she had copied the poem. Taking out one book after another, she shook her head and looked at her hands—these shelves were very dusty; that told a housekeeping story that was disgraceful, she said to herself, gayly. Well, she would look after Jane, now that she could think and breathe again! So, poking about, pulling out one flexible, leather-covered volume after another, her fate fell upon her. . . .

The book looked like her own Commonplace Book; Tom had more than once given her blank-books just like his own—bound in red morocco, with mottled edges, and stamped, "*Diary, 18——.*"

There was a whole row of these books on one of the bottom shelves of the bookcase that ran round three sides of the room, and she had been looking at them, one by one, hurriedly, for she knew she needed that rest upstairs before the company came. She pulled the books out, impatiently, fluttering the leaves over, and putting them back. One or two were her own notebooks; but the rest were Tom's memoranda—accounts, notes, etc., etc., back to— "Why, dear me!" said Amy to herself, "they go back to before we were married!"

There was one date that caught her eye; she had heard it repeated and repeated in the last few weeks; she had heard it that very morning in court, when Thomas Fleming had said: "In March, 1887, L. F. Smith paid me in one check $17,400; $14,400 for a piece of land belonging to the Hammond estate, and $3,000 which he owed my personal account."

The flexible, red-covered diary marked 1887 drew her hand with the fascination which comes with remembered pain. Ah! how she had suffered every time that date fell like a scalding drop of fear upon her heart! It is not true of spiritual pain that one remembereth no more the anguish for joy that a blessing has been born into the soul! She shivered as she opened the book. It occurred to her, with vague surprise, that this book would probably have settled the whole matter, if Tom had only remembered it. He had shown in court that records of that year had been among certain office books burned in the great March fire, when the building in which he had his office had been destroyed. Yes, this book might have cleared the whole matter up, easily and quickly, for, as she saw at a glance, here were entries about the Hammond Trust. She forgot her fatigue, and the nap she ought to have; she forgot the poem altogether; she sat down on the floor, running the pages over eagerly. It occurred to her, as a climax of the successful day, that she would bring this book out at dinner (if she could only find something about the $14,400) and show it as her final triumph. Then her eyes fell on the figures $17,400.

"Received from L. H. Smith, to-day, $17,400 for Hammond property, in Linden Hill." Then the comment, "A whacking good price. I hardly expected to get so much." The significance of this brief statement did not penetrate her joy. She began eagerly to look again for the other figures—and then turned back, perplexed. $17,-400 for the Hammond property? Suddenly her eye caught another familiar sum—$3,000. Ah, now she would find it! Yes, verily, so she did. . . . "Borrowed $3,000 from Hammond Estate to pay back money borrowed from Ropes Estate."

Suddenly it seemed to this poor woman, sitting on the floor in the dark corner of the library, her fingers dusty, her whole slender body tingling with fatigue—it seemed as if something fell, shuddering, down and down, and down in her breast. Strangely enough, this physical recognition informed her soul. She heard herself speak, as one falling into the unconsciousness of an anæsthetic hears, with vague astonishment, words faltering unbidden from the lips. "No. No. No," came the body's frightened denial. "Then, in silence, the Soul: "He—did it. He did it."

It was characteristic of Amy that she sought no loophole of escape. It never occurred to her that there could be an explanation. There were the figures; and the figures meant the facts. *"A certain man named Ananias"* (so suddenly, the words ran in her mind) *"sold a possession . . . and kept back part of the price."*

Out in the hall the half-hour struck, muffled and mellow. Then silence.

"God, if he did it, I can't live—can't live. *God?"*

Suddenly the happenings of the day seemed to blur and run together, and there was a moment, not of unconsciousness, but of profound indifference. Her capacity for feeling snapped. But when she tried to rise, her whole being was sick; so sick that again the soul forgot or did not understand, and heard, with dull curiosity, the body saying, "No. No." She steadied herself by holding on to the bookshelves; and then, somehow, she got upstairs. It was the sight of the

89

soft, gray dress, with its pretty laces, that stung her awake. That dress: was it hers? Was she to put it on? Was she to go and sit at the head of that shining table down in the dining-room?

"But, you know, I—*can't*," she said aloud, her voice hoarse and falling.

. . . . .

But she did.

By the time Fleming and his counsel came tramping up from the gate, at a quarter past seven, and stopped hilariously, to kick the snow off their boots before entering the hall, Amy Fleming had arisen to meet the summons of Life. She called Jane to fasten her dress, and when the woman, startled and shocked at the shrunken face, cried out:

"Oh, good land! what's wrong wi' ye, Mrs. Fleming?" she was able to say, quietly:

"Jane, when Mr. Fleming comes in, tell him I've had to go down to the kitchen to see about some things. And say I put his dress suit out on the sofa in my room. Tell him the studs are in his shirt."

Jane, silenced, went back to the kitchen. "Say, Mary Ann," she said, "look-a-here; there's something the matter upstairs." The presence of the accommodating waitress checked further confidences; but, indeed, when Amy Fleming, ghastly, in her pretty dinner dress, sought refuge in the kitchen (the one spot where her husband would not be apt to pursue her), and stood listening to the voices of the two men going upstairs, Mary Ann needed no information that there was "something the matter."

"She looks like she was dead," the frightened women told each other.

"Jane," her mistress said, "I wish you would open a bottle of champagne; one of the pints, not one of the big bottles, and give—me—a glass;" her voice was faint. Jane obeyed hurriedly, and as the cork popped one man upstairs called out gayly to the other, "Hullo! has it begun already?"

Amy drank the wine and handed the glass back to the anxious woman. "I was feeling faint, Jane. I am all right now, thank you. Oh, there's the door bell! I'll go into the library." And when the two rather early comers had taken off their wraps and made their way downstairs again, they found their hostess smiling whitely at them from the hearthrug.

"Oh, Amy *dear!*" the wife said, dismayed, "what is the matter?" And the husband protested in a friendly way that he was afraid Mrs. Fleming was tired out. "Of course it has been a wearing week for you, in spite of its triumph," he said, delicately.

Then Thomas Fleming and his lawyer came downstairs, and there was more handshaking and congratulations, and it was not until he looked at his wife at dinner that Fleming really saw her face; its haggard pallor struck him dumb in the midst of some gay story to the pretty neighbor on his right. He had been dull, just at first, and his gayety was a little forced, but after his first glass of champagne he brightened up very much, and had begun to tell a funny story. "And so the automobilist," he was saying—and broke off, staring blankly at Amy. "I'm afraid my wife is not well," he said, anxiously. But the pretty neighbor reassured him.

"Oh, it's the reaction. Mr. Fleming. Amy has been perfectly splendid; but now, naturally, she feels the reaction."

Somehow or other, with its gayety and good fellowship, that dreadful evening passed. When the friendly folk streamed out into the starry winter night, there was some anxious comment.

"How badly she looked!"

"My dear, can you wonder? Think what she's been through!"

But one woman, on her husband's arm, murmured a question: "You don't suppose he *could* have—done anything?"

"Twelve good men and true have said he didn't; your remark is out of order."

"But tell me, honestly, do you suppose it is possible that—that?"

"I don't know anything about it, Helen. I would bank on Tom Fleming as soon as on any man I know. But I don't know any man (myself included) who is not human. So, if you ask about 'possibilities'—but no! honestly, as you

92

"MANY WATERS"

say, I'm sure Fleming is all right. And his wife is a noble woman. I've always admired Mrs. Fleming."

"She is the best woman in the world!" Amy's friend said, warmly. But in her own heart she was thinking that if it came to possibilities, she knew *one* man to whom wrongdoing was impossible! And, happily, she squeezed his arm, and brushed her cold, rosy cheek against his shoulder.

IV

When Fleming closed the door upon the last lingering guest, he turned anxiously to his wife. "Amy, I haven't had a chance to speak to you! You are worn out. Bates, look at her—she's worn out!"

Bates, lounging in the library doorway, agreed. "Indeed she is; Mrs. Fleming, you ought not to have attempted a dinner party. I believe it's all my fault, because I suggested it."

"It's your fault because you got me off," Fleming said, jocosely. The dulness of the first part of the evening had quite disappeared; he was rather flushed and inclined to laugh buoyantly at everything; but his face was anxious when he looked at his wife. "Amy, you must go right straight to bed!"

"I am going now," she said, pulling and straightening the fingers of her long gloves.

"Good-night, Mr. Bates. I—will copy that poem for you—sometime," she ended faintly.

Her husband put his arm about her to help her upstairs, but she drew away. "No; stay down and smoke with Mr. Bates." Then, as he insisted on coming up with her, she stopped on the first landing, and pushed his arm away, sharply. "Please—*don't?* My head aches. Please—go away."

Thomas Fleming, dumfounded, could not find his wits for a reply before she had slipped away from him, and he heard the door of their bed-room close behind her. He stood blankly upon the stairs for a moment, and then went back to Bates.

"I never knew Amy so upset," he said, stu-pidly. And, indeed, there are few things more bewildering than sudden irrational irritation in a sweet and reasonable soul.

"It's been a hard week for her," Bates ex-plained, easily. But Fleming smoked morosely; he was plainly relieved when his guest said he thought he would go to bed. He suggested, in a perfunctory way, a last visit to the dining-room for a drink of whiskey, and when this was declined, arose with alacrity to conduct the sleepy lawyer to the spare-room door.

"We'll take the eight-fifteen in the morning, Bates," he said; and Bates, yawning, agreed.

Fleming went softly into his own room, and was half disappointed, half relieved, to find his wife lying motionless, with closed eyes. "A good night's sleep will set her up," he thought, tenderly. For himself, he stopped in the process of pulling off his boots, and, shutting his lips hard together, stared at the floor. . . After a while he drew a long breath;—"Well, thank the eternal Powers," he said; and pulled off his boots softly—Amy must have a good night's sleep. Fleming himself had a good night's sleep. That Amy's eyes opened painfully to the dark, when all the house had sunk into silence, of course he did not know. She seemed to be sleeping soundly when he awoke the next morning; and again he crept about, not even daring to kiss her, lest she might be disturbed. Just before he and Bates made a dash for the eight-fifteen, he told Jane to ask Mrs. Fleming to call him up on the telephone when she came downstairs, so he might know how she was.

As for Amy, when she heard the front door close behind the two hurrying men, she got up and sat wearily on the side of the bed.

"Now, I've got time to think," she said. There was a certain relief in the consciousness of silence and of time. She could think all day; she could think until half-past six; how many hours? Ten! Ten hours—in which to take up a new life. Ten hours in which to become acquainted with her husband.

"I have never known him," she said feebly to herself. Well, now she must think. . . . No doubt he had loved her; she was not questioning that. She was dully indifferent to the whole matter of love. The question was, what was she going to do? After restitution was made, what was she going to do? How were they to go on living? Mere restitution—(which must be made on Monday. No, Monday was a holiday; they would have to wait until Tuesday. Oh, how could she bear the delay?) Well, on Tuesday, then, the money would be given to Mr. Hammond. But mere restitution would not change the fact of what he was. She dropped back against her pillows, hiding her face. "I never knew him."

Oh, this would *not* do! She must think.

Poor soul! She had no thoughts but that one. Over and over the words repeated themselves, until her very mind was sore. But she did her best; the habit of common-sense was a great help. She had some coffee, and dressed and went down to the library—recoiling, involuntarily, at the sight of that corner where the books were still in some slight disorder. She even called Jane and bade her bring her duster. When the dusting was done, she told the woman that she would not see any one, all day. "I have a headache," she explained; "don't let any one in." And when Jane left her, she drew her little chair up to the hearth; "Now, I'll think," she said. But her eye caught the flash of sunlight on a crystal ball on the mantelpiece, and it seemed as if her mind broke into a glimmering kaleidoscope: those partridges had been a little overcooked last night . . . the gilt on the narrow, old-fashioned mirror over the mantel was tarnishing . . . the $3,000 had been "borrowed" from one Trust to pay another. . . . Borrowing from Peter to pay Paul. . . . How clear the crystal was. . . Two thefts. . . . Jane must dust those shelves better. . . . Then she started with dismay—she was not thinking! Well, restitution, first of all;—on Tuesday. They would sell a bond, and take some money out of the bank. But after restitution they must go on living. She must try to understand him, to help him to be good, to be patient with him. "But I don't know him," came over and over the dreadful refrain, checked by the instant determination: "Oh, I *must* think!"

So the day passed. She told Jane to telephone her husband that she was up and feeling better; and he sent back some anxious message—she must rest, she must not overdo. He could not, unfortunately, come out on an early train, as he had hoped to do, being detained by some business matters, so he would have to dine in town. He would come out on the eight-thirty. She grasped at the delay with passionate relief; two hours more to think. Then it came over her that she was glad not to see him. What did that mean? She wondered, vaguely, if she had stopped loving him? Not that it made any difference whether she loved him or not. Love had no meaning to her. "Perhaps this is the way people who are dead feel about us," she thought. Then she wondered if she hated him, this stranger, this—thief? No, she did not hate him either. But when respect, upon which love is built, is wrenched away, what happens? There is no love, of course. She thought, vaguely, that she had pitied Mrs. Hammond. And yet she herself did not care, apparently. How strange not to care! Pulling her wedding-ring off, slipping it on, pulling it off again, she said to herself, numbly, that she did not understand why she did not care. However, she could not go into this question of love and hate. Neither mattered. She beat her poor mind back to its task of "thinking."

The long, sunny winter afternoon faded into the dusk; a gleam of sunset broke yellow across the pleasant room, and catching with a glimmering flash on the crystal, melted into a bloom of gray, with the fire, like the spark of an opal, shifting and winking on the hearth.

When Fleming came hurriedly up the garden path to his own door, he had to pull out his latch-key to let himself into the house. This slight happening made him frown; so she was not well enough to come down? He took off his coat and started immediately upstairs, then he caught sight of her in the library, standing motionless, her back to the door, one hand resting on the mantelpiece, the other drooping at her side, the fingers between the pages of a book. He came in quickly, with a gayly derisive laugh.

"You didn't hear me?" Then, as she did not turn, he sobered. "Amy, what is it? Why, Amy! Is there anything the matter? Is anything wrong?" His face was keenly disturbed, and he put his hand on her shoulder to make her look at him, but she lifted it away, gently, still keeping her eyes fastened on the fire.

"Yes. There is something—wrong."

"Amy!" he said, now thoroughly alarmed, "what is the matter? Tell me!"

"I will tell you. Sit down. There: at the library table. I will—show you."

He sat down, blankly, his lower-lip falling open with perplexity. She sighed once, and brushed her hand over her eyes; then came, quietly, away from the hearth, and, going round the table, stood behind him and laid the book down beside him. She pressed it open, and in silence ran her finger down the page.

V

The fire sputtered a little; then everything was still. She had left him, and had gone back to the hearthrug, and stood as before, one hand on the mantelpiece, the other, listless, at her side. The silence was horrible.

Then, suddenly, Thomas Fleming ripped and tore the pages out of the book, and threw them on the logs: the quick leap of the flames shone on his white face and his furious eyes. A minute afterward he spoke. . . . Under that storm of outrageous words she bent and shrunk a little, silently. Once she looked at him with a sort of curiosity. So this was her husband? Then she looked at the fire.

When, choking with anger, he paused, she said, briefly, that she had been hunting for her Commonplace Book, down on that lower shelf, and had found—this.

"What the devil were my diaries doing on your lower shelf? One of those damned women of yours poking—"

"When we moved they were put there. They had been in your old desk in the other house. They were locked up there. I suppose you forgot to lock them up here," she ended, simply.

That next hour left its permanent mark on those two faces; agony and shame were cut into the wincing flesh, as by some mighty die. At first Fleming was all rage; then rage turned into sullenness, and sullenness to explanation and excuse. But as he calmed down, shame, an old, old shame, that he had loathed and lived with for a dozen years, a shame that, except when Amy was too tenderly proud of him, he was sometimes able for days, or even weeks, to forget—this old shame reared its deadly head, and looked out of his abased and shifting eyes. Yet he had his glib excuses and explanations. Amy, in the midst of them, sat down in her little low chair by the fire. She did not speak. She had her handkerchief in her hand, and kept pulling it out on her knee; smoothing it; then folding it; and a minute later, spreading it out again. At last, after a labored statement—how he had only borrowed it; how it had been at a time when he had been horribly pressed; how he had always meant to return it, of course; how, in fact, he had returned it by giving an enormous amount of work for which he had never had any credit, or any money, either! (though, as it happened, he had never been in a position to pay it back in actual cash); after this miserable and futile explanation had been repeated and repeated, he stopped to get his breath; and then, still pulling the hem of her handkerchief straight on her knee, his wife said, in a lifeless voice:

"Need we talk about it any more? On Tuesday we will send it back. (Monday is a holiday. You can't send it until Tuesday.) Then we will never talk about it any more."

"Send what back?"

"The money. To Mr. Hammond!"

"Are you out of your senses?" he said roughly. "You can't send it until Tuesday," she repeated, mechanically.

He brought his fist down violently on the table. "I will never send it back! Never! You are insane! Why, it would be acknowl-edging——"

"It would be confession," she agreed.
"Well! that would be ruin."

"Ruin?"

"Why, if people knew——" he began.

"It is ruin, anyhow," she said, dully. "Don't you see? The only thing left is restitution."

"I can't make what you call—'restitution,' without—ruin; absolute ruin! Do you realize what it would mean to me, in this town, to have it known that I—borrowed from the Trust, and —and had not yet returned it? On the stand, of course, I had to protect myself; and that would be—against me. And it *would* be known. Hammond would never let it be settled privately! He couldn't prosecute me on the old charge; but I suppose he might make a claim of—of perjury. Anyhow, just the publicity would ruin me. And he would make it public. Trust Hammond! Besides, I've given it back ten times over in unpaid-for work to the Estate——" He stopped abruptly. Amy had fainted. . . .

Sunday was a long day of struggle. The immediate hour of violence was over; he was ashamed; and he loved her; and he was frightened. But he was immovable. His hardness was worse than his violence.

"I can not do it, Amy; I will not do it. The thing is done. It's over. It's settled. I'm sorry; I—regret it; nobody regrets it as much as I do. But I will not destroy myself, and destroy you—you, too!—by returning it." Then, sullenly, "Anyway, I don't owe it, morally. I've more than made it up to them."

Monday, the holiday (and holidays had always been such joy to them; a whole day at home together!)—Monday, they struggled to the death.

It was in the afternoon that she suddenly flagged. She had been kneeling beside him, entreating him; and he had been hard and violent and childish by turns; but he would not. And toward dusk there came a dreadful pause. Partly, no doubt, it was because she was exhausted; but it was more than that. It was a sudden blasting consciousness that the man must save or lose his own soul. If she forced him to make restitution, the restitution would not be his, but hers. If she pushed him into honesty, he would still be dishonest. If he preferred the mire, he would be filthy if plucked out against his will and set on clean ground. A prisoner in heaven is in hell! No, he must save himself. She could not save him.

She drew away and looked at him; then she covered her face with her hands. "I am done," she said, faintly.

The suddenness of her capitulation left him open-mouthed. But before he could speak she went away and left him. He heard her slip the bolt of their bedroom door; and then he heard her step overhead. After that all was still.

The afternoon was very long; once he went and walked drearily about the snowy lanes,

103

avoiding passersby as well as he could. But for the most part he sat in the library and tried to read or smoke; but he forgot to turn over the pages, and he had to keep reaching for a match to relight his cigar. He said to himself that his life was over. Amy would leave him, of course; she had said as much. Well, he couldn't help it. Better the misery of a broken home than public shame, and disgrace, and ruin. And he had made restitution (as she called it); he had made it many times over!

It was late at night, as he was saying something like this to himself for the hundredth time, that his wife came back into the room. She stood up in the old place, on the hearthrug. Very gently she told him what she had to say. She did not look at him; her eyes were fixed on the Japanese crystal resting in its jade bowl on the mantelpiece; once she took it up, and turned it over and over in the palm of her hand, looking at it intently as she spoke. But probably she did not even see it.

"I have thought it all out," she began in a low voice; "and I see I was wrong——" He started. "I was wrong. You must save your own soul. I can't do it for you. Oh, I would! but I can't. I shall not ever again insist. Yes, the Kingdom of God must be within you. I never understood that before."

"Amy," he began, but she checked him.

"Please!—I am not through yet. I shall pay

the money back, somehow, sometime. (Oh, wait
—wait; *don't* interrupt me!) Of course, I shall
not betray you. My paying it shall not tell the
truth, because, unless the truth is from you, it
can not help you. It must be your truth, not
mine. But I shall save, and save, and save, and
pay it back—to clear my own soul. For I—I
have lived on that three thousand dollars too,"
she said with a sick look. She put the crystal
back into its bowl. "It will take—a long time,"
she said, faintly.

She stopped, trembling from the effort of so
many calm words. Thomas Fleming, looking
doggedly at the floor, said: "I suppose you'll get
a separation?"

"Get a separation?" she glanced at him for an
instant. "Why, we are separated," she said.
"We can't be any more separated than we are.
I suppose we have never been together. But I
won't leave you, if that is what you mean."

"You'll stay with me?" he burst out; "I thought
you despised me!"

"Why, no," she said, slowly; "I don't think I
despise you. I don't think I do. But of
course—" She looked away, helplessly. "Of
course, I have no respect for you."

"Well," he said, "I'm sorry. But there's nothing I can do about it."

Amy turned, listlessly, as if to go upstairs
again; but he caught her dress.

"You really mean you won't—leave me?"

105

"No, I won't leave you."

"Of course," he said, roughly, "you don't love me; but—" His voice faltered into a sort of question.

She turned sharply from him, hiding her face in her arm, moving blindly, with one hand stretched out to feel her way, toward the door.

"Oh," she said; "oh—I'm afraid—I—"

And at that he broke. . . . Poor, weak Love, poor Love that would have denied itself for very shame; Love brought him to his knees; his arms around her waist, his head against her breast, his tears on her hand.

"Amy! *I will do it. I will give it back.* Oh, Amy, Amy—"

"TO MAKE A HOOSIER HOLIDAY"

BY GEORGE ADE

"TO MAKE A HOOSIER HOLIDAY"

BY GEORGE ADE

IF you will take a map of the State of Indiana and follow with your pencil one of the many railway lines radiating from Indianapolis, you will find, if you are extremely diligent in your search, a black speck marked "Musselwhite." It is not an asterisk, meaning a county seat—simply a speck on the enameled surface. Furthermore, it is one of many specks. A map which shows all of the towns of the Musselwhite kind looks like a platter of caviare—a mere scramble of dark globules, each the same as the others.

As a matter of fact, Musselwhite seemed one of a thousand to the sleepy travelers in the parlor cars. Lying back on their upholstered griddles, slowly baking to a crisp, they would be aroused by a succession of jolts and grinds and would look out with torpid interest at a brindle-colored "depot," a few brick stores ornately faced with cornices of galvanized iron, a straggling row of frame houses, prigged out with scallops and protuberant bay windows, a few alert horses at the

Reprinted, by permission of the author, from Collier's Weekly for December 17, 1904. Copyright, 1904, by P. F. Collier & Son.

hitch-rack and a few somnolent Americans punctuated along the platform. Then the train would laboriously push this panorama into the background and whisk away into the cornfields, and the travelers would never again think of Musselwhite. Certainly they would never think of it as a hotbed of politics, an arena of social strivings, a Mecca for the remote farmhand and a headquarters for religious effort. Yet Musselwhite was all of these—and more.

The town had two wings of the Protestant faith, but they did not always flap in unison. They were united in the single belief that the Catholic congregation at the other end of town was intent on some dark plan to capture the government and blow up the public school system.

The Zion Methodist Church stood across the street from the Campbellite structure. Each had a high wooden steeple and a clangorous bell. Zion Church had an undersized pipe-organ which had to be pumped from behind. The Campbellites had merely an overgrown cottage organ, but they put in a cornet to help out—this in the face of a protest from the conservative element that true religion did not harmonize with any "brass-band trimmings."

In the Campbellite Church the rostrum was movable, and underneath was a baptismal pool wherein the newly converted were publicly immersed. Whenever there was to be a Sunday night "baptizing" at the Campbellite Church, the

"A HOOSIER HOLIDAY"

attendance was overflowing. The Methodists could offer no ceremony to compare with that of a bold descent into the cold plunge, but every winter they had a "protracted meeting," which kept the church lighted and warmed for seven nights in the week. During this "revival" period the Campbellites were in partial eclipse.

It must not be assumed that there was any petty rivalry between the two flocks. It was the strong and healthy competition between two laborers in the vineyard, each striving to pick the larger bunch of grapes. If the Zion Church gave a mush-and-milk sociable, it was only natural that the Campbellites, in their endeavor to retain a hold on the friendly sympathies of Musselwhite, should almost immediately make announcement of a rummage party or an old people's concert. The Campbellites had their Sunday-school in the morning, preceding the regular service, and the Methodists had theirs in the afternoon. The attendance records and missionary collections were zealously compared. Unusual inducements were offered to the growing youth of Musselwhite to memorize the golden text and fight manfully for the large blue card which was the reward for unbroken attendance. In Musselwhite, as in many other communities, there were parents who believed in permitting the children to attend two religious services every Sunday, thereby establishing a good general average for the family, even if the parents remained at

111

home to read the Sunday papers. The children found no fault with this arrangement. The morning Sunday-school was a sort of full-dress rehearsal for the afternoon service, to which the children flocked in confident possession of those hidden meanings of the Scripture which can always be elucidated by a hardware merchant who wears dark clothes once a week.

At Christmas time the "scholars" found themselves in a quandary. Each church had exercises Christmas Eve. A child can not be in two places at the same time, no matter how busy his effort or how earnest his intention. And so it came about that the congregation offering the more spectacular entertainment and the larger portion of mixed candy drew the majority of the lambkins. The rivalry between the Methodists and the Campbellites touched perihelion on Christmas Eve. An ordinary Christmas tree studded with tapers, festooned with popcorn, and heavy with presents no longer satisfied the junior population, for it had been pampered and fed upon novelty. The children demanded a low-comedy Santa Claus in a fur coat. They had to be given star parts in cantatas, or else be permitted to speak "pieces" in costume. One year the Campbellites varied the programme by having a scenic chimney-corner erected back of the pulpit. There was an open fireplace glowing with imitation coals. In front of the fireplace was a row of stockings, some of which were of most mirth-provoking length and capacity, for the sense of humor was rampant in Musselwhite. A murmur of impatient and restless curiosity rather interfered with the recitations and responsive readings which opened the programme. It rose to a tiptoe of eager anticipation when Mr. Eugene Robinson, the Superintendent of the Sunday-school, arose and, after a few felicitous remarks, which called forth hysterical laughter, read a telegram from Kriss Kringle saying that he would arrive in Musselwhite at 8:30 sharp. Almost immediately there was heard the jingle of sleighbells. The older and more sophisticated boys identified the tone as coming from a strand of bells owned by Henry Boardman, who kept the livery barn, but the minds of the younger brood were singularly free from all doubt and questioning. A distinct "Whoa!" was heard, and then the Saint, swaddled in furs and with a most prodigious growth of cotton whiskers, came right out through the fireplace with his pack on his back and asked in a loud voice, "Is this the town of Musselwhite?" His shaggy coat was sifted with snow, in spite of the fact that the night was rather warm and muggy, and his whole appearance tallied so accurately with the pictures in the books that the illusion was most convincing until "Tad" Saulsbury, aged twelve, piped in a loud voice: "I know who it is. It's Jake Francis."

His mother moved swiftly down the aisle and

"churned" him into silence, after which the distribution of presents proceeded with triumphant hilarity.

It was generally conceded that the Campbellite chimney-corner entertainment rather laid over and topped and threw into the shade any other Christmas doings that had been witnessed in Musselwhite. That is why the Methodists were spurred to unusual effort one year later, and that is why "Doc" Silverton, Sam Woodson, and Orville Hufty, as a special committee on arrangements, met in the doctor's office one evening in November to devise ways and means.

"They're goin' to give another chimney-corner show," said "Doc" Silverton. "We've got to do something to offset it. I claim that the Christmas tree is played out. Since they've started shippin' in these evergreen trees from Chicago, a good many people have their own trees right at home. We can't very well take up the chimney-corner idee. It's too much like trailin' along behind the Campbellites and takin' their dust."

"We've got to give 'em something new and different," said Orville Hufty. "I sent and got a book that's supposed to tell how to get up shows for Christmas, but it's all about singin' songs and speakin' pieces, and we know by experience that such things don't ketch the crowd here in Musselwhite."

"I've been thinkin'," said Sam Woodson, very slowly, "that we might do this: Go to the Campbellites and segest that we take turn about in givin' exhibitions. That is, if they hold off this year, we'll give them a clear field next year."

"Not much!" exclaimed "Doc" Silverton, with great decision. "That'd look like a clean back-down. Don't give 'em anything to crow about. Let's beat 'em at their own game. We can do it if you'll help me on a little scheme that I've been layin' awake nights and thinkin' about. Don't laugh when I tell you what it is. It's nothin' more or less than a weddin'."

"You mean to have somebody get married on Christmas Eve?" asked Mr. Hufty, looking at him coldly.

"That's it exactly," replied "Doc" with a grin of enthusiasm.

"What's gettin' married got to do with Christmas?" asked Sam Woodson.

"People get married every day," added Mr. Hufty.

"Not the people that I'm thinkin' about," said "Doc," leaning back and looking at them serenely. "Can you imagine what kind of a crowd we'll have in that church if we advertise that old 'Baz' Leonard is goin' to get married to Miss Wheatley?"

The other two committeemen gazed at "Doc" in sheer amazement, stunned by the audacity of his suggestion. "Baz" Leonard and Miss Wheatley! It took several moments for them to grasp the Napoleonic immensity of the proposition.

"Well, I'll be jiggered!" said Mr. Hufty. "How did you come to think of anything like that?"

"Is 'Baz' goin' to marry her?" asked Sam Woodson.

"He is," replied "Doc," "but he don't know it—yet. I'm bankin' on the fact that he won't overlook a chance to show off in public, and that Miss Wheatley is about due to get married to some one."

"I think you'd be doin' her a favor if you picked out somebody besides 'Baz,'" suggested the cold and unresponsive Woodson.

"'Baz' is the man," said "Doc" firmly. "If we've got a public character in this town it's 'Baz' Leonard. If there's a woman in town that's supposed to be out of the marryin' class, it's Miss Wheatley. Her gettin' married to any one would be about the biggest piece of news you could spring on Musselwhite. But gettin' married to 'Baz' Leonard! Say! They won't have a handful of people at their chimney-corner show. And you can bet they'll never keep Jake Francis over there to play Santa Claus. Any time that old 'Baz' gets married again, Jake'll want to be there to see it."

"I don't see how you're goin' to work it in on a Christmas Eve exhibition," said Woodson, but even as he spoke he chuckled reflectively, and it was evident that the beautiful possibilities of the plan were beginning to ramify his understanding.

"Simplest thing in the world," said "Doc." "We announce that we're goin' to give Miss Wheatley a Christmas present."

"You'd better postpone the show till April 1," suggested Mr. Hufty, and then all three committeemen leaned back in their chairs, exchanged glances, and roared with laughter. It was evident that no vote would be necessary.

"I've thought it all out," continued "Doc." "We can have the regular entertainment, then the distribution of presents. We'll have Santy Claus bring in the marriage license and present it to 'Baz.' Then we'll lead the happy couple to the altar, and after Brother King has done a scientific job of splicin', we'll give them their combination Christmas and weddin' presents. The different Sunday-school classes can chip in and buy presents for them. They'll be glad to do it."

"It sounds all right, but can we talk 'em into it?" asked Mr. Hufty. "'Baz' has fooled around her a little, but I never thought he wanted to marry her."

"I'll guarantee to have him on hand when the time comes," said "Doc" confidently. "I want you two fellows to have the women go after Miss Wheatley. We must take it for granted that they're already engaged. Have the women go

117

over and congratulate her, and then convince her that if she has a church weddin' she'll get a raft of presents. It's the third and last call with her, and I don't think we'll have to use blinkers or a curb bit."

And so, next day, there began the strangest campaign that ever Cupid waged by Proxy. Rumor—strong, persistent, undeniable—had it that "Baz" Leonard and Miss Beulah Wheatley were to become as one, indivisible. "United in the holy bonds of wedlock" is the way it was put by the editor of the "Courier."

Unless you, indulgent reader, have lived in a Musselwhite, you can not fully comprehend how convulsing was the excitement that laid hold upon the whole township when the story went jumping from house to house, across farm lots, over ditches, through the deep woods, until it was gleefully discussed around the lamplight as far away as Antioch and Burdett's Grove. For "Baz" Leonard was a man who had posed in the fierce light of publicity for many years. In Rome he would have been a senator. In Musselwhite he was a constable. As a war veteran, as a member of the Volunteer Fire Department, as a confirmed juror, as custodian of a bass drum, as judge of elections, as something-or-other, he contrived to be where the common run of mortals had to look at him and rather admire his self-possession and dignified bearing. To be in the foreground of activities, to be in some way connected with every event which partook of the ceremonial, this was the one gnawing ambition of Ballantyne Leonard. His front name, by some system of abbreviation known only to small towns, had been condensed to "Baz." His wife had died soon after the war. He lived in a small frame house, more thoroughly covered by mortgage than by paint. A pension and the occasional fee coming to a constable provided him with the essentials of life—tobacco and one or two other items less important. As a factor in the business life of Musselwhite he was a comparative cipher, but at public functions he shone. Take it on the Fourth of July. On a borrowed horse, with a tri-colored sash once around his waist and once over the shoulder, he led the parade. On election nights he read the returns. The job of pumping the organ in the Zion Church he refused because he could not perform his duties in view of the congregation. Every winter, when the Methodist revival had stirred the town to a high-strung fervor, he walked up the main aisle and joined the church, becoming for a few nights the nucleus of a shouting jubilation. Every summer he attended a soldiers' reunion, drank to the memory of blood-stained battlefields, and was let out of the church as a backslider. If a traveling magician or hypnotist requested "some one from the audience to kindly step upon the stage," "Baz" was always the first to respond. The happiness of his life came from now and then being on a pedestal. "Doc" Silverton knew what he was talking about when he said that on Christmas Eve he would have his man on hand, ready to be married.

As for Miss Beulah Wheatley, she was a small, prim, and exceedingly antique maiden lady who looked out at the world through a pair of bull's-eye spectacles. Those whose memories extended back far enough testified that, as a girl, she had been "not bad lookin'," and they could account for her having been marooned all these years only on the cruel theory that some marry and some don't. Miss Wheatley was a pocket edition of Joan of Arc when it came to church activities, her efforts being concentrated on foreign missionary work. She was a landmark of Zion. "Doc" Silverton once calculated that she had embroidered twenty-seven pairs of slippers for the coming and going preachers. It was known that she owned the house in which she lived, and it was vaguely rumored that she had money invested. In Musselwhite, fitting about like a lonesome and unmated bird among the satisfied and well-fed domestic pigeons, she was a pathetic joke. People respected her because she was pious and a good housekeeper, but likewise they poked fun at her, for the "old maid" is always a fair target.

No two people in Musselwhite were more surprised by the announced engagement than Mr. "Baz" Leonard and Miss Beulah Wheatley.

"A HOOSIER HOLIDAY"

"Baz" met the first congratulations with good nature, his only sensation being one of gratification that the public should be interested in his private affairs. Later on, when his denials were pooh-poohed into silence, and he was given positive proof that Miss Wheatley had been up to Babcock's store, picking out dress goods, he became alarmed. Even this alarm was tempered by the joy of being the most-talked-about man in Musselwhite, and "Doc" Silverton never lost faith. At the first opportunity he called "Baz" into the office and gave him a long and violent handshaking. It's somethin' you ought to have done years ago, 'Baz,' " he said, leading his visitor over to an operating chair. "She's a fine woman, and she's got a little property, and I don't see that that you could do better."

"I'd like to know how them reports got started," said "Baz." "I ain't seen Miss Wheatley for goin' on six weeks, and when I did see her we didn't talk about nothin' except them Plymouth Rock chickens she bought from——"

"That's all right, 'Baz,' " said "Doc," patting him on the shoulder. "You kept it quiet as long as you could, but Miss Wheatley's a woman, you know, and she was so proud of gettin' you away from all these widows around town, you can't blame her for braggin' a little. Now that it's all settled, we're going to give you the biggest weddin' that was ever seen in this neck of the woods."

Thereupon he outlined the plans for Christmas

121

Eve, minimizing the fact that Miss Wheatley would be a party to the exercises, and enlarging upon the glory that would come to the groom. He told how the organ would thunder, how the church would be jammed, how the infant class would strew flowers in the pathway of the hero, and "Baz," listening, was lost.

In the meantime Mrs. Woodson and Mrs. Hufty had been working on Miss Wheatley. They did not falsify to her, but they led her to believe that Mr. Leonard had said many things that were really said by "Doc" Silverton, and they did it in such a way that the feminine conscience did not suffer a single pang. Miss Wheatley gathered, from the nature of their conversation, that they were the emissaries of the would-be groom. Certainly their assurances were emphatic, and she, as if in a dream, permitted herself to be measured for a wedding gown.

And so Miss Wheatley and "Baz" Leonard were engaged, and neither had spoken to the other a word that was even remotely suggestive of matrimony. "Doc" Silverton, past-master at politics and all manner of deep scheming, "clinched" the matter by giving a supper at the Commercial Hotel. "Baz" was present and Miss Wheatley was present and many witnesses were present. When the pie had been served, "Doc" arose and made a speech of congratulation to the couple. He referred to the undying splendor of Mr. Leonard's war record, his long and honorable career as a public servant, and the high esteem in which he was held by the beautiful little city of Musselwhite. It was meet and proper, said "Doc," that such a man should choose for his companion and helpmate an estimable lady whose light had never been hidden under a bushel, etc.

"Baz" and Miss Wheatley looked at each other across the celery tops, bewildered, but lacking the moral courage to arise and protest. They were being carried along on a wave of popular enthusiasm. It seemed exhilarating to Miss Wheatley. "Baz" wore an air of melancholy doubt, especially after the supper at the Commercial Hotel, when he had been given the privilege of taking a long, hard, and critical look at Miss Wheatley in her best clothes.

Word came to the committee that the groom was weakening. "Baz" had been meditating and gazing upon two pictures. One was pleasant— he at the church with a yellow rose in his coat and hundreds of people looking at him. The other was a long-drawn vista of straight and narrow matrimony under the supervision of a small but determined woman.

"I guess we'll have to call it off," he said, as he met "Doc" Silverton in front of the post-office, and he looked across the street in a guilty and shamefaced manner.

"You can't call it off," said "Doc." "You've

announced your engagement in the presence of witnesses and we've fixed up the whole programme."

"I didn't announce it—you did."

"Well, you were present, and silence gives consent. If you try to back out now she can sue you for breach of promise."

"What'll she git?"

"I'm surprised at you, 'Baz'—after all that your friends have done for you in this thing."

"Baz" studied a display of Christmas goods in a window and rubbed his chin reflectively. Finally he said, "I ain't got any clothes that's fit to wear."

"Doc" hesitated. The committee had not undertaken to outfit the bridegroom. But he knew that the failure of his pet enterprise would fill the town with Campbellite hilarity, so he said, "We'll see that you get a new suit."

Christmas Eve came. It found Musselwhite keyed up to the highest pitch of glad expectation. Every aspiring comic in the town had exhausted his stock of inventive humor in thinking up presents to give to "Baz" and Miss Wheatley. From cardboard mottoes of satirical character to a nickel-plated kitchen stove, the gifts, large and small, were waiting behind the pulpit of the Zion Church. As many people as could elbow their way into the seats and aisles and corners of the church were waiting. Miss Wheatley, all in white, with smelling salts, also six married women to give her courage, waited in the pastor's study. And down the street, in a small frame house, a grizzled veteran, who had faced death on many fields of carnage, lay back on his bed and told a despairing committee that he was ill, even to the point of death, and that there could be no wedding. He had put on the new black suit. The black bow tie had been carefully balanced by Sam Woodson. "Baz," with the dull horror of impending calamity numbing his resolution, had even combed his hair, and then, when Mr. Hufty looked at his watch and said, "It's about time to start," "Baz" had been stricken.

"Where does it seem to hurt you?" asked Sam Woodson.

"All over," said "Baz," looking steadfastly at the ceiling. "I'm as weak as a kitten."

"Your pulse is all right," said "Doc" Silverton," "and you've got a good color. Was Freeman Wheatley over to see you to-day?"

"Baz" rolled over and looked at the wall, and then answered hesitatingly, "Yes, I seen him for a little while."

"What did he say to you?"

"He said she didn't have as much property as most people think, and that no livin' man could get along with her."

"I thought you was slick enough to see through Freeman Wheatley," said Mr. Hufty. "He wants to sidetrack this thing so he'll come into her property."

"This is no time for foolin'," said "Doc" Silverton, arising and rolling up his sleeves. "There's nothin' the matter with 'Baz' except he's a little overheated by the pleasure of this gladsome occasion. I'll bleed him and cool him off a little and he'll be all O. K."

Saying which he produced a pocket surgical case and took out a long, glittering knife.

"Don't you go to cuttin' into me," said "Baz," sitting up in the bed.

"Then you quit this tomfoolin' and come along with us," said "Doc" sternly. "We ain't got a minute to spare."

"Baz" thereupon showed immediate improvement. With a deep sigh he stood up and they bundled him into his overcoat.

The moonlit street was quite deserted. It seemed that every one in town was waiting at the church. "Doc" Silverton walked ahead with the silent victim. Behind, Mr. Hufty and Sam Woodson executed quiet dance steps in the snow, indicative of their joy.

In front of the Gridley house, "Baz" stopped. "I need a drink of water," he said. "I think it'd brace me up."

"You can get one at the church," said "Doc." "I'd rather step in to the Gridley well here. It's the best water in town."

The committee waited at the front gate. "Baz" disappeared around the corner of the house and they heard the dry clanking of the

126

iron pump and the splatter of water, and then there was silence and a pause, but no "Baz" appeared.

"Mebbe he's slipped out the back way," suggested Mr. Hufty in a frightened whisper, and the committee ran for the pump. The Gridley back yard lay quiet in the moonlight and there was neither sound nor sight of bridegroom.

"He couldn't get away so soon," said "Doc."

"I don't see any tracks in the snow."

"D'you s'pose——" began Sam Woodson, looking upward, and then he pointed to where Mr. "Baz" Leonard sat in the high crotch of a cherry tree.

"This is a put-up job," said Mr. Leonard.

"I'm just gettin' on to it."

"'Baz,' you're actin' like a child," began Mr. Hufty. "Come on, now; they're waitin' for you."

"Let him stay up there and freeze," said "Doc." "I'm done with him. I didn't think an old soldier would be afraid to face a crowd of people."

"I ain't afraid," said "Baz," shifting his position. "I've had the cards stacked on me, that's all."

"Go over to the church, Sam," said "Doc" Silverton, after an awkward pause. "Tell the whole crowd to come over here and take a look at the bridegroom that's gone to roost like a chicken." Sam started.

127

"Don't you bring no crowd here," shouted "Baz" as he began to descend. "This is the lowest trick that was ever put up on a human bein'."

Thus ended his resistance. They led him like a lamb to the slaughter.

People in Musselwhite said it was the making of "Baz" Leonard. For years after that he walked a chalk mark and his habits seemed to improve, for he was afraid to attend a soldiers' reunion. He should have been happy, for he lived in a cottage that was spick and span, and had a capable woman to tell him what to do at every turn. And yet there were times when, at Sunday morning services, he would look across at "Doc" Silverton with a reproachful light in his eyes, as if to say, "You did this to me."

A CHRISTMAS PRESENT FOR A LADY

BY MYRA KELLY

A CHRISTMAS PRESENT FOR A LADY

BY MYRA KELLY

IT was the week before Christmas, and the First Reader Class, in a lower East Side school, had, almost to a man, decided on the gifts to be lavished on "Teacher." She was quite unprepared for any such observance on the part of her small adherents, for her first study of the roll book had shown her that its numerous Jacobs, Isidores, and Rachels belonged to a class to which Christmas Day was much as other days. And so she went serenely on her way, all unconscious of the swift and strict relation between her manner and her chances. She was, for instance, the only person in the room who did not know that her criticism of Isidore Belchatosky's hands and face cost her a tall "three for ten cents" candlestick and a plump box of candy. But Morris Mogilewsky, whose love for Teacher was far greater than the combined loves of all the other children, had as yet no present to bestow. That his "kind feeling" should be without proof when the lesser loves of Isidore Wishnewsky, Sadie Gonorowsky, and Bertha

131

Binderwitz were taking the tangible but surprising forms which were daily exhibited to his confidential gaze was more than he could bear. The knowledge saddened all his hours, and was the more maddening because it could in no wise be shared by Teacher, who noticed his altered bearing and tried with all sorts of artful beguilements to make him happy and at ease. But her efforts served only to increase his unhappiness and his love. And he loved her! Oh, how he loved her! Since first his dreading eyes had clung for a breath's space to her "like man's shoes" and had then crept timidly upward past a black skirt, a "from silk" apron, a red "jumper," and "from gold" chain to her "light face," she had been mistress of his heart of hearts. That was more than three months ago. How well he remembered the day!

His mother had washed him horribly, and had taken him into the big red schoolhouse, so familiar from the outside, but so full of unknown terrors within. After his dusty little shoes had stumbled over the threshold he had passed from ordeal to ordeal until, at last, he was torn in mute and white-faced despair from his mother's skirts.

He was then dragged through long halls and up tall stairs by a large boy, who spoke to him disdainfully as "greenie," and cautioned him as to the laying down softly and taking up gently of those poor, dusty shoes, so that his spirit was quite broken and his nerves were all unstrung when he was pushed into a room full of bright sunshine and of children who laughed at his frightened little face. The sunshine smote his timid eyes, the laughter smote his timid heart, and he turned to flee. But the door was shut, the large boy gone, and despair took him for its own.

Down upon the floor he dropped, and wailed, and wept, and kicked. It was then that he heard, for the first time, the voice which now he loved. A hand was forced between his aching body and the floor, and the voice said:

"Why, my dear little chap, you mustn't cry like that. What's the matter?"

The hand was gentle and the question kind, and these, combined with a faint perfume suggestive of drug stores and barber shops—but nicer than either—made him uncover his hot little face. Kneeling beside him was a lady, and he forced his eyes to that perilous ascent; from shoes to skirt, from skirt to jumper, from jumper to face, they trailed in dread uncertainty, but at the face they stopped—they had found rest.

Morris allowed himself to be gathered into the lady's arms and held upon her knee, and when his sobs no longer rent the very foundations of his pink and wide-spread tie, he answered her question in a voice as soft as his eyes, and as gently sad.

"I ain't so big, and I don't know where is my mama."

So, having cast his troubles on the shoulders of the lady, he had added his throbbing head to the burden, and from that safe retreat had enjoyed his first day at school immensely.

Thereafter he had been the first to arrive every morning, and the last to leave every afternoon; and under the care of Teacher, his liege lady, he had grown in wisdom and love and happiness, but the greatest of these was love. And now, when the other boys and girls were planning surprises and gifts of price for Teacher, his hands were as empty as his heart was full. Appeal to his mother met with denial prompt and energetic.

"For what you go and make, over Christmas, presents? You ain't no Krisht; you should better have no kind feelings over Krishts, neither; your papa could to have a mad."

"Teacher ain't no Krisht," said Morris stoutly; "all the other fellows buys her presents, und I'm loving mit her; it's polite I gives her presents the while I'm got such a kind feeling over her."

"Well, we ain't got no money for buy nothing," said Mrs. Mogilewsky sadly. "No money, und your papa, he has all times a scare he shouldn't to get no more, the while the boss"— and here followed incomprehensible, but depressing, financial details, until the end of the interview found Morris and his mother sobbing and rocking in one another's arms. So Morris was

A CHRISTMAS PRESENT

helpless, his mother poor, and Teacher all unknowing.

.   .   .   .   .   .

And now the great day, the Friday before Christmas, has come, and the school is, for the first half hour, quite mad. Doors open suddenly and softly to admit small persons, clad in wondrous ways and bearing wondrous parcels. Room 18, generally so placid and so peaceful, is a howling wilderness full of brightly colored, quickly changing groups of children, all whispering, all gurgling, and all hiding queer bundles. A new-comer invariably causes a diversion; the assembled multitude, athirst for novelty, falls upon him and clamors for a glimpse of his bundle and a statement of its price.

Teacher watches in dumb amaze. What can be the matter with the children? They can't have guessed that the shrouded something in the corner is a Christmas tree? What makes them behave so queerly, and why do they look so strange? They seem to have grown stout in a single night, and Teacher, as she notes this, marvels greatly. The explanation is simple, though it comes in alarming form. The sounds of revelry are pierced by a long, shrill yell, and a pair of agitated legs spring suddenly into view between two desks. Teacher, rushing to the rescue, notes that the legs form the unsteady stem of an upturned mushroom of brown flannel and green braid, which she recognizes as the outward seem-

135

ing of her cherished Bertha Binderwitz; and yet, when the desks are forced to disgorge their prey, the legs restored to their normal position are found to support a fat child—and Bertha was best described as "skinny"—in a dress of the Stuart tartan tastefully trimmed with purple. Investigation proves that Bertha's accumulative taste in dress is an established custom. In nearly all cases the glory of holiday attire is hung upon the solid foundation of every-day clothes as bunting is hung upon a building. The habit is economical of time, and produces a charming embonpoint.

Teacher, too, is more beautiful than ever. Her dress is blue, and "very long down, like a lady," with bands of silk and scraps of lace distributed with the eye of art. In her hair she wears a bow of what Sadie Gonorowsky, whose father "works by fancy goods," describes as "black from plush ribbon—costs ten cents."

Isidore Belchatosky, relenting, is the first to lay tribute before Teacher. He comes forward with a sweet smile and a tall candlestick—the candy has gone to its long home—and Teacher for a moment can not be made to understand that all that length of bluish-white china is really hers "for keeps."

"It's to-morrow holiday," Isidore assures her; "and we gives you presents, the while we have a kind feeling. Candlesticks could to cost twenty-five cents."

A CHRISTMAS PRESENT

"It's a lie. Three for ten," says a voice in the background, but Teacher hastens to respond to Isidore's test of her credulity:

"Indeed, they could. This candlestick could have cost fifty cents, and it's just what I want. It is very good of you to bring me a present."

"You're welcome," says Isidore, retiring; and then the ice being broken, the First Reader Class in a body rises to cast its gifts on Teacher's desk, and its arms round Teacher's neck.

Nathan Horowitz presents a small cup and saucer; Isidore Applebaum bestows a large calendar for the year before last; Sadie Gonorowsky brings a basket containing a bottle of perfume, a thimble, and a bright silk handkerchief; Sarah Schodsky offers a penwiper and a yellow celluloid collar-button, and Eva Kidansky gives an elaborate nasal douche, under the pleasing delusion that it is an atomizer.

Once more sounds of grief reach Teacher's ears. Rushing again to the rescue, she throws open the door and comes upon woe personified. Eva Gonorowsky, her hair in wildest disarray, her stocking fouled, ungartered, and down-gyved to her ankle, appears before her teacher. She bears all the marks of Hamlet's excitement, and many more, including a tear-stained little face and a gilt saucer clasped to a panting breast.

"Eva, my dearest Eva, what's happened to you *now?*" asks Teacher, for the list of ill chances which have befallen this one of her charges is very long. And Eva wails forth that a boy, **a** very big boy, had stolen her golden cup "what I had for you by present," and has left her only the saucer and her undying love to bestow.

Before Eva's sobs have quite yielded to Teacher's arts, Jacob Spitsky presses forward with a tortoise-shell comb of terrifying aspect and hungry teeth, and an air showing forth a determination to adjust it in its destined place. Teacher meekly bows her head; Jacob forces his offering into her long-suffering hair, and then retires with the information, "Costs fifteen cents, Teacher," and the courteous phrase—by etiquette prescribed—"Wish you health to wear it."

Here a big boy, a very big boy, enters hastily. He does not belong to Room 18, but he has long known Teacher. He has brought her a present; he wishes her a merry Christmas. The present, when produced, proves to be a pretty gold cup, and Eva Gonorowsky, with renewed emotion, recognizes the boy as her assailant and the cup as her property. Teacher is dreadfully embarrassed; the boy not at all so. His policy is simple and entire denial, and in this he perseveres, even after Eva's saucer has unmistakably proclaimed its relationship to the cup.

Meanwhile the rush of presentation goes steadily on. Other cups and saucers come in wild profusion. The desk is covered with them, and their wrappings of purple tissue paper require a monitor's whole attention. The soap, too, becomes urgently perceptible. It is of all sizes, shapes, and colors, but of uniform and dreadful power of perfume. No other teacher has so many helps to the toilet. None other is so beloved.

Teacher's aspect is quite changed, and the "blue long down like a lady dress" is almost hidden by the offerings she has received. Jacob's comb has two massive and bejeweled rivals in the "softy hair." The front of the dress, where aching or despondent heads are wont to rest, is glittering with campaign buttons of American celebrities, beginning with James G. Blaine and extending into modern history as far as Patrick Divver, Admiral Dewey, and Captain Dreyfus. Outside the blue belt is a white one, nearly clean, and bearing in "sure 'nough golden words" the curt, but stirring, invitation, "Remember the Maine." Around the neck are three chaplets of beads, wrought by chubby fingers and embodying much love, while the waist-line is further adorned by tiny and beribboned aprons. Truly, it is a day of triumph.

When the waste-paper basket has been twice filled with wrappings and twice emptied; when order is emerging out of chaos; when the Christmas tree has been disclosed and its treasures distributed, a timid hand is laid on Teacher's knee and a plaintive voice whispers, "Say, Teacher, I got something for you"; and Teacher turns quickly to see Morris, her dearest boy charge, with his poor little body showing quite plainly between his shirtwaist buttons and through the gashes he calls pockets. This is his ordinary costume, and the funds of the house of Mogilewsky are evidently unequal to an outer layer of finery.

"Now, Morris, dear," says Teacher, "you shouldn't have troubled to get me a present; you know you and I are such goods friends that—"

"Teacher, yis, ma'am," Morris interrupts, in a bewitching rising inflection of his soft and plaintive voice; "I know you got a kind feeling by me, and I couldn't to tell even how I'm got a kind feeling by you. Only it's about that kind feeling I should give you a present. I didn't"—with a glance at the crowded desk—"I didn't to have no soap nor no perfumery, and my mama, she couldn't to buy none by the store; but, Teacher, I'm got something awful nice for you by present."

"And what is it, deary?" asks the already rich and gifted young person. "What is my new present?"

"Teacher, it's like this: I don't know; I ain't so big like I could to know"—and, truly, God pity him! he is passing small—"It ain't for boys —it's for ladies. Over yesterday on the night comes my papa on my house, and he gives my mama the present. Sooner she looks on it, sooner she has a awful glad; in her eye stands tears, und she says, like that—out of Jewish—'Thanks,' un' she kisses my papa a kiss. Und my papa, how he

A CHRISTMAS PRESENT

is polite! he says—out of Jewish, too—'You're welcome, all right,' un' he kisses my mama a kiss. So my mama, she sets and looks on the present, und all the time she looks she has a glad over it. Und I didn't to have no soap, so you could to have the present."

"But did your mother say I might?"

"Teacher, no ma'am; she didn't say like that un' she didn't to say *not* like that. She didn't to know. But it's for ladies, un' I didn't to have no soap. You could to look on it. It ain't for boys."

And here Morris opens a hot little hand and discloses a tightly-folded pinkish paper. As Teacher reads it he watches her with eager, furtive eyes, dry and bright, until hers grow suddenly moist, when his promptly follow suit. As she looks down at him, he makes his moan once more:

"It's for ladies, und I didn't to have no soap."

"But, Morris, dear," cries Teacher unsteadily, laughing a little, and yet not far from tears, "this is ever so much nicer than soap—a thousand times better than perfume; and you're quite right, it is for ladies, and I never had one in all my life before. I am so very thankful."

"You're welcome, all right. That's how my papa says; it's polite," says Morris proudly. And proudly he takes his place among the very little boys, and loudly he joins in the ensuing song. For the rest of that exciting day he is a shining point of virtue in a slightly confused class. And at three o'clock he is at Teacher's desk again, carrying on the conversation as if there had been no interruption.

"Und my mama," he says insinuatingly—"she kisses my papa a kiss."

"Well?" says Teacher.

"Well," says Morris, "you ain't never kissed me a kiss, und I seen how you kissed Eva Gonorowsky. I'm loving mit you too. Why don't you never kiss me a kiss?"

"Perhaps," suggests Teacher mischievously, "perhaps it ain't for boys."

But a glance at her "light face," with its crown of surprising combs, reassures him.

"Teacher, yis, ma'am; it's for boys," he cries as he feels her arms about him, and sees that in her eyes, too, "stands tears."

"It's polite you kisses me a kiss over that for ladies' present."

Late that night Teacher sat in her pretty room —for she was, unofficially, a great pampered young person—and reviewed her treasures. She saw that they were very numerous, very touching, very whimsical, and very precious. But above all the rest she cherished a frayed pinkish paper, rather crumpled and a little soiled. For it held the love of a man and woman and a little child, and the magic of a home, for Morris Mogilewsky's Christmas present for ladies was the receipt for a month's rent for a room on the top floor of a Monroe Street tenement.

THE OUTCASTS OF POKER FLAT

BY FRANCIS BRET HARTE

THE OUTCASTS OF POKER FLAT

BY FRANCIS BRET HARTE

AS Mr. John Oakhurst, gambler, stepped into the main street of Poker Flat on the morning of the twenty-third of November, 1850, he was conscious of a change in its moral atmosphere since the preceding night. Two or three men, conversing earnestly together, ceased as he approached, and exchanged significant glances. There was a Sabbath lull in the air, which, in a settlement unused to Sabbath influences, looked ominous.

Mr. Oakhurst's calm, handsome face betrayed small concern of these indications. Whether he was conscious of any predisposing cause, was another question. "I reckon they're after somebody," he reflected; "likely it's me." He returned to his pocket the handkerchief with which he had been whipping away the red dust of Poker Flat from his neat boots, and quietly discharged his mind of any further conjecture.

In point of fact, Poker Flat was "after somebody." It had lately suffered the loss of several thousand dollars, two valuable horses, and a prominent citizen. It was experiencing a spasm of virtuous reaction quite as lawless and ungovernable as any of the acts that had provoked it. A secret committee had determined to rid the town of all improper persons. This was done permanently in regard to two men who were then hanging from the boughs of a sycamore in the gulch, and temporarily in the banishment of certain other objectionable characters. I regret to say that some of these were ladies. It is but due to the sex, however, to state that their impropriety was professional, and it was only in such easily established standards of evil that Poker Flat ventured to sit in judgment.

Mr. Oakhurst was right in supposing that he was included in this category. A few of the committee had urged hanging him as a possible example, and a sure method of reimbursing themselves from his pockets of the sums he had won from them. "It's agin justice," said Jim Wheeler, "to let this yer young man from Roaring Camp—an entire stranger—carry away our money." But a crude sentiment of equality residing in the breasts of those who had been fortunate enough to win from Mr. Oakhurst overruled this narrower local prejudice.

Mr. Oakhurst received his sentence with philosophic calmness, none the less coolly that he was aware of the hesitation of his judges. He was too much of a gambler not to accept Fate. With him life was at best an uncertain game, and he recognized the usual percentage in favor of the dealer.

A body of armed men accompanied the deported wickedness of Poker Flat to the outskirts of the settlement. Besides Mr. Oakhurst, who was known to be a coolly desperate man, and for whose intimidation the armed escort was intended, the expatriated party consisted of a young woman familiarly known as "The Duchess"; another, who had gained the infelicitous title of "Mother Shipton"; and "Uncle Billy," a suspected sluice-robber and confirmed drunkard. The cavalcade provoked no comments from the spectators, nor was any word uttered by the escort. Only, when the gulch which marked the uttermost limit of Poker Flat was reached, the leader spoke briefly and to the point. The exiles were forbidden to return at the peril of their lives.

As the escort disappeared, their pent-up feelings found vent in a few hysterical tears from the Duchess, some bad language from Mother Shipton, and a Parthian volley of expletives from Uncle Billy. The philosophic Oakhurst alone remained still. He listened calmly to Mother Shipton's desire to cut somebody's heart out, to the repeated statements of the Duchess that she would die on the road, and to the alarming oaths that seemed to be bumped out of Uncle Billy as he rode forward. With the easy good humor characteristic of his class, he insisted upon exchanging his own riding-horse, Five Spot, for the sorry mule which the Duchess rode. But even this act did not draw the party into any closer sympathy. The young woman readjusted her somewhat draggled plumes with a feeble, faded coquetry; Mother Shipton eyed the possessor of Five Spot with malevolence, and Uncle Billy included the whole party in one sweeping anathema.

The road to Sandy Bar—a camp that, not having as yet experienced the regenerating influences of Poker Flat, consequently seemed to offer some invitation to the emigrants—lay over a steep mountain range. It was distant a day's severe journey. In that advanced season, the party soon passed out of the moist temperate regions of the foothills into the dry, cold bracing air of the Sierras. The trail was narrow and difficult. At noon the Duchess, rolling out of her saddle upon the ground, declared her intention of going no farther, and the party halted.

The spot was singularly wild and impressive. A wooded amphitheater, surrounded on three sides by precipitous cliffs of naked granite, sloped gently toward the crest of another precipice that overlooked the valley. It was undoubtedly the most suitable spot for a camp, had camping been advisable. But Mr. Oakhurst knew that scarcely half the journey to Sandy Bar was accomplished, and the party were not equipped or provisioned for delay. This fact he pointed out to his companions curtly, with a philosophic commentary on the folly of "throwing up their hand before the game was played out." But they were furnished with liquor, which in this emergency stood them in place of food, fuel, rest, and prescience. In spite of his remonstrances, it was not long before they were more or less under its influence. Uncle Billy passed rapidly from a bellicose state into one of stupor, the Duchess became maudlin, and Mother Shipton snored. Mr. Oakhurst alone remained erect, leaning against a rock, calmly surveying them.

Mr. Oakhurst did not drink. It interfered with a profession which required coolness, impassiveness, and presence of mind, and, in his own language, he "couldn't afford it." As he gazed at his recumbent fellow-exiles, the loneliness begotten of his pariah-trade, his habits of life his very vices, for the first time seriously oppressed him. He bestirred himself in dusting his black clothes, washing his hands and face, and other acts characteristic of his studiously neat habits, and for a moment forgot his annoyance. The thought of deserting his weaker and more pitiable companions never perhaps occurred to him. Yet he could not help feeling the want of that excitement which, singularly enough, was most conducive to that calm equanimity for which he was notorious. He looked at the gloomy walls that rose a thousand feet sheer above the circling pines around him; at the sky, ominously clouded; at the valley below, already deepening into shadow.

149

And, doing so, suddenly he heard his own name called.

A horseman slowly ascended the trail. In the fresh, open face of the newcomer Mr. Oakhurst recognized Tom Simson, otherwise known as "The Innocent" of Sandy Bar. He had met him some months before over a "little game," and had, with perfect equanimity, won the entire fortune —amounting to some forty dollars—of that guileless youth. After the game was finished, Mr. Oakhurst drew the youthful speculator behind the door and thus addressed him: "Tommy, you're a good little man, but you can't gamble worth a cent. Don't try it over again." He then handed him his money back, pushed him gently from the room, and so made a devoted slave of Tom Simson.

There was a remembrance of this in his boyish and enthusiastic greeting of Mr. Oakhurst. He had started, he said, to go to Poker Flat to seek his fortune. "Alone?" No, not exactly alone; in fact—a giggle—he had run away with Piney Woods. Didn't Mr. Oakhurst remember Piney? She that used to wait on the table at the Temperance House? They had been engaged a long time, but old Jake Woods had objected, and so they had run away, and were going to Poker Flat to be married, and here they were. And they were tired out, and how lucky it was they had found a place to camp and company. All this the Innocent delivered rapidly, while Piney

—a stout, comely damsel of fifteen—emerged from behind the pine tree, where she had been blushing unseen, and rode to the side of her lover.

Mr. Oakhurst seldom troubled himself with sentiment, still less with propriety; but he had a vague idea that the situation was not felicitous. He retained, however, his presence of mind sufficiently to kick Uncle Billy, who was about to say something, and Uncle Billy was sober enough to recognize in Mr. Oakhurst's kick a superior power that would not bear trifling. He then endeavored to dissuade Tom Simson from delaying further, but in vain. He even pointed out the fact that there was no provision, nor means of making a camp. But, unluckily, the Innocent met this objection by assuring the party that he was provided with an extra mule loaded with provisions, and by the discovery of a rude attempt at a log-house near the trail. "Piney can stay with Mrs. Oakhurst," said the Innocent, pointing to the Duchess, "and I can shift for myself."

Nothing but Mr. Oakhurst's admonishing foot saved Uncle Billy from bursting into a roar of laughter. As it was, he felt compelled to retire up the canyon until he could recover his gravity. There he confided the joke to the tall pine trees, with many slaps of his leg, contortions of his face, and the usual profanity. But when he returned to the party, he found them seated by a fire—for the air had grown strangely chill and the sky overcast—in apparently amicable conversation. Piney was actually talking in an impulsive, girlish fashion to the Duchess, who was listening with an interest and animation she had not shown for many days. The Innocent was holding forth, apparently with equal effect, to Mr. Oakhurst and Mother Shipton, who was actually relaxing into amiability. "Is this yer a d—d picnic?" said Uncle Billy, with inward scorn, as he surveyed the sylvan group, the glancing fire-light, and the tethered animals in the foreground. Suddenly an idea mingled with the alcoholic fumes that disturbed his brain. It was apparently of a jocular nature, for he felt impelled to slap his leg again and cram his fist into his mouth.

As the shadows crept slowly up the mountain a slight breeze rocked the tops of the pine trees, and moaned through their long and gloomy aisles. The ruined cabin, patched and covered with pine boughs, was set apart for the ladies. As the lovers parted, they unaffectedly exchanged a kiss, so honest and sincere that it might have been heard above the swaying pines. The frail Duchess and the malevolent Mother Shipton were probably too stunned to remark upon this last evidence of simplicity, and so turned without a word to the hut. The fire was replenished, the men lay down before the door, and in a few minutes were asleep.

Mr. Oakhurst was a light sleeper. Toward

morning he awoke benumbed and cold. As he stirred the dying fire, the wind, which was now blowing strongly, brought to his cheek that which caused the blood to leave it—snow!

He started to his feet with the intention of awakening the sleepers, for there was no time to lose. But turning to where Uncle Billy had been lying, he found him gone. A suspicion leaped to his brain and a curse to his lips. He ran to the spot where the mules had been tethered; they were no longer there. The tracks were already rapidly disappearing in the snow.

The momentary excitement brought Mr. Oakhurst back to the fire with his usual calm. He did not waken the sleepers. The Innocent slumbered peacefully, with a smile on his good-humored, freckled face; the virgin Piney slept beside her frailer sisters as sweetly as though attended by celestial guardians, and Mr. Oakhurst, drawing his blanket over his shoulders, stroked his mustachios and waited for the dawn. It came slowly in the whirling mist of snowflakes, that dazzled and confused the eye. What could be seen of the landscape appeared magically changed. He looked over the valley, and summed up the present and future in two words —"Snowed in!"

A careful inventory of the provisions, which, fortunately for the party, had been stored within the hut, and so escaped the felonious fingers of Uncle Billy, disclosed the fact that with care and prudence they might last ten days longer. "That is," said Mr. Oakhurst, *sotto voce* to the Innocent, "if you're willing to board us. If you ain't—and perhaps you'd better not—you can wait till Uncle Billy gets back with provisions." For some occult reason, Mr. Oakhurst could not bring himself to disclose Uncle Billy's rascality, and so offered the hypothesis that he had wandered from the camp and had accidentally stampeded the animals. He dropped a warning to the Duchess and Mother Shipton, who of course knew the facts of their associate's defection. "They'll find out the truth about us *all*, when they find out anything," he added, significantly, "and there's no good frightening them now."

Tom Simson not only put all his worldly store at the disposal of Mr. Oakhurst, but seemed to enjoy the prospect of their enforced seclusion. "We'll have a good camp for a week, and then the snow'll melt, and we'll all go back together." The cheerful gayety of the young man and Mr. Oakhurst's calm infected the others. The Innocent, with the aid of pine boughs, extemporized a thatch for the roofless cabin, and the Duchess directed Piney in the rearrangement of the interior with a taste and tact that opened the blue eyes of that provincial maiden to their fullest extent.

"I reckon now you're used to fine things at Poker Flat," said Piney. The Duchess turned away sharply to conceal something that reddened her cheek through its professional tint, and Mother Shipton requested Piney not to "chatter." But when Mr. Oakhurst returned from a weary search for the trail, he heard the sound of happy laughter echoed from the rocks. He stopped in some alarm, and his thoughts first naturally reverted to the whisky, which he had prudently *cached.* "And yet it don't somehow sound like whisky," said the gambler. It was not until he caught sight of the blazing fire through the still blinding storm: and the group around it, that he settled to the conviction that it was "square fun."

Whether Mr. Oakhurst had *cached* his cards with the whisky as something debarred the free access of the community, I cannot say. It was certain that, in Mother Shipton's words, he "didn't say cards once" during the evening. Haply the time was beguiled by an accordion produced somewhat ostentatiously by Tom Simson, from his pack. Notwithstanding some difficulties attending the manipulation of this instrument, Piney Woods managed to pluck several reluctant melodies from its keys, to an accompaniment by the Innocent on a pair of bone castinets. But the crowning festivity of the evening was reached in a rude camp-meeting hymn, which the lovers, joining hands, sang with great earnestness and vociferation. I fear that a certain defiant tone and Covenanter's swing to its chorus, rather than any devotional quality,

155

caused it speedily to infect the others, who at last joined in the refrain:

> I'm proud to live in the service of the Lord,
> And I'm bound to die in His army.

The pines rocked, the storm eddied and whirled above the miserable group, and the flames of their altar leaped heavenward, as if in token of the vow.

At midnight the storm abated, the rolling clouds parted, and the stars glittered keenly above the sleeping camp. Mr. Oakhurst, whose professional habits had enabled him to live on the smallest possible amount of sleep, in dividing the watch with Tom Simson, somehow managed to take upon himself the greater part of that duty. He excused himself to the Innocent, by saying that he had "often been a week without sleep." "Doing what?" asked Tom. "Poker!" replied Oakhurst, sententiously; "when a man gets a streak of luck—nigger-luck—he don't get tired. The luck gives in first. Luck," continued the gambler, reflectively, "is a mighty queer thing. All you know about it for certain is that it's bound to change. And it's finding out when it's going to change that makes you. We've had a streak of bad luck since we left Poker Flat—you come along, and slap you get into it, too. If you can hold your cards right along you're all right. For," added the gambler, with cheerful irrelevance,

OUTCASTS OF POKER FLAT

The third day came, and the sun, looking through the white-curtained valley, saw the outcasts divide their slowly decreasing store of provisions for the morning meal. It was one of the peculiarities of that mountain climate that its rays diffused a kindly warmth over the wintry landscape, as if in regretful commiseration of the past. But it revealed drift on drift of snow piled high around the hut; a hopeless, uncharted, trackless sea of white lying below the rocky shores to which the castaways still clung. Through the marvelously clear air, the smoke of the pastoral village of Poker Flat rose miles away. Mother Shipton saw it, and from a remote pinnacle of her rocky fastness, hurled in that direction a final malediction. It was her last vituperative attempt, and perhaps for that reason was invested with a certain degree of sublimity. It did her good, she privately informed the Duchess, "Just to go out there and cuss, and see." She then set herself to the task of amusing "the child," as she and the Duchess were pleased to call Piney. Piney was no chicken, but it was a soothing and ingenious theory of the pair thus to account for the fact that she didn't swear and wasn't improper.

When night crept up again through the gorges, the reedy notes of the accordion rose and fell in fitful spasms and long-drawn gasps by

157

the flickering camp-fire. But music failed to fill entirely the aching void left by insufficient food, and a new diversion was proposed by Piney—story-telling. Neither Mr. Oakhurst nor his female companions caring to relate their personal experiences, this plan would have failed, too, but for the Innocent. Some months before he had chanced upon a stray copy of Mr. Pope's ingenious translation of the Iliad. He now proposed to narrate the principal incidents of that poem—having thoroughly mastered the argument and fairly forgotten the words—in the current vernacular of Sandy Bar. And so for the rest of that night the Homeric demigods again walked the earth. Trojan bully and wily Greek wrestled in the winds, and the great pines in the canyon seemed to bow to the wrath of the son of Peleus. Mr. Oakhurst, listened with quiet satisfaction. Most especially was he interested in the fate of "Ash-heels," as the Innocent persisted in denominating the "swift-footed Achilles."

So with small food and much of Homer and the accordion, a week passed over the heads of the outcasts. The sun again forsook them, and again from leaden skies the snowflakes were sifted over the land. Day by day closer around them drew the snowy circle, until at last they looked from their prison over drifted walls of dazzling white, that towered twenty feet above their heads. It became more and more difficult to replenish their fires, even from the fallen trees beside them, now half-hidden in the drifts. And yet no one complained. The lovers turned from the dreary prospect and looked into each other's eyes, and were happy. Mr. Oakhurst settled himself coolly to the losing game before him. The Duchess' more cheerful than she had been, assumed the care of Piney. Only Mother Shipton —once the strongest of the party—seemed to sicken and fade. At midnight on the tenth day she called Oakhurst to her side. "I'm going," she said, in a voice of querulous weakness, "but don't say anything about it. Don't waken the kids. Take the bundle from under my head and open it." Mr. Oakhurst did so. It contained Mother Shipton's rations for the last week, untouched. "Give 'em to the child," she said, pointing to the sleeping Piney.

"You've starved yourself," said the gambler.

"That's what they call it," said the woman, querulously, as she lay down again, and, turning her face to the wall, passed quietly away.

The accordion and the bones were put aside that day, and Homer was forgotten. When the body of Mother Shipton had been committed to the snow, Mr. Oakhurst took the Innocent aside, and showed him a pair of snowshoes, which he had fashioned from the old pack-saddle.

"There's one chance in a hundred to save her yet," he said, pointing to Piney; "but it's there," he added, pointing toward Poker Flat. "If you can reach there in two days she's safe."

"And you?" asked Tom Simson.

"I'll stay here," was the curt reply.

The lovers parted with a long embrace. "You are not going, too?" said the Duchess, as she saw Mr. Oakhurst apparently waiting to accompany him.

"As far as the canyon," he replied. He turned suddenly, and kissed the Duchess, leaving her pallid face aflame, and her trembling limbs rigid with amazement.

Night came, but not Mr. Oakhurst. It brought the storm again and the whirling snow. Then the Duchess, feeding the fire, found that some one had quietly piled beside the hut enough fuel to last a few days longer. The tears rose to her eyes, but she hid them from Piney.

The women slept but little. In the morning, looking into each other's faces, they read their fate. Neither spoke; but Piney, accepting the position of the stronger, drew near and placed her arm around the Duchess's waist. They kept this attitude for the rest of the day. That night the storm reached its greatest fury, and, rending asunder the protecting pines, invaded the very hut.

Toward morning they found themselves unable to feed the fire, which gradually died away. As the embers slowly blackened, the Duchess crept closer to Piney, and broke the silence of many hours:

"Piney, can you pray?"

"No, dear," said Piney, simply.

The Duchess, without knowing exactly why, felt relieved, and, putting her head upon Piney's shoulder, spoke no more. And so reclining, the younger and purer pillowing the head of her soiled sister upon her virgin breast, they fell asleep.

The wind lulled as if it feared to waken them. Feathery drifts of snow, shaken from the long pine boughs, flew like white-winged birds, and settled about them as they slept. The moon through the rifted clouds looked down upon what had been the camp. But all human stain, all trace of earthly travail, was hidden beneath the spotless mantle mercifully flung from above.

They slept all that day and the next, nor did they waken when voices and footsteps broke the silence of the camp. And when pitying fingers brushed the snow from their wan faces, you could scarcely have told from the equal peace that dwelt upon them, which was she that had sinned. Even the Law of Poker Flat recognized this, and turned away, leaving them still locked in each other's arms.

But at the head of the gulch, on one of the largest pine trees, they found the deuce of clubs pinned to the bark with a bowie knife. It bore the following, written in pencil, in a firm hand:

161

♣

BENEATH THIS TREE
LIES THE BODY
OF
JOHN OAKHURST
WHO STRUCK A STREAK OF BAD LUCK
ON THE 23D OF NOVEMBER, 1850,
AND
HANDED IN HIS CHECKS
ON THE 7TH OF DECEMBER, 1850.

♣

And pulseless and cold, with a Derringer by his side and a bullet in his heart, though still calm as in life, beneath the snow lay he who was at once the strongest and yet the weakest of the outcasts of Poker Flat.

PURPLE-EYES

BY JOHN LUTHER LONG

PURPLE-EYES

BY JOHN LUTHER LONG

I—THE FEVER JAPONICA

GARLAND was charmed with his reception. Before he could open his head (in his own perhaps too picturesque phrase) the two girls had buried their delightful noses in the mats, and were bobbing vividly up and down, sibilating honorifics at him in the voice and manner used only to personages. The mother joined them an instant later, making a phalanx; and she was nearly as beautiful, and quite as graceful, as her daughters. So that at one moment he would have presented to him the napes of three pretty necks, and at the next, with a conjurer's quick change, three pairs of eyes that smiled always, and three mouths that did their best (which was very well indeed) to assist the eyes. At first, I say, he was charmed, then a little bewildered, then bewitched. And perhaps it was well that his conversation-book was the only thing about him that spoke Japanese; for Garland's vocabulary, even when it was fairly accurate, had grown indiscreet since coming to Japan.

He perceived, however, by a surreptitious glance at the conversation-book when the napes of the necks were in view, that they were addressing him as "Augustness" and "Excellency," and that the mother was insisting that he should take immediate possession of her "miserable" house and its contents. He wondered dreamily—and he drifted into dreams with the most curious ease —whether the girls would be included.

Finally he began to feel it his duty to be tired of this fawning, as his refluent American democracy insisted upon naming it—though, personally, he liked it—and all the clever pretences of the Japanese. He sat bolt upright and frowned. But the charming kotowing did not in the least abate. He had heard somewhere that the only way to stop this sort of thing short of apoplexy was to compete in it.

He tried to reach the mats with his own nose. It seemed easy, but it was a disaster. There is a trick in·it. He plunged forward helplessly almost into the lap of one of his hostesses. Garland sat up, with their joint assistance, very red in the face, but quite cheerful; for though the mother looked greatly pained, the girls were smiling like two Japanese angels. (The phrase is again Garland's: there are no Japanese angels.) Garland had the instant intelligence to perceive that this had at once stopped the kotowing, and precipitated a piquant intimacy. "I say," said he, idiomatically, "I nearly broke my neck trying to say howdy-do in your way. Now won't you kindly say it in mine, without the least danger to life and limb?"

He held out his hand invitingly, and the one on his right went into debate as to which one to give him. She knew there was some foreign etiquette in the matter.

"In doubt, shake both," said Garland, doing it.

The one on his left emulated her sister to the last particular (the mother had retired for refreshments), but he noticed that the hands she gave him were long and white. He glanced up, and found himself looking into a pair of blue eyes. He followed the forehead to the brassy hair above. Then he began furiously to turn the leaves of the conversation-book. The one on his right laughed a little, and said:

"What you lig as', please?"

Garland closed the book, and stared. He did not ask what he had meant to, because of something he saw in the questioner's face.

"Ah, if you lig more bedder for do so, speak the English," she said, with a quiet flourish that was lost upon Garland.

He flung the conversation-book into a corner. Black-Eyes, as he had mentally named her, in despair of her Japanese name, which was Meadowsweet, smiled ecstatically.

"Ah-h-h! You lig those—those English?"

"Like it? It's heavenly! I say, fancy, if you can—but you can't—depending upon a dictionary for your most sacred sentiments for three months."

Wherein it will be perceived that Garland had learned the whole art of Japanese politeness—gentle prevarication.

"*How* that is nize!" breathed the blue-eyed one, fervently.

Garland turned suddenly upon her, then questioned her with his eyes. She understood.

"Those—thing—you—speak-ing," she barely breathed once more, in explanation.

"Oh!" said Garland. But it meant more than print can express. "Tell me, if you please, what your name is."

It was Miss Purple-Wistaria; but the Japanese of this was quite as impossible as the other.

"Do you mind me calling you Blue-Eyes?" asked Garland. "When it comes to Japanese proper names—I have already taken the liberty of mentally calling your sister Black-Eyes, and if you don't mind—"

"You call those blue-eye?" asked Miss Meadowsweet.

"Why, yes," said Garland. "What do you call them?"

"Purple-eye."

"Well, I like that better, anyhow. It shall be Purple-Eyes."

"She got other already English name," confided Black-Eyes, with the manner for her sister he did not like.

"Oh! What is it?"

"Sarann," laughed the dark one. "Tha' 's jus' joke her fadder. He all times joke upon her." Garland did not quite understand. He decided that he did not wish to, for the blue-eyed one looked very uncomfortable.

"I shall call her Purple-Eyes," he said.

The disagreeableness of the other continued.

"Yaes: tha' 's good name—for her," she added, with an intention that was distinctly odious.

"In America that would be the most beautiful name a man could give a beautiful woman," said Garland, severely.

The dark one looked a bit frightened. The blonde one gave him the merest horizon of her eyes as she raised her head. Gratitude was in them.

"Now, won't you go on, and tell me how you knew me before I opened my blooming head?"

He had again addressed himself to Purple-Eyes, but Black-Eyes answered:

"What is that—open you' head, an' blooming you' head?"

Garland informed her.

"Oh-h-h!" laughed the dark one. "Tha' 's way know yo' 'fore open you' *bloom*-ing head!"

She suddenly reached into the bosom of the kimono of the blue-eyed one, and brought forth a photograph of Garland; whereat Garland got red again, and again the blue-eyed one drooped her head.

"Oh, I say," Garland began, without a very distinct idea of what he was going to say, "Brownie sent you that—aha, ha, ha!"—he had happily drifted into the very thing—"and wrote you that I would arrive with a letter from him; so that you would know me—you know; and of course when I arrived—of course when I arrived—why, of *course*—oh, hang it!"

They both waited breathlessly upon his words.

"*Of* course," echoed Black-Eyes, sympathically—"of course—tha' 's correc', an' tha' 's also —*nize.* Of course—you arrive when you arrive."

Garland wondered whether she was guying him.

"Yes—why, of course,' said he once more, and a laugh *en masse* cleared the air.

Garland, in a panic, was searching his pockets.

"What lot pockets!' sighed Black-Eyes, insidiously desiring to compose his nerves.

"Sixteen," admitted Garland. "I wish they were only one, just now. By Jove, I've lost that letter!"

The graceful mother arrived with the tobacco *bon* (there appeared to be no servant'), and Garland, professing an ignorance which seems problematical after three months in Japan, desired to be initiated into the art and mystery of the Japanese pipe. The tender was made to Purple-Eyes, but Black-Eyes undertook it.

"*So,*" she said, rolling a pellet of the tobacco, and putting it into the pipe; "an' *so,*" as she fearlessly put a live coal upon it with her fingers; "*so*," as she put it to her own lips and sent out a tiny puff; "an'—an'—an' *so!*" as she laughed and put it to his. And yet Garland found himself wishing that the other one had done it, and believing that she could do it better! And this, you perceive, was already perilous business.

It was afternoon when Garland arrived, and the mother's actions, though covered by diplomatic entrances and exits, with a view to impressing him to the contrary, indicated to him that she was cooking. And presently Purple-Eyes got up and lighted the *andon*. Garland, who delighted in her grace of motion, had not yet learned that each movement was the result of much study and the practice of many stoical rules of decorum. However, he rose as far as his knees, and said he must go. A glance of alarm passed between the girls, and both stiffened in consternation.

"Sa-ay—tha' 's not nize for us," accused the dark one, with valor. "Brownie he write unto us that you so kine with him, you give him you' las' pair boots, an' go naked on you' both feet. Tha' 's way we got do you. *But*—account you go'n' go 'way, we can not. Hence we got be always 'shamed 'fore Brownie—an' *aeverybody*. Tha' 's not nize—for us." Garland haᴅ not risen above his knees, and she came hopefully forward. "Please don' go 'way!" She turned to Purple-Eyes in the peremptory way that

171

Garland resented. "Sa-ay—why *you* don' as' him stay among us? Sa-ay—don' you wish?" Garland's eyes followed. Unconsciously they besought her.

"We *lig*—if you stay—among us," said Purple-Eyes, haltingly.

But there was something else—just the timid lifting of an eyelid. Garland answered this with a rift of pleasure which shot across his face.

"Me? *I* lig also if you stay among us—I." But now it was spoken to the mats. There was the edge of a smile visible, nevertheless, and Garland felt the courage it took for this.

"Well, if *you* like," said Garland—he laughed suddenly—"*I* like too."

"Thangs!"

They both said it at once; but some splendid reward passed from Purple-Eyes to Garland.

So presently they had a feast, in which four little tables stood in a circle—one for each. There would have been only three had not Garland insisted that the mother should dine with them. He had not the least idea how fearfully he had disarranged domestic matters, for the mother, of course, instantly did as he requested. And then the three of them served him, and cunningly joined in engaging him while one or the other prepared the viands. But finally it was a very joyous meal; and only when the Osaka beer came on did Garland at all suspect how much out of the ordinary it was for them. They had forgotten to be taught how to open the bottles!

II—THE SHADOW OF THE SHOJI

And he went to sleep that night, when sleep came, on a floor that was as dainty as any bed, in a huge wadded overcoat called a *futon*, on a wooden pillow that rocked and screeched a little (as if afraid to screech more) when he turned. An *andon* burned dimly behind a screen, and he was aware of the slumberous aroma Japonica, as he characterized it. But he could not sleep—of course not. For, less than six feet away, behind the translucent walls of paper, he could hear the melodious dithyrambics of the three voices. He could catch a sleepy word now and then, which he knew came from the blue-eyed one. They were much fewer than those of the other two. Some vague picture of those eyes, patiently sad, as he had conceived them, kept itself between him and sleep, until finally it was sudden morning, and the splendid light of Japan, subdued by the *shoji*, was shining in his face.

He lay indolently awake for a long time. Presently a noise not much greater than the alighting of a fly upon a stretched screen drew his attention. He perceived a dampened finger slowly working against the other side of the *shoji*, until presently the paper parted, and the finger came through. It was very pink at the tip. Slowly it reamed the hole larger, then disappeared, to be replaced by an eye. And the eye was blue. Garland nearly laughed aloud, until he remembered that he was the objective of the eye. Then unconsciously he arranged his hair a little, and began to pose. But the humor of it came down upon him again, and he laughed. The eyes instantly disappeared, and he could see the shadow of its owner gliding away, and he could see the shadow of its owner gliding away. **In a panic of regret, Garland called out:**

"Don't go, Purple-Eyes!"

The shadow hesitated, and then returned.

"How you know tha'a's Purple-Eyes?"

"By her own confession—now."

Her pretty laugh sifted through the *shoji*.

"You want me come unto you?" asked the voice beyond. "That''s what I dunno."

Garland was (in his own phrase again) quite paralyzed. He might have thought, but he did not, that she was only tendering the offices of the servant they did not have; but he called out, with a mixture of bravado and trembling which alarmed them both:

"Yes; come in!"

The damaged *shoji* slid haltingly aside, and she entered very slowly and softly, and he thought of the pictures of the returning Sun-Goddess as she came through the opening and down the burst of light it let in. As she prostrated herself Garland noticed that her hair had been newly dressed (an operation of several hours), and that she wore a dainty blue kimono, too gay for any but a geisha to wear. But it became her royally.

"You look more than ever like a picture on a fan," greeted Garland, with even more admiration in his eyes than in his voice.

Instead of being pleased, as any other Japanese girl would have been, Purple-Eyes slowly shook her head.

"Alas! you naever see no picture on fan lig unto me."

"But I have,' insisted Garland.

She shook her head again.

"Well, then, if not, why not?"

"They got not those purple eye—an' pink face —an' flaming hair——,"

She sighed, and looked askance at Garland. He seemed fully to agree with her. She changed her tone to one of resigned solicitude and ceremony.

"You sleeping well—all those night?"

"Well, by the great Jehovah and the Continental Congress, if I were a Japanese artist, that is the kind of eyes and face and hair they should all have! Yes, sir!—every blamed one of them!"

The girl caught her breath, and something flamed up her face and lighted her splendid eyes anew. She dared to look at him. It had all sounded quite true. Wistfully she dissembled—this at least was truly Japanese.

"You sleeping well all"—she lost her purpose for a moment—"all those night—all?"

"Blue eyes for me, every day in the week."

"You sleeping well?" Joy was all too plainly in her voice now—irrepressible joy.

He laughed, and caught her hands rapturously. She did not deny him, and he kissed them.

"Oh, you are delightful!" said he.

"Me? *I* don' sleep—moach."

"You look as fresh as new porcelain."

"Yaes; I been fix up."

She consciously let him look her over.

"No; I didn't sleep at first. I was listening to your voice," Garland confessed, quite without reservation.

The girl was confused a little.

"You don' lig be annoy with those voice?"

"Why, it is divine!"

A white shaft of fear crossed her face.

"Tha'.'s—jus'—fun—I egspeg?"

"Tha'.'s ver' earnest," he gayly mocked.

He was pleasing her now. She even went with his mood a little way. Joy was such a beautiful and tempting and elusive thing!

"Lig goddess, mebby?"

Garland nodded seriously.

"Tha'.'s *nize*—for *me*."

"An' for *me*"—in quite her own manner.

"But not the goddesses?"

They laughed together, and she drew confidently a little closer to him.

PURPLE-EYES

"Listen; I go'n' tell you a thing. You *not* in fun—*not?*"

"I mean every word," declared Garland, "and more than I have words to mean."

"An' you lig be tell?"

"That is what I am waiting so impatiently for —to be tell."

"Tha' 's nize. Eijinsan 'most always fun. Nobody but you aever lig those hair an' eye. Aeverybody hate me. *Why?* Account they say I b'long pink-face people. Account my fadder he sei yo jin—a west-ocean mans. *I* di'n' do so unto those hair an' eye! I can *not* help. *Me?* When I see you got those purple eye lig unto me, an' also those yellow hairs, an' all pink in the face, I thing mebby you go'n' lig me liddle— lig I was brodder an' fadder with you. Also, I thing mebby you go'n' take me away with you—beyond those west-ocean, where pink-face people live. *Me?* Don' you thing those pink-face people lig me liddle if I come unto them?"

"God bless you—yes," said Garland, with something suspiciously tender in voice and eyes. He still had her hands, delighting in them, caressing them. The girl's face was irradiated. She poured out all her soul for him.

"*Me?* Listen 'nother time. Before I know you' eyes purple an' you' hair yellow lig unto me, I lig you? *Me?* Sa-ay—I lig jus' your *picture!*" She laughed, confused, and shifted a

177

little closer. "You don' hate me account I do-ing those?"

"No," said Garland, guiltily—"no, I don't hate you."

"Sa-ay—you go'n' take me at those pink-face people?"

Garland was silent.

"If you don', I got go myself. Me? I got go!" Garland nodded, and she understood him to have assented. This was wrong. But her joy was superb, and Garland had a very soft heart.

"Oh—how that is nize! Me? I got so. I dunno—all times seem lig I b'long 'cross west-ocean. Seem lig I different from aeverybody else. Me? I got have somebody lig me—some-body touch me—hole my hands—so—so—so!" She illustrated fervidly.

Garland, alarmed at her dynamic emotion, re-leased them. She returned them to him.

"But—nobody don' wish. Others—Japan people—they don' lig be ligued. But me? I got be—else I got pain in my heart an' am ill. You aever have those pain at you' heart—lig you all times falling down—down—down? Tha' 's mos' tarrible. Tha' 's lone-some-ness. Me? I thing I go'n' die sometime account that. Tha' 's lone-some-ness to cross west-ocean to pink-face peo-ple. Yaes; tha' 's why I got do those. Oku-Sama—tha' 's my modder—she saying 'most all times, 'Jus' lig pink-face people. Always got be lig by 'nother—touch by 'nother—speak sof' by 'nother.' An' tha' 's *you*—yaes! You lig me, an' you touch me, an' you speak sof' unto me the ver' first time I seeing you. *Me?* I *know*, those time I first seeing you, that you don' hate me ac-count I got those pink face upon me."

"No," admitted Garland, seriously.

"*How* that is nize! It make something rest—go 'sleep inside me. I got that peace. Jus' when you touch my hand at first I got some happiness. But *now*—I got that peace."

She began regretfully to detach herself. Gar-land detained her. She was very dainty and very confiding—very wise. She had uncon-sciously got very close to him. And Garland had vanquished his alarm of her.

"*Me?* I don' wish; but I got git you some-things eat. Soon you starve. I *got*."

But Garland would not let her go—and she was a willing captive, though she dissembled an urgent necessity.

"Where is Black-Eyes—and your mother?" asked Garland.

The girl seemed reluctant, but told him that they all worked in the neighboring silk-mill, the pulsations of which he had heard in the night.

"Never mind. I'd rather famish," said the im-pulsive Garland, with a strange remorse. "Will you assist?"

"Yaes," laughed the girl. "*Me?* I been fam-ish—many times."

"Heavens!" breathed Garland, inventorying

179

all her daintiness once more. "How much do your mother and sister earn?"

The girl seemed quite indifferent as to this.

"Sometime fi' sen; sometime ten—fifteen; one times, twenty-two."

"And you?"

"Me? Oh, jus' liddle."

She earned more than the other two.

"And what does it cost you to live?"

"Live? Half those fi'—ten—fifteen sen."

"And you save the rest? That is very prudent."

The girl looked bewildered; then she explained:

"Other half sen' Brownie."

He suddenly let her go. She leaned over him bewitchingly.

"Firs' some breakfas'; then I go'n' help you fanish—all day! What you thing?"

She came back in a moment. The sleeves of her kimono were tucked out of the way, and there was rice-flour on her pretty arms.

"You go'n' to naever tell—'bout those fi'—ten—fifteen sen, an' all those?"

"No," said Garland; "I will never tell."

"Else they go'n' kill me," she threatened gayly.

"I prefer to have you live," he laughed, as brightly as he could.

"Tha' 's secret among jus' you an' me?"

"Yes," said Garland.

She started away, then came back.

"*Me?* I lig—I *lig*—have secret among jus' you an' me." With a radiant face she fled.

And here was Brownie's poor little skeleton stripped naked. He had lived at the university like a gentleman. He was still living in Philadelphia like a gentleman. Garland wondered whether it would make any difference in Philadelphia if it were known that it was the pitiful "fi"—ten—fifteen sen" that his mother and sisters earned each day that supported him. A great disgust for Brownie and a great pity for Purple-Eyes were the immediate postulates. And is not pity akin to love?

III—THE DANCE OF THE RED MAPLE-LEAVES

The question of making one's toilet in the interior of Japan is still a serious one for the American who lives behind closed doors and cherishes his divine right of privacy. Garland had solved the vexation for all his contemporaries (according to Garland) by making his toilet as to half or quarter of his sacred person at a time (depending somewhat upon the danger of surprise), thus reducing the chances of exposure by one-half or three-quarters. Purple-Eyes brought him the requisites for his toilet, and the moment she was gone he bared his shoulders and chest, and plunged into the delightful water, perfumed, like everything else, with the aroma

181

Japonica. But his pretty hostess reappeared through the movable walls at an unwatched place.

He abandoned a momentary impulse to scuttle behind the screen because of the admiration he saw in her eyes, and then he half turned that she might see the muscles of his back.

"*How* you are beau-ti-ful!" she said slowly, as her eyes traveled, quite without embarrassment, over his athletic uppers.

"Thanks," he laughed, with pleasure in the little incident.

Garland turned a little further, and raised his arms above his head in the way of athletes.

She handed him a towel he had dropped.

"I thing I come tell you we got large tub for bath," she said then.

"Where is it?" asked Garland, suspiciously.

"There."

She pointed.

"That's what I thought. You must excuse me. I can't perform that sacred rite in the fierce light that beats upon a front porch."

"Yaes? Eijinsan don' lig?" She did not understand.

"No," admitted Garland.

"Also, you lig for me go 'way liddle?" Garland said yes, and she went.

When she returned, it was with a delightful breakfast of fish, rice, and persimmons. She put the little table between them, and on her knees, on the other side, taught him how to eat as a Japanese should. This is really not difficult, except the chopsticks; and with these she had to help him so often that their fingers were in almost constant contact. Alas! Garland made it as difficult as possible. And, alas! Garland was glad of the chopsticks!

Her joy overflowed the mouth and eyes which it seemed should know nothing but tears.

Afterward he helped her, with masculine joy of his own ineptitude, to reform the apartment, and secrete the things which had made it successively a reception-room, sleeping-chamber, and breakfast-room. You may judge whether or not this was delightful to a fellow like Garland, and also whether it was perilous.

It is not often that one has the felicity of ending one's breakfast with a song, and then of ending the song with a dance. Purple-Eyes brought her samisen quite without suggestion from Garland, and said with naïveté:

"I go'n' sing you a song. You lig me sing?"

"Try me!" challenged Garland, with an admiration in his eyes which pleased her greatly.

"Long down behine the Suwanee River" was the curious song she sang, in Japanese English.

Garland laughed.

"Don' you lig those?" she pouted. "I learn it for you."

He said it was lovely, and begged her to go on. But his eyes wandered from the fingers on the

strings to those on the plectrum, and then away
to the lips above; and when she turned into the
chorus he joined her with his inconstant eyes still
there. It was only an indifferent tenor, but the
girl thought it full of fervor. It was only that
it joined and mingled with hers—as she fancied
their spirits doing and might always do.

How that is nize!" she breathed in frank
ecstasy. "You got voice lig—lig—"

But there was nothing at hand to compare it
with, and she laughed confessingly.

"Nothing," said Garland. "It's original."

"Yaes—nothing original," she admitted.

"Sing another," begged Garland, with enthusiasm.

She did—"When the swallows flying home";
and then still another—"'Tis the last rosebud
summer."

"Where did you learn them?" asked he.

"That day when I got you' picture. *Me?* I
thing you lig me sing, mebby. Well, I git those
song; I make them United States' language, so
you comprehend."

"God bless you!" said Garland.

The girl leaned forward with dewy eyes.

"Sa-ay—you lig me also dance—jus' one—
liddle—dance—for *you?*"

She came bewitchingly nearer. Garland
glanced again at her geisha-like costume. Had
she thought all this out for his entertainment, he
wondered.

"Yes," he said.

"But—you naev—*naever* go'n' tell?"

She raised her brows, and held up a finger archly.

"On my sacred honor!" laughed Garland.

"No one?"

"Not a soul."

"Tha''s go'n' be 'nother secret among jus' you an' me foraever an' aever?"

"Forever and ever," announced Garland, as if it were the Service.

"Account if you aever do, they go'n' kill me!"

"What! Kill you?"

"Dade!" She nodded ominously.

"Who?"

"Black-Eyes an' those modder."

"Oh!" said Garland. He understood.

He was left to guess that this dainty flower had been taught the arts of a geisha to assist also in keeping up Brownie's state.

"I lig dance for *you*," confessed the girl, joyously. "Others? No; I do not lig. They *as'* me, 'Where you got those pink face?' *Me?* I don', lig those. I rather work in those mill. My modder an' my sister getting all times an-gery—account I don' dance. *But*—tha''s in-sult upon me! I don't *lig* be insult. So! *Me?* I jus' don' dance for no one—but—but—jus'—*you!*"

She vanished through the *shoji*, and presently returned, a symphony in autumnal reds and browns.

"I go'n' dance for you that red maple-leaf dance. Me? I am that leaf."

"You look it," said Garland, more tenderly than he knew.

The girl spread her garments that he might inspect her.

"This is a forest," she went on; "an' you— sa-ay—you a *tree!* Aha, ha, ha!"

She laughed, made him a noble courtesy, and murmured a little tune to which she floated down from the top of a maple-tree. For a while she lay quite still, shivering a little. Then the wind stirred her, and she rose, and swept down upon Garland, then back and into a whirl of other leaves. Then hither and thither, merrily, like an autumn leaf, until she shivered down at his feet, with bowed head.

She was making it more and more perilous for Garland.

IV—"HOW THAT IS NIZE!"

That night they had a gay little supper, with a tiny servant, who, Garland guessed, with entire accuracy, had been borrowed for the occasion.

"You got nize day?" asked Black-Eyes.

Garland caught a startled glance from Purple-Eyes, and answered discreetly that he had had—oh, yes; a very pleasant day, giving no damaging particulars.

But Black-Eyes fancied from the blankness of his countenance that he was indulging in the same kind of prevarication with which she would have met such a question. She devoted herself to him all the rest of the evening. As he retired for the night, the last thing she said to him, with a reproachful glance at Purple Eyes, was:

"To-morrow you go'n have mos' bes' nize times. *I* go'n' stay home with you!"

And she did, making it a very dreary day for Garland. He could not help thinking of Purple-Eyes at the factory, with her dainty hands begrimed.

But presently, when she returned, there was no grime upon her hands. She was dainty and smiling.

"You got nize day?" she asked, with her head coyly down. She knew he had not. And she purposely quoted her sister.

"No," he said savagely. "I'm glad it's over."

The flame was in her face again. But she kept it down.

"I think Black-Eyes ver' be-witch-ing."

"But she is not—*you*," he said.

She looked slowly up. The little weariness which had been limned upon her face by the day's drudgery was gone, and in its stead was a vague glory reflected from within.

"*How* that is nize," she whispered — "for *me!*"

"For me," said Garland, approaching her threateningly. She did not retreat. She subsided a little toward him—just a little—that he

187

might know she would never retreat from him. Her eyes smiled confidently.

He stopped where he was.

"Who is to be chatelaine to-morrow?"

"What is that chat—?" she asked.

"Who is to keep the house?"

"Me. Me one day, Black-Eyes next."

She saw his face lighten.

"You lig that?"

"I like half of it."

She thought a moment until she understood; then she lifted her shining face.

"Ah, Eijinsan, how be-witch-ing *you* are!"

v—THE PLAINTIVE TEMPLE BELLS

The next day they went up to the temple on the mountain-side, the plaintive bells of which Garland had heard. Purple-Eyes was tall, and walked with less difficulty than most Japanese girls, so they walked. It was a day of dreams. Garland remembered afterward the smell of the incense, the voices of the chanting *bonzes*, that the tea-house on the mountain-side where they rested called itself the House of the Seven Golden Crystals; the rest was Purple-Eyes— and happiness. Japan had been growing upon him for three months, and now unhappiness made but little impression.

The day remained in his mind with the sum of his dreams—this lotus-eating, nectar-drinking, happy-go-lucky Garland!

Thus it curiously went on. One day it was Black-Eyes, and the true Japan, and the real Garland. The next it was Purple-Eyes, and the ideal Japan, and the lotus-eating Garland. What is more like lotus-eating than being adored? At first Garland used to smile at the strange dual life which circumstances had wrought out for him. Then he used to wonder which was better. Later he tried to decide only which he liked better. Now he no longer differentiated at all. His analytical edge was quite dulled. Still, he had heard that this fever of Japan always wore off. Some said it lasted as long as two years, some said five; no one had said ten. And what then?

"Why, then? *Me!*"

He had spoken the last three words aloud, and they had been answered by the laughing, dewy-eyed subject of them.

He looked at her.

"Well, one ought to be content," he laughed.

"An' you—content?" she smiled back.

He did not answer at once.

"Do you know that you have been growing more bewitching every day since——"

"Sinze *you*—an' *joy*—came at Japan?"

From the opened *shoji* she flung him the gay greeting he had taught her, and disappeared; for it was Black-Eyes' day, and she had yet to dress for her work.

That day he harbored madly the notion of marriage with Purple-Eyes and a residence in Japan. It had quite infected him before night, and was distinctly, but less and less strongly, in his mind for several days. But then came a letter from his elder brother, in answer to his own of a rather confessional and emotional sort, asking him what he meant by living upon three working-women. It told him to go away—to the devil—anywhere —but away from there. It was like a cold douche. The fever Japonica, as every one had said, was at last gone. So small a thing as his brother's letter had cured it. Now he smiled. He had meant to write to Miss Warburton, offering to release her.

VI—"SAYONARA?"

I know not what he said to Purple-Eyes, but with her tears there was a certain buoyancy that had not been there but for some hope. And why not? For Garland was a very sweet and gentle fellow, who abhorred pain. The three went to see him off, and he tried desperately to be gay; but something was pulling at his heart-strings, and there were tears perilously near his eyes. Black-Eyes did not marvel at this. She had always understood that it was the way of west-ocean men. But they were only too evidently ready to be answered by other tears in the dewy eyes that were blue. And *this* was annoying to Black-Eyes. She made her sister tremble by a look. So she of the blue eyes could only grasp and hold

190

Garland's big hand in both her own exquisite ones when the others looked away. When their eyes returned hers looked off to the big funnels of the ship, though she still held the hand. But when she looked at Garland again he had his handkerchief to his eyes; something inside had given way. Then hers came from her sleeve, too. So at last it was quite a little tragedy.

Sad it is that one forgets that one has eaten of the lotus; but thus it is with the lotus, and thus did Garland.

That night, in bed, Black-Eyes undertook some criticism of Garland. Her sister flared up in a way that was new and superb.

"Tha' 's a lie! He's the mos' bes' nize gent in the whole worl'." And she fell to sobbing.

"What is the matter?" asked the mother, who was kinder than Black-Eyes.

"I got that lone-some-ness," sobbed the girl, in answer.

"Poor little pink-face!" said the mother, touching her cheek. "Always must be touch by some one!"

"*Me?*" said Purple-Eyes, with a power and assurance which were startling. "I am glad I have that pink face!" She laughed. "And I am glad I have *not* that brown face! Aha!"

The mother asked in alarm:

"Has the Eijinsan told you strange things?"

"The strangest and most beautiful things in all the world!" breathed Purple-Eyes. "Not *told* them, but looked them—thought them—to me."

"And you believed?"

"I believed."

"That is very sad," said the mother. "It is the way of the west-ocean men."

"Ah, it *is* his way, thank Shaka! and it is *not* sad. It is very joyous."

"Shaka grant that it is not, my daughter. To the Eijinsan you are only a plaything, I fear."

"He may have me for a plaything," said the girl, defiantly. "Who has not playthings?"

"When a plaything becomes shabby—"

"But I am not, and I never shall be."

"In a little while we shall know," said the mother, finally.

"In a little while we shall know," repeated the girl, joyously.

VII—"WHAT YOU BED?"

Later they found the letter—in the discarded conversation-book. It said that Garland was having his final outing before becoming a Benedick; and the missionary on the hill told them that that meant that he was to be married upon his return to America. Purple-Eyes drew a sharp breath, then faced the other two savagely. She was able to laugh presently; but it was a very piteous laugh.

"Tha's what I know! Aha, ha, ha! He—he —tell me all those." But the pitiful lie stuck in her throat, and her lips were dry. "He tell me *aevery*-thing! Yaes,"—to a look of doubt from Black-Eyes—"he go'n' marry that other for jus' liddle—"

"Speak Japanese," said her mother, who was not so clever at English as her daughters; but the request fell like a lash upon Purple-Eyes' heart.

"I will not!" she flamed forth. "I will speak his language. He will come for me. If he do not come, I shall go to him. He go'n marry that other—*if* he marry her—*if*—jus' liddle— *Me?* He go'n' marry me las' an' foraever!"

Suddenly she became aware that she had betrayed her secret.

"Oh, all the gods in the sky!" she cried in anguish. "Tha',s lie. He *not* go'n' marry me. He *don'* say. Jus' I thing so—jus' I—," She had to debase herself still further, if she would be shriven. "He *not* go'n' come for me. I *not* go'n' go at him. *Me?* Tha',s correc', Oku-San; I jus' his liddle plaything. He don't say naw-thing. Jus' I thing so."

Her mother nodded.

"And when he tires of the plaything—"

She threw an imaginary something into the air.

"Yaes," whispered Purple-Eyes, humbly bowing her head; but when her face was down she smiled. It was all very sure to her. As she looked up she saw something like malevolence upon the face of her sister.

"*But*—also he not *go'n'* marry that other foraever!" Her sister smiled unbelievingly.

"I bed you don'?"

"Ah! *what* you bed?" challenged Black-Eyes.

"That heart in my bosom!" answered Purple-Eyes.

VIII—LONE-SOME-NESS

Garland did not reach the end of his ante-Benedick wanderings until a year later. Then he found, among other letters awaiting him, one in a long, dainty envelope addressed in English and Japanese. He knew it was from Purple-Eyes before he opened it. It was seven months old.

As he read, all her little tricks of inflection came back upon him. He knew that her long white hands were waving emphases at him—very gently. The questioning which her eyes had learned after his coming—as if she were not quite sure of something—was upon him out of the shadows beyond the lamp. The subtle aromas which always exhaled from her garments were distinct enough to startle him. He looked quickly back and about the room. Then he laughed softly. But his face had flushed, and gladness had lit his eyes. The fever Japonica was once more in his veins—and it was his own room—and America—with only her pictured face (fallen from the envelope) before him—herself on the other side of the world. Uncon-sciously he read aloud—in her voice and manner:

PURPLE-EYES

"That is ledder from me, Miss Purple-Eyes, unto you, Mister J. F. Garland. That is nize day in Japan. I lig if you hoarry soon coming at Japan 'nother time. You been 'way ver' long time. I lig if you hoarry account aeverybody hating me more an' more. I got those feeling again 'bout somethings I want an' have not got it. That is lone-some-ness. That is to cross west-ocean. You have also got those? Me? I been that sad aever sinze you gone me away from. I been that ill. I thing mebby I go'n' die soon. *Aexcep'* you come? Say you go'n' come, that I don' die? Black-Eyes she all times make amusement 'bout you don' come. That is a liar. She don' know you who you are. She don' know you that you go'n' come soon as you kin. Mebby you go'n' marry with those pink-face for liddle while? Me? I study those conversation-book so I kin write unto you. Also, I fine those ledder you lose when you first arrive among us at Japan. You desire those ledder? Me? I keep it upon my bosom among those photograph of you. Mister J. F. Garland, I don' keer you do marry those other for liddle while. Then you go'n' marry me las' an' foraever. Jus' hoarry. Yit I am not gay. I can not be gay until you come again. That is sad for me. Also, you do not lig for me be gay, but lig unto widow till you come. Then, Mister J. F. Garland, I shall be that happy. Mebby you ill an' can not come unto me? Then I come unto you, if you wish me. What you thing? That is a picture of me lig I promise. I fix up same lig those day you hol' my hands. How that was nize! That is first time I aever been my hands hol' so nize—so sof'. Mister J. F. Garland, that is you hol' my hands that sof'. Me? I don' let no one else do those unto my hands—lig you wishing, mebby. Jus' you. Mister J. F. Garland, you go'n' hol' my hands all times this afterwhile? Say, don't stay marry with that other so ver' long. Account those lone-some-ness. Please sen' me picture of those other you marry unto. If you marry unto them. I lig see how she is that beautiful. Please write me letter aevery day. Please come back that soon. So I kin be joyous. It is that sad for me."

Every laboriously formed letter, printed like the first copy of a child at school, told him what this had cost her; and the little flourishes at the end, where she had grown more certain, what pride she had in them! The picture was exquisitely colored, as only the Japanese can color them, and had been very costly to her. He set it before him, and with his head in his hands studied it. The eyes were very blue, but no bluer than her own. They looked into his half sadly, half gayly, tempting him again. The Japan fever had its way with him, and for a moment—ten—he lived that lotus life with her over again. Then came a great upheaval inside which was yearning. He was tired. He had been tired ever since leaving Japan. In those eyes he saw again the invitation to rest. The hair, with its brassy lustre—he could see the sun on it again —smell its perfume—feel it under his hands. The lips were parted a little, as they nearly always were, and within showed the brilliant teeth. "Oh," he cried out, as he rose, "get thee behind me—moon-goddess—get thee behind me!" He laughed wofully, and took up the picture again. "I thought it gone—the fever—the dreaming—the lotus-eating."

There was a knock on the door, and a messenger-boy handed in the answer to a note.

"Yes," it ran; "I shall be home at eight—*and so glad!*"

It was twenty minutes to eight.

Garland hurried into his evening clothes and hastened away, leaving the rest of the letters unopened. But he came back, from down the stairs, and again set the picture up before him. Then he strode softly up and down the apartment, a smile half sad, half gay, upon his face. The little clock chimed the few notes which told him it was a quarter past eight. He smiled—another kind of smile. He had forgotten—that she would be at home at eight and would be glad! He looked again briefly at the picture of Purple-Eyes. There was moisture in his own. Then softly, as if it were sentiment, he turned it face down and went out.

THE RUN OF THE YELLOW MAIL

BY FRANK H. SPEARMAN

THE RUN OF THE YELLOW MAIL

BY FRANK H. SPEARMAN

THERE wasn't another engineer on the division who dared talk to Doubleday the way Jimmie Bradshaw did.

But Jimmie had a grievance, and every time he thought about it, it made him nervous.

Ninety-six years. It seemed a good while to wait; yet in the regular course of events on the mountain division there appeared no earlier prospect of Jimmie's getting a passenger run.

"Got your rights, ain't you?" said Doubleday, when Jimmie complained.

"I have and I haven't," grumbled Jimmie, winking hard; "there's younger men than I am on the fast runs."

"They got in on the strike; you've been told that a hundred times. We can't get up another strike just to fix you out on a fast run. Hang on to your freight. There's better men than you in Ireland up to their belt in the bog, Jimmie."

"It's a pity they didn't leave you there, Doubleday."

"You'd have been a good while hunting for a freight run if they had."

Then Jimmie would get mad and shake his finger and talk fast: "Just the same, I'll have a fast run here when you're dead."

"Maybe; but I'll be alive a good while yet, my son," the master mechanic would laugh. Then Jimmie would walk off very warm, and when he got into private with himself he would wink furiously and say friction things about Doubleday which needn't now be printed, because it is different. However, the talk always ended that way, and Jimmie Bradshaw knew it always would end that way.

The trouble was, no one on the division would take Jimmie seriously, and he felt that the ambition of his life would never be fulfilled; that he would go plugging to gray hairs and the grave on an old freight train; and that even when he got to the right side of the Jordan there would still be something like half a century between him and a fast run. It was funny to hear him complaining about it, for everything, even his troubles, came funny to him, and in talking he had an odd way of stuttering with his eyes, which were red. In fact, Jimmie was nearly all red; hair, face, hands—they said his teeth were freckled.

When the first rumors about the proposed Yellow Mail reached the mountains Jimmie was running a new ten-wheeler; breaking her in on a freight "for some fellow without a lick o' sense to use on a limited passenger run," as Jimmie observed bitterly. The rumors about the mail came at first like stray mallards—opening signs of winter—and as the season advanced flew thicker and faster. Washington never was very progressive in the matter of improving the transcontinental service, but they once put in a postmaster-general down there, by mistake, who wouldn't take the old song. When the bureau fellows that put their brains up in curl papers told him it couldn't be done he smiled softly, but he sent for the managers of the crack lines across the continent, without suspecting how it bore incidentally on Jimmie Bradshaw's grievance against his master mechanic.

The postmaster-general called the managers of the big lines, and they had a dinner at Chamberlain's, and *they* told him the same thing. "It has been tried," they said in the old, tired way; "really it can't be done."

"California has been getting the worst of it for years on the mail service," persisted the postmaster-general moderately. "But Californians ought to have the best of it. We don't think anything about putting New York mail in Chicago in twenty hours. It ought to be simple to cut half a day across the continent and give San Francisco her mail a day earlier. Where's the fall-down?" he asked, like one refusing no for an answer.

The general managers looked at our representative sympathetically, and coughed cigar smoke his way to hide him.

"West of the Missouri," murmured a Pennsylvania swell, who pulled indifferently at a fifty-cent cigar. Everybody at the table took a drink on the *exposé*, except the general manager, who sat at that time for the Rocky Mountains.

The West End representative was unhappily accustomed to facing the finger of scorn on such occasions. It had become with our managers a tradition. There was never a conference of continental lines in which we were not scoffed at as the weak link in the chain of everything—mail, passenger, specials, what not—the trouble was invariably laid at our door.

But this time there was a new man sitting for the line at the Chamberlain dinner; a youngish man with a face that set like cement when the West End was trod upon.

The postmaster-general was inclined, from the reputation we had, to look on our chap as a man looks at a dog without a pedigree, or at a dray horse in a bunch of standard breeds. But something in the mouth of the West End man gave him pause; since the Rough Riders, it has been a bit different about verdicts on things Western. The postmaster-general suppressed a rising sarcasm with a sip of Chartreuse, for the dinner was ripening, and waited; nor did he mistake—the West Ender *was* about to speak.

"Why west of the Missouri?" he asked, with a lift of the face that was not altogether candid. The Pennsylvania man shrugged his brows; to explain might have seemed indelicate.

"If it is put through, how much of it do you propose to take yourself?" inquired our man, looking evenly at the Alleghany official.

"Sixty-five miles, including stops from New York post-office to Canal Street," replied the Pennsylvania man, and his words flowed with irritating smoothness and ease.

"What do you take?" continued the man with the jaw, turning to the Burlington representative, who was struggling, belated, with an artichoke.

"*About* seventy from Canal to Tenth and Mason. Say, seventy," repeated the "Q" manager, with the lordliness of a man who has miles to throw at almost anybody, and knows it.

"Then suppose we say sixty-five from Tenth and Mason to Ogden," suggested the West Ender. There was a well-bred stare the table round, a lifting of glasses to mask expressions that might give pain. Sixty-five miles an *hour?* Through the *Rockies?*

But the postmaster-general struck the table quickly and heavily; he didn't want to let it get away. "Why, hang it, Mr. Bucks," he exclaimed with emphasis, "if you will say sixty, the business is done. We don't ask you to do the Rockies in the time these fellows take to cut the

Alleghanies. Do sixty, and I will put mail in 'Frisco a day earlier every week in the year."

"Nothing on the West End to keep you from doing it," said General Manager Bucks. He had been put up then only about six months. "But——"

Every one looked at the young manager. The Pennsylvania man looked with confidence, for he instantly suspected there must be a string to such a proposition, or that the new representative was "talking through his hat."

"But what?" asked the Cabinet member, uncomfortably apprehensive.

"But we are not putting on a sixty-five mile schedule just because we love our country, you understand, nor to lighten an already glorious reputation. Oh, no," smiled Bucks faintly, "we are doing it for 'the stuff.' You put up the money; we put up the speed. Not sixty miles; sixty-five—from the Missouri to the Sierras. No; no more wine. Yes, thank you, I will take a cigar."

The trade was on from that minute. Bucks said no more then; he was a good listener. But next day—when it came to talking money—he talked more money into the West End treasury for one year's running than was ever talked before on a mail contract for the best three years' work we ever did.

When they asked him how much time he wanted to get ready, and told him to take plenty, three months were stipulated. The contracts were drawn, and they were signed by our people without hesitation because they knew Bucks. But while the preparations for the fast schedule were being made, the Government weakened on signing. Nothing ever got through a Washington department without hitch, and they said our road had so often failed on like propositions that they wanted a test. There was a deal of wrangling, then a test run was agreed upon by all the roads concerned. If it proved successful—if the mail was put to the Golden Gate on the second of the schedule—public opinion and the interests in the Philippines, it was concluded, would justify the heavy premium asked for the service.

In this way the dickering and the figuring became, in a measure, public, and keyed up everybody interested to a high pitch. We said nothing for publication, but under Bucks' energy sawed wood for three whole months. Indeed, three months goes as a day getting a system into shape for an extraordinary schedule. Success meant with us prestige; but failure meant obloquy for the road and for our division chief who had been so lately called to handle it.

The real strain, it was clear, would come on his old—the mountain—division; and to carry out the point rested on the motive power of the mountain division; hence, concretely, on Doubleday, master mechanic of the hill country.

In thirty days Neighbor, superintendent of

the motive power, called for reports from the division master mechanics on the preparations for the Yellow Mail run, and they reported progress. In sixty days he called again. The subordinates reported well except Doubleday. Doubleday said merely "Not ready"; he was busy tinkering with his engines. There was a third call in eighty days, and on the eighty-fifth a peremptory call. Everybody said ready except Doubleday. When Neighbor remonstrated sharply, he would say only that he would be ready in time. That was the most he would promise, though it was generally understood that if he failed to deliver the goods he would have to make way for somebody who could.

The plains division of the system was marked up for seventy miles an hour, and, if the truth were told, a little better; but, with all the help they could give us, it still left sixty for the mountains to take care of, and the Yellow Mail proposition was conceded to be the toughest affair the motive power at Medicine Bend ever faced. However, forty-eight hours before the mail left the New York post-office Doubleday wired to Neighbor, "Ready"; Neighbor to Bucks, "Ready"; and Bucks to Washington, "Ready" —and we were ready from end to end.

Then the orders began to shoot through the mountains. The test run was of especial importance, because the signing of the contract was believed to depend on the success of it. Once signed, accidents and delays might be explained; for the test run there must be no delays. Despatches were given the 11, which meant Bucks; no lay-outs, no slows for the Yellow Mail. Road masters were notified: no track work in front of the Yellow Mail. Bridge gangs were warned, yard masters instructed, section bosses cautioned, track walkers spurred—the system was polished like a barkeeper's diamond, and swept like a parlor car for the test flight of the Yellow Mail.

Doubleday, working like a boiler washer, spent all day Thursday and all Thursday night in the roundhouse. He had personally gone over the engines that were to take the racket in the mountains. Ten-wheelers they were, the 1012 and the 1014, with fifty-six-inch drivers and cylinders big enough to sit up and eat breakfast in. Spick and span both of them, just long enough out of the shops to run smoothly to the work; and on Friday Oliver Sollers, who, when he opened a throttle, blew miles over the tender like feathers, took the 1012, groomed as you'd groom a Wilkes mare, down to Piedmont for the run up to the Bend.

Now Oliver Sollers was a runner in a thousand, and steady as a clock; but he had a fireman who couldn't stand prosperity, Steve Horigan, a cousin of Johnnie's. The glory was too great for Steve, and he spent Friday night in Gallagher's place celebrating, telling the boys what the 1012 would do to the Yellow Mail. Not a thing, Steve claimed after five drinks, but pull the stamps clean off the letters the minute they struck the foothills. But when Steve showed up at five A. M. to superintend the movement, he was seasick. The instant Sollers set eyes on him he objected to taking him out. Mr. Sollers was not looking for any unnecessary chances on one of Bucks' personal matters, and for the general manager the Yellow Mail test had become exceedingly personal. Practically everybody East and West had said it would fail; Bucks said no.

Neighbor himself was on the Piedmont platform that morning, watching things. The Mc-Cloud despatchers had promised the train to our division on time, and her smoke was due with the rise of the sun. The big superintendent of motive power, watching anxiously for her arrival, and planning anxiously for her outgoing, glared at the bunged fireman in front of him, and, when Sollers protested, Neighbor turned on the swollen Steve with sorely bitter words. Steve swore mightily he was fit and could do the trick —but what's the word of a railroad man that drinks? Neighbor spoke wicked words, and while they poured on the guilty Steve's crop there was a shout down the platform. In the east the sun was breaking over the sand-hills, and below it a haze of black thickened the horizon. It was McTerza with the 808 and the Yellow Mail. Neighbor looked at his watch; she was, if anything, a minute to the good, and before the car tinks could hustle across the yard, a streak of gold cut the sea of purple alfalfa in the lower valley, and the narrows began to smoke with the dust of the race for the platform.

When McTerza blocked the big drivers at the west end of the depot, every eye was on the new equipment. Three standard railway mail cars, done in varnished buttercup, strung out behind the sizzling engine, and they looked pretty as cowslips. While Neighbor vaguely mediated on their beauty and on his boozing fireman, Jimmie Bradshaw, just in from a night run down from the Bend, walked across the yard. He had just seen Steve Horigan making a "sneak" for the bath-house, and from the yard gossip Jimmie had guessed the rest.

"What are you looking for, Neighbor?" asked Jimmie Bradshaw.

"A man to fire for Sollers—up. Do you want it?"

Neighbor threw it at him across and carelessly, not having any idea Jimmie was looking for trouble. But Jimmie surprised him; Jimmie did want it.

"Sure, I want it. Put me on. Tired? No. I'm fresh as rainwater. Put me on, Neighbor; I'll never get fast any other way. Doubleday wouldn't give me a fast run in a hundred years. Neighbor," exclaimed Jimmie, greatly wrought, "put me on, and I'll plant sunflowers on your grave."

There wasn't much time to look around; the 1012 was being coupled on to the mail for the hardest run on the line.

"Get in there, you blamed idiot," roared Neighbor presently at Jimmie. "Get in and fire her; and if you don't give Sollers 210 pounds every inch of the way I'll set you back wiping."

Jimmie winked furiously at the proposition while it was being hurled at him, but he lost no time climbing in. The 1012 was drumming then at her gauge with better than 200 pounds. Adam Shafer, conductor for the run, ran backward and forward a minute examining the air. At the final word from his brakeman he lifted two fingers at Sollers; Oliver opened a notch, and Jimmie Bradshaw stuck his head out of the gangway. Slowly, but with swiftly rising speed, the yellow string began to move out through the long lines of freight cars that blocked the spurs; and those who watched that morning from the Piedmont platform thought a smoother equipment than Bucks' mail train never drew out of the mountain yards.

Jimmie Bradshaw jumped at the work in front of him. He had never in his life lifted a pick in as swell a cab as that. The hind end of the 1012 was as big as a private car; Jimmie had never seen so much play for a shovel in his life, and he knew the trick of his business better than most men even in West End cabs—the trick of holding the high pressure every minute, of feeling

212

the draughts before they left the throttle; and as Oliver let the engine out very, very fast, Jimmie Bradshaw sprinkled the grate bars craftily and blinked at the shivering pointer, as much as to say, "It's you and me now for the Yellow Mail, and nobody else on earth."

There was a long reach of smooth track in front of the foothills. It was there the big start had to be made, and in two minutes the bark of the big machine had deepened to a chest tone full as thunder. It was all fun for an hour, for two hours. It was that long before the ambitious fireman realized what the new speed meant: the sickening slew, the lurch on lurch so fast the engine never righted, the shortened breath along the tangent, the giddy roll to the elevation and the sudden shock of the curve, the roar of the flight on the ear, and, above and over it all, the booming purr of the maddened steel. The canoe in the heart of the rapids, the bridge of a liner at sea, the gun in the heat of the fight, take something of this—the cab of the mail takes it all.

When they struck the foothills, Sollers and Jimmie Bradshaw looked at their watches and looked at each other, but like men who had turned their backs on every mountain record. There was a stop for water—speed drinks so hard—an oil round, an anxious touch on the journals; then the Yellow Mail drew reeling into the hills. Oliver eased her just a bit for the heavier curves, but for all that the train writhed frantically as it cut the segments, and the men thought, in spite of themselves, of the mountain curves ahead. The worst of the run lay ahead of the pilot, because the art in mountain running is not alone or so much in getting up hill; it is in getting down hill. But by the way the Yellow Mail got that day up hill and down, it seemed as if Steve Horigan's dream would be realized, and that the 1012 actually would pull the stamps off the letters. Before they knew it they were through the gateway, out into the desert country, up along the crested buttes, and then, sudden as eternity, the wheel-base of the 1012 struck a tight curve, a pent-down rail sprang out like a knitting-needle, and the Yellow Mail shot staggering off the track into a gray borrow-pit.

There was a crunching of truck and frame, a crashing splinter of varnished cars, a scream from the wounded engine, a cloud of gray ash in the burning sun, and a ruin of human effort in the ditch. In the twinkle of an eye the mail train lay spilled on the alkali; for a minute it looked desperately bad for the general manager's test.

It was hardly more than a minute, though; then like ants from out a trampled hill men began crawling from the yellow wreck. There was more—there was groaning and worse, yet little for so frightful a shock. And first on his feet, and quickest back with no more than scratches, and quickest back under the cab after his engineer, was Jimmie Bradshaw, the fireman.

Sollers, barely conscious, lay wedged between the tank and the footboard. Jimmie, all by himself, eased him away from the boiler. The conductor stood with a broken arm directing his brakeman how to chop a crew out of the head mail car, and the hind crews were getting out themselves. There was a quick calling back and forth, and the cry, "Nobody killed!" But the engineer and the conductor were put out of action. There was, in fact, but one West End man unhurt; yet that was enough—for it was Jimmie Bradshaw.

The first wreck of the fast mail—there have been worse since—took place just east of Crockett's siding. A west-bound freight lay at that moment on the passing track waiting for the mail. Jimmie Bradshaw cast up the possibilities of the situation the minute he righted himself.

Before the freight crew had reached the wreck, Jimmie was hustling ahead to tell them what he wanted. The freight conductor demurred; and when they discussed it with the freight engineer, Kingsley, he objected. "My engine won't never stand it; it'll pound her to pieces," he argued. "I reckon the safest thing to do is to get orders."

"Get orders!" stormed Jimmie Bradshaw, pointing at the wreck. "Get orders! Are you running an engine on this line and don't know the orders for those mail bags? The orders is to move 'em! That's orders enough. Move 'em! Uncouple three of those empty box-cars and hustle 'em back. By the Great United States! any man that interferes with the moving of this mail will get his time—that's what he'll get. That's Doubleday, and don't you forget it. The thing is to move the mail—not stand here chewing about it!"

"Bucks wants the stuff hustled," put in the freight conductor, weakening before Jimmie's eloquence. "Everybody knows that."

"Uncouple there!" cried Jimmie, climbing into the Mogul cab. "I'll pull the bags, Kingsley; you needn't take any chances. Come back there, every mother's son of you, and help on the transfer."

He carried his points with a gale. He was conductor and engineer and general manager all in one. He backed the boxes to the curve below the spill, and set every man at work piling the mail from the wrecked train to the freight cars. The wounded cared for the wounded, and the dead might have buried the dead; Jimmie moved the mail. Only one thing turned his hair gray; the transfer was so slow, it looked as if it would defeat his plan. As he stood fermenting, a stray party of Sioux bucks on a vagrant hunt rose out of the desert passes, and halted to survey the confusion. It was Jimmie Bradshaw's opportunity. He had the blanket men in council in a trice. They talked for one minute, in two he had them regularly sworn in and carrying second-class. The registered stuff was jealously guarded by those of the mail clerks who could still hobble—and who, head for head, leg for leg, and arm for arm, can stand the wrecking that a mail clerk can stand? The mail crews took the registered matter; the freight crews and Jimmie, dripping sweat and anxiety, handled the letter bags; but second and third class were temporarily hustled for the Great White Father by his irreverent children of the Rockies.

Before the disabled men could credit their senses the business was done, themselves made as comfortable as possible, and with the promise of speedy aid back to the injured, the Yellow Mail, somewhat disfigured, was again heading westward in the box-cars. This time Jimmie Bradshaw, like a dog with a bone, had the throttle. Jimmie Bradshaw for once in his life had the coveted fast run, and till he sighted Fort Rucker he never for a minute let up.

Meantime there was a desperate crowd around the despatcher at Medicine Bend. It was an hour and twenty minutes after Ponca Station reported the Yellow Mail out, before Fort Rucker, eighteen miles farther west, reported the box-cars and Jimmie Bradshaw in, and followed with a wreck report from the Crockett siding. When that end of it began to tumble into the Wickiup office Doubleday's face went very hard —fate was against him, the contract was gone glimmering, he didn't feel at all sure his own head and the roadmaster's wouldn't follow it. Then the Rucker operator began again to talk about Jimmie Bradshaw, and "Who's Bradshaw?" asked somebody; and Rucker went on excitedly with the story of the Mogul and of three box-cars, and of a war party of Sioux squatting on the brake-wheels; it came so mixed that Medicine Bend thought everybody at Rucker Station had gone mad.

While they fumed, Jimmie Bradshaw was speeding the mail through the mountains. He had Kingsley's fireman, big as an ox and full of his own enthusiasm. In no time they were flying across the flats of the Spider Water, threading the curves of the Peace River, and hitting the rails of the Painted Desert, with the Mogul sprinting like a Texas steer, and the box-cars leaping like yearlings at the points. It was no case of scientific running, no case of favoring the roadbed, of easing the strain on the equipment; it was simply a case of galloping to a Broadway fire with a Silsby rotary on a 4—11 call. Up hill and down, curve and tangent, it was all one. There was speed made on the plains with that mail, and there was speed made in the foothills with the fancy equipment, but never the speed that Jimmie Bradshaw made when he ran the mail through the gorges in three box-cars; and frightened operators and paralyzed station-agents all the way up the line watched the fear-

218

ful and wonderful train jump the switches with Bradshaw's red head sticking out of the cab window.

Medicine Bend couldn't get the straight of it over the wires. There was an electric storm in the mountains, and the wires went bad in the midst of the confusion. They knew there was a wreck, and supposed there was mail in the ditch, and, with Doubleday frantic, the despatchers were trying to get the track to run a train down to Crockett's. But Jimmie Bradshaw had asked at Rucker for rights to the Bend, and in an unguarded moment they had been given; after that it was all off. Nobody could get action on Jimmie Bradshaw to head him off. He took the rights, and stayed not for stake and stopped not for stone. In thirty minutes the operating department was ready to kill him, but he was making such time it was concluded better to humor the lunatic than to try to hold him up anywhere for a parley. When this was decided Jimmie and his war party were already reported past Bad Axe, fifteen miles below the Bend, with every truck on the box-cars smoking.

The Bad Axe run to the Bend was never done in less than fourteen minutes until Bradshaw that day brought up the mail. Between those two points the line is modeled on the curves of a ram's horn, but Jimmie with the Mogul found every twist on the right of way in eleven minutes; that particular record is good yet. Indeed, before Doubleday, then in a frenzied condition, got his cohorts fairly on the platform to look for Jimmie, the hollow scream of the big freight engine echoed through the mountains. Shouts from below brought the operators to the upper windows; down the Bend they saw a monster locomotive flying from a trailing horn of smoke. As the stubby string of freight cars slewed quartering into the lower yard, the startled officials saw them from the Wickup windows wrapped in a stream of flame. Every journal was afire, and the blaze from the boxes, rolling into the steam from the stack, curled hotly around a bevy of Sioux Indians, who clung sternly to the footboards and brake-wheels on top of the box-cars. It was a ride for the red men that is told around the council fires yet. But they do not always add in their traditions that they were hanging on, not only for life, but also for a butt of plug tobacco promised for their timely help at Crockett siding.

By the time Jimmie slowed up his amazing equipment the fire brigade was on the run from the roundhouse. The Sioux warriors climbed hastily down the fire escapes, a force of bruised and bareheaded mail clerks shoved back the box-car doors, the car tinks tackled the conflagration, and Jimmie Bradshaw, dropping from the cab with the swing of a man who has done it, waited at the gangway for the questions to come to him, and for a minute they came hot.

RUN OF THE YELLOW MAIL

"What the blazes do you mean by bringing in an engine in that condition?" yelled Doubleday, pointing to the blown machine.

"I thought you wanted the mail," winked Jimmie.

"How the devil are we to get the mail with you blocking the track for two hours?" demanded Calahan insanely.

"Why, the mail's here—in these box-cars," responded Jimmie Bradshaw, pointing to his bobtail train. "Now don't look daffy like that; every sack is right here. I thought the best way to get the mail here was to bring it. Hm! We're forty minutes late, ain't we?"

Doubleday waited to hear no more. Orders flew like curlews from the superintendent and the master mechanic. They saw there was a life for it yet. A string of new mail cars was backed down beside the train before the fire brigade had done with the trucks. The relieving mail crews waiting at the Bend took hold like cats at a pudding, and a dozen extra men helped them sling the pouches. The 1014, blowing porpoisewise, was backed up just as Benedict Morgan's train pulled down for Crockett's siding, and the Yellow Mail, rehabilitated, rejunevated, and exultant, started up the gorge for Bear Dance, only fifty-three minutes late, with Hanksworth in the cab.

"And if you can't make that up, Frank, you're no good on earth," spluttered Doubleday at the engineer he had put in for that special endeavor. And Frank Hawksworth did make it up, and the Yellow Mail went on and off the West End on the test, and into the Sierras for the coast, *on time.*

"There's a butt of plug tobacco and transportation to Crockett's coming to these bucks, Mr. Doubleday," winked Jimmie Bradshaw uncertainly, for with the wearing off of the strain came the idea to Jimmie that he might have to pay for it himself. "I promised them that," he added, "for helping with the transfer. If it hadn't been for the blankets we wouldn't have got off for another hour. They chew Tomahawk—rough and ready preferred—Mr. Doubleday. Hm!"

Doubleday was looking off into the mountains.

"You've been on a freight run some time, Jimmie," said he tentatively after a while.

The Indian detachment was crowding in pretty close on the red-headed engineer. He blushed. "If you'll take care of my tobacco contract, Doubleday, we'll call the other matter square. I'm not looking for a fast run as much as I was."

"If we get the mail contract," resumed Doubleday reflectively, "and it won't be your fault if we don't—hm!—we may need you on one of the runs. Looks to me like you ought to have one."

Jimmie shook his head. "I don't want one—don't mind me; just fix these gentlemen out with some tobacco before they scalp me, will you?"

The Indians got their leaf, and Bucks got his contract, and Jimmie Bradshaw got the pick of the runs on the Yellow Mail, and ever since he's been kicking to get back on a freight. But they don't call him Bradshaw any more. No man in the mountains can pace him on a dare-devil run. And when the head brave of the hunting party received the butt of tobacco on behalf of his company, he looked at Doubleday with dignity, pointed to the sandy engineer, and spoke freckled words in the Sioux.

That's the way it came about. Bradshaw holds the belt for the run from Bad Axe to Medicine Bend; but he never goes by the name of Bradshaw any more. West of McCloud, everywhere up and down the mountains, they give him the name that the Sioux gave him that day—Jimmie the Wind.

MRS. PROTHEROE

BY BOOTH TARKINGTON

MRS. PROTHEROE

BY BOOTH TARKINGTON

WHEN Alonzo Rawson took his seat as the Senator from Stackpole in the upper branch of the General Assembly of the State, an expression of pleasure and of greatness appeared to be permanently imprinted upon his countenance. He felt that if he had not quite arrived at all which he meant to make his own, at least he had emerged upon the arena where he was to win it, and he looked about him for a few other strong spirits with whom to construct a focus of power which should control the Senate. The young man had not long to look, for within a week after the beginning of the session these others showed themselves to his view, rising above the general level of mediocrity and timidity, party leaders and chiefs of factions, men who were on their feet continually, speaking half a dozen times a day, freely and loudly. To these, and that house at large, he felt it necessary to introduce himself by a speech which must prove him one of the elect, and he awaited impatiently an opening.

Alonzo had no timidity himself. He was not one of those who first try their voices on motions

From "In the Arena." Copyright, 1905, by McClure, Phillips & Co.

to adjourn, written in form and handed out to
novices by presiding officers and leaders. He
was too conscious of his own gifts, and he had
been "accustomed to speaking" ever since his
days in the Stackpole City Seminary. He was
under the impression, also, that his appearance
alone would command attention from his colleagues and the gallery. He was tall; his hair
was long, with a rich waviness, rippling over both
brow and collar, and he had, by years of endeavor,
succeeded in molding his features to present an
aspect of stern and thoughtful majesty whenever he "spoke."

The opportunity to show his fellows that new
greatness was among them was delayed not over-
long, and Senator Rawson arose, long and bony in
his best clothes, to address the Senate with a huge
voice in denunciation of the "Sunday Baseball
Bill," then upon second reading. The classical
references, which, as a born orator, he felt it
necessary to introduce, were received with accla-
mations which the gavel of the Lieutenant-Governor had no power to still.

"What led to the De-cline and Fall of the
Roman Empire?" he exclaimed. "I await an answer from the advocates of this *de*-generate
measure! I *demand* an answer from them! Let
me hear from them on *that* subject! Why don't
they speak up? They can't give one. Not because they ain't familiar with history—no, sir!
That's not the reason! It's because they *daren't*,

228

because their answer would have to go on record *against* 'em! Don't any of you try to raise it against me that I ain't speaking to the point, for I tell you that when you encourage Sunday Baseball, or any kind of Sabbath-breakin' on Sunday you're tryin' to start the State on the downward path that beset Rome! *I'll* tell you what ruined it. The Roman Empire started out to be the greatest nation on earth, and they had a good start, too, just like the United States has got to-day. Then what happened to 'em? Why, them old ancient fellers got more interested in athletic games and gladiatorial combats and racing and all kinds of outdoor sports, and bettin' on 'em, than they were in oratory, or literature, or charitable institutions and good works of all kinds. At first they were moderate and the country was prosperous. But six days in the week wouldn't content 'em, and they went at it all the time, so that at last they gave up the seventh day to their sports, the way this bill wants *us* to do, and from that time on the result was *de*-generacy and *de*-gradation! You better remember *that* lesson, my friends, and don't try to sink this State to the level of Rome!"

When Alonzo Rawson wiped his dampened brow, and dropped into his chair, he was satisfied to the core of his heart with the effect of his maiden effort. There was not one eye in the place that was not fixed upon him and shining with surprise and delight, while the kindly Lieutenant-Governor, his face very red, rapped for order. The young Senator across the aisle leaned over and shook Alonzo's hand excitedly.

"That was beautiful, Senator Rawson!" he whispered. "I'm *for* the bill, but I can respect a masterly opponent."

"I thank you, Senator Truslow," Alonzo returned graciously. "I am glad to have your good opinion, Senator."

"You have it, Senator," said Truslow enthusiastically. "I hope you intend to speak often."

"I do, Senator. I intend to make myself heard," the other answered gravely, "upon all questions of moment."

"You will fill a great place among us, Senator!"

Then Alonzo Rawson wondered if he had not underestimated his neighbor across the aisle; he had formed an opinion of Truslow as one of small account and no power, for he had observed that, although this was Truslow's second term, he had not once demanded recognition nor attempted to take part in a debate. Instead, he seemed to spend most of his time frittering over some desk work, though now and then he walked up and down the aisles talking in a low voice to various Senators. How such a man could have been elected at all, Alonzo failed to understand. Also, Truslow was physically inconsequent, in his colleague's estimation—"a little, insignificant, dudish kind of a man," he had thought; one whom he would have darkly suspected of cigarettes had he not been dumfounded to behold Truslow smoking an old black pipe in the lobby. The Senator from Stackpole had looked over the other's clothes with a disapproval that amounted to bitterness. Truslow's attire reminded him of pictures in New York magazines, or the dress of boys newly home from college, he didn't know which, but he did know that it was contemptible. Consequently, after receiving the young man's congratulations, Alonzo was conscious of the keenest surprise at his own feeling that there might be something in him after all.

He decided to look him over again, more carefully to take the measure of one who had shown himself so frankly an admirer. Waiting, therefore, a few moments until he felt sure that Truslow's gaze had ceased to rest upon himself, he turned to bend a surreptitious but piercing scrutiny upon his neighbor. His glance, however, sweeping across Truslow's shoulder toward the face, suddenly encountered another pair of eyes beyond, so intently fixed upon himself that he started. The clash was like two searchlights meeting—and the glorious brown eyes that shot into Alonzo's were not the eyes of Truslow.

Truslow's desk was upon the outer aisle, and along the wall were placed comfortable leather chairs and settees, originally intended for the use of members of the upper house, but nearly always occupied by their wives and daughters, or "lady-lobbyists," or other women spectators.

Leaning back with extraordinary grace, in the chair nearest Truslow, sat the handsomest woman Alonzo had ever seen in his life. Her long coat of soft gray fur was unrecognizable to him in connection with any familiar breed of squirrel; her broad flat hat of the same fur was wound with a gray veil, underneath which her heavy brown hair seemed to exhale a mysterious glow, and never, not even in a lithograph, had he seen features so regular or a skin so clear! And to look into her eyes seemed to Alonzo like diving deep into clear water and turning to stare up at the light.

His own eyes fell first. In the breathless awkwardness that beset him they seemed to stumble shamefully down to his desk, like a country boy getting back to his seat after a thrashing on the teacher's platform. For the lady's gaze, profoundly liquid as it was, had not been friendly.

Alonzo Rawson had neither the habit of petty analysis, nor the inclination toward it; yet there arose within him a wonder at his own emotion, at its strangeness and the violent reaction of it. A moment ago his soul had been steeped in satisfaction over the figure he had cut with his speech and the extreme enthusiasm which had been accorded it—an extraordinarily pleasant feeling: suddenly this was gone, and in its place he found himself almost choking with a dazed sense of having been scathed, and at the same time understood in a way in which he did not understand himself. And yet—he and this most unusual lady had been so mutually conscious of each other in their mysterious interchange that he felt almost acquainted with her. Why, then, should his head be hot with resentment? Nobody had *said* anything to him!

He seized upon the fattest of the expensive books supplied to him by the State, opened it with emphasis and began not to read it, with abysmal abstraction, tinglingly alert to the circumstance that Truslow was holding a low-toned but lively conversation with the unknown. Her laugh came to him, at once musical, quiet, and of a quality which irritated him into saying bitterly to himself that he guessed there was just as much refinement in Stackpole as there was in the Capital City, and just as many old families! The clerk calling his vote upon the "Baseball Bill," at that moment, he roared "No!" in a tone which was profane. It seemed to him that he was avenging himself upon somebody for something and it gave him a great deal of satisfaction.

He returned immediately to his imitation of Archimedes, only relaxing the intensity of his attention to the text (which blurred into jargon before his fixed gaze) when he heard that light laugh again. He pursed his lips, looked up at the ceiling as if slightly puzzled by some profound question beyond the reach of womankind; solved it almost immediately; and, setting his hand to pen and paper, wrote the capital letter "O" several hundred times on note paper furnished by the State. So oblivious was he, apparently, to everything but the question of statecraft which occupied him that he did not even look up when the morning's session was adjourned and the law-makers began to pass noisily out, until Truslow stretched an arm across the aisle and touched him upon the shoulder.

"In a moment, Senator!" answered Alonzo in his deepest chest tones. He made it a very short moment, in deed, for he had a wild, breath-taking suspicion of what was coming.

"I want you to meet Mrs. Protheroe, Senator," said Truslow, rising, as Rawson, after folding his writings with infinite care, placed them in his breast pocket.

"I am pleased to make your acquaintance, ma'am," Alonzo said in a loud, firm voice, as he got to his feet, though the place grew vague about him when the lady stretched a charming, slender, gloved hand to him across Truslow's desk. He gave it several solemn shakes.

"We shouldn't have disturbed you, perhaps?" she asked, smiling radiantly upon him. "You were at some important work, I'm afraid."

He met her eyes again, and their beauty and the thoughtful kindliness of them fairly took his breath. "I am the chairman, ma'am," he replied, swallowing, "of the committee on drains and dikes."

"I knew it was something of great moment," she said gravely, "but I was anxious to tell you that I was interested in your speech."

A few minutes later, without knowing how he had got his hat and coat from the cloak-room, Alonzo Rawson found himself walking slowly through the marble vistas of the State-house to the great outer doors with the lady and Truslow. They were talking inconsequently of the weather, and of various legislators, but Alonzo did not know it. He vaguely formed replies to her questions, and he hardly realized what the questions were; he was too stirringly conscious of the rich quiet of her voice and of the caress of the gray fur of her cloak when the back of his hand touched it—rather accidentally—now and then, as they moved on together.

It was a cold, quick air to which they emerged, and Alonzo, daring to look at her, found that she had pulled the veil down over her face, the color of which, in the keen wind, was like that of June roses seen through morning mists. At the curb a long, low, rakish black automobile was in waiting, the driver a mere indistinguishable cylinder of fur.

Truslow, opening the little door of the tonneau, offered his hand to the lady. "Come over to the club, Senator, and lunch with me," he said.

"Mrs. Protheroe won't mind dropping us there on her way."

That was an eerie ride for Alonzo, whose feet were falling upon strange places. His pulses jumped and his eyes swam with tears of unlawful speed, but his big ungloved hand tingled not with the cold so much as with the touch of that divine gray fur upon his little finger.

"You intend to make many speeches, Mr. Truslow tells me," he heard the rich voice saying.

"Yes, ma'am," he summoned himself to answer.

"I expect I will. Yes, ma'am." He paused, and then repeated, "Yes, ma'am."

She looked at him for a moment. "But you will do some work, too, won't you?" she asked slowly.

Her intention in this passed by Alonzo at the time. "Yes, ma'am," he answered. "The committee work interests me greatly, especially drains and dikes."

"I have heard," she said, as if searching his opinion, "that almost as much is accomplished in the committee-rooms as on the floor? There—and in the lobby and in the hotels and clubs?"

"I don't have much to do with that!" he returned quickly. "I guess none of them lobbyists will get much out of me! I even sent back all their railroad tickets. They needn't come near me!"

After a pause which she may have filled with unexpressed admiration, she ventured, almost timidly: "Do you remember that it was said that Napoleon once attributed the secret of his power over other men to one quality?"

"I am an admirer of Napoleon," returned the Senator from Stackpole. "I admire all great men."

"He said that he held men by his reserve."

"It can be done," observed Alonzo, and stopped, feeling that it was more reserved to add nothing to the sentence.

"But I suppose that such a policy," she smiled upon him inquiringly, "wouldn't have helped him much with women?"

"No," he agreed immediately. "My opinion is that a man ought to tell a *good* woman everything. What is more sacred than—"

The car, turning a corner much too quickly, performed a gymnastic squirm about an unexpected street-car and the speech ended in a gasp, as Alonzo, not of his own volition, half rose and pressed his cheek closely against hers. Instantaneous as it was, his heart leaped violently, but not with fear. Could all the things of his life that had seemed beautiful have been compressed into one instant it would not have brought him even the suggestion of the wild shock of joy of that one, wherein he knew the glamourous perfume of Mrs. Protheroe's brown hair and felt her cold cheek firm against his, with only the gray veil between.

"I'm afraid this driver of mine will kill me

some day," she said, laughing and composedly straightening her hat. "Do you care for big machines?"

"Yes, ma'am," he answered huskily. "I haven't been in many."

"Then I'll take you again," said Mrs. Protheroe. "If you like I'll come down to the State-house and take you out for a run in the country."

"When?" said the lost young man, staring at her with his mouth open. "When?"

"Saturday afternoon if you like. I'll be there at two."

They were in front of the club and Truslow had already jumped out. Mrs. Protheroe gave him her hand and they exchanged a glance significant of something more than a friendly good-by. Indeed, one might have hazarded that there was something almost businesslike about it. The confused Senator from Stackpole, climbing out reluctantly, observed it not, nor could he have understood, even if he had seen, that delicate signal which passed between his two companions.

When he was upon the ground, Mrs. Protheroe extended her hand without speaking, but her lips formed the word "Saturday." Then she was carried away quickly, while Alonzo, his heart hammering, stood looking after her, born into a strange world, the touch of the gray fur upon his little finger, the odor of her hair faintly about him, one side of his face red, the other pale.

MRS. PROTHEROE

"To-day is Wednesday," he said, half aloud. "Come on, Senator." Truslow took his arm and turned him toward the club doors.

The other looked upon his new friend vaguely. "Why, I forgot to thank her for the ride," he said.

"You'll have other chances, Senator," Truslow assured him. Mrs. Protheroe has a hobby for studying politics and she expects to come down often. She has plenty of time—she's a widow, you know."

"I hope you didn't think," exclaimed Alonzo indignantly, "that I thought she was a married woman!"

After lunch they walked back to the State-house together, Truslow regarding his thought-ful companion with sidelong whimsicalness. Mrs. Protheroe's question, suggestive of a differ-ence between work and speechmaking, had re-curred to Alonzo, and he had determined to make himself felt, off the floor as well as upon it. He set to this with a fine energy that afternoon in his committee-room, and the Senator from Stack-pole knew his subject. On drains and dikes he had no equal. He spoke convincingly to his col-leagues of the committee upon every bill that was before them, and he compelled their hum-blest respect. He went earnestly at it, indeed, and sat very late that night in his room at a nearby boarding-house, studying bills, trying to keep his mind upon them and not to think of his strange morning and of Saturday. Finally his neighbor in the next room, Senator Ezra Trumbull, long abed, was awakened by his praying and groaned slightly. Trumbull meant to speak to Rawson about his prayers, for Trumbull was an early one to bed and they woke him every night. The partition was flimsy and Alonzo addressed his Maker in the loud voice of those accustomed to talking across wide out-of-door spaces. Trumbull considered it especially unnecessary in the city; though, as a citizen of a county which loved but little his neighbor's district, he felt that in Stackpole there was good reason for a person to shout his prayers at the top of his voice and even then have small chance to carry through the distance. Still, it was a delicate matter to mention, and he put it off from day to day.

Thursday passed slowly for Alonzo Rawson, nor was his voice lifted in debate. There was little but routine; and the main interest of the chamber was in the lobbying that was being done upon the "Sunday Baseball Bill," which had passed to its third reading and would come up for final disposition within a fortnight. This was the measure which Alonzo had set his heart upon defeating. It was a simple enough bill: it provided, in substance, that baseball might be played on Sunday by professionals in the State capital, which was proud of its league team. Naturally, it was denounced by clergymen, and deputations of ministers and committees from women's religious societies were constantly arriving at the State-house to protest against its passage. The Senator from Stackpole reassured all of these with whom he talked, and was one of their staunchest allies and supporters. He was active in leading the wavering among his colleagues, or even the inimical, out to meet and face the deputations. It was in this occupation that he was engaged, on Friday afternoon, when he received a shock.

A committee of women from a church society was waiting in the corridor, and he had rounded up a reluctant half-dozen senators and led them forth to be interrogated as to their intentions regarding the bill. The committee and the law-makers soon distributed themselves into little argumentative clumps, and Alonzo found himself in the centre of these, with one of the ladies who had unfortunately—but, in her enthusiasm, without misgivings—begun a reproachful appeal to an advocate of the bill whose name was Goldstein.

"Senator Goldstein," she exclaimed, "I could not believe it when I heard that you were in favor of this measure! I have heard my husband speak in the highest terms of your old father. May I ask you what *he* thinks of it? If you voted for the desecration of Sunday by a low baseball game, could you dare go home and face that good old man?"

"Yes, madam," said Goldstein mildly; "we are *both* Jews."

A low laugh rippled out from near-by, and Alonzo, turning almost violently, beheld his lady of the furs. She was leaning back against a broad pilaster, her hands sweeping the same big coat behind her, her face turned toward him, but her eyes, sparklingly delighted, resting upon Goldstein.

Under the broad fur hat she made a picture as engaging, to Alonzo Rawson, as it was be-witching. She appeared not to see him, to be quite unconscious of him—and he believed it. Truslow and five or six members of both houses were about her, and they all seemed to be bend-ing eagerly toward her. Alonzo was furious with her.

Her laugh lingered upon the air for a moment, then her glance swept round the other way, omitting the Senator from Stackpole, who, imme-diately putting into practice a reserve which would have astonished Napoleon, swung about and quitted the deputation without a word of farewell or explanation. He turned into the cloak-room and paced the floor for three minutes with a malevolence which awed the colored at-tendants into not brushing his coat; but, when he returned to the corridor, cautious inquiries addressed to the tobacconist elicited the informa-tion that the handsome lady with Senator Trus-low had departed.

MRS. PROTHEROE

Truslow himself had not gone. He was lounging in his seat when Alonzo returned and was genially talkative. The latter refrained from replying in kind, not altogether out of reserve, but more because of a dim suspicion (which rose within him the third time Truslow called him "Senator" in one sentence) that his first opinion of the young man as a light-minded person might have been correct.

There was no session the following afternoon, but Alonzo watched the street from the windows of his committee-room, which overlooked the splendid breadth of stone steps leading down from the great doors to the pavement. There were some big bookcases in the room, whose glass doors served as mirrors in which he more and more sternly regarded the soft image of an entirely new gray satin tie, while the conviction grew within him that (arguing from her behavior of the previous day) she would not come, and that the Stackpole girls were nobler by far at heart than many who might wear a king's-ransom's-worth of jewels round their throats at the opera-house in a large city. This sentiment was heartily confirmed by the clock when it marked half-past two. He faced the bookcase doors and struck his breast, his open hand falling across the gray tie with tragic violence; after which, turning for the last time to the windows, he uttered a loud exclamation and, laying hands upon an ulster and a gray felt hat, each as new as the satin tie, ran hurriedly from the room. The black automobile was waiting.

"I thought it possible you might see me from a window," said Mrs. Protheroe as he opened the little door.

"I was just coming out," he returned, gasping for breath. "I thought—from yesterday—you'd probably forgotten."

"Why 'from yesterday'?" she asked.

"I thought—I thought—" He faltered to a stop as the full glorious sense of her presence overcame him. She wore the same veil.

"You thought I did not see you yesterday in the corridor?"

"I thought you might have acted more— more—"

"More cordially?"

"Well, he said, looking down at his hands, "more like you knew we'd been introduced."

At that she sat silent, looking away from him, and he, daring a quick glance at her, found that he might let his eyes remain upon her face. That was a dangerous place for eyes to rest, yet Alonzo Rawson was anxious for the risk. The car flew along the even asphalt on its way to the country like a wild goose on a long slant of wind, and, with his foolish fury melted inexplicably into honey, Alonzo looked at her—and looked at her—till he would have given an arm for another quick corner and a street-car to send his cheek against that veiled, cold cheek of hers again. It was not until they reached the alternate vacant lots and bleak Queen Anne cottages of the city's ragged edge that she broke the silence.

"You were talking to some one else," she said almost inaudibly.

"Yes, ma'am, Goldstein, but——"

"Oh, no!" She turned toward him, lifting her hand. "You were quite the lion among ladies."

"I don't know what you mean, Mrs. Protheroe," he said, truthfully.

"What were you talking to all those women about?"

"It was about the 'Sunday Baseball Bill.'"

"Ah! The bill you attacked in your speech last Wednesday?"

"Yes, ma'am."

"I hear you haven't made any speeches since then," she said indifferently.

"No, ma'am," he answered gently. "I kind of got the idea that I'd better lay low for a while, at first, and get in some quiet, hard work."

"I understand. You are a man of intensely reserved nature."

"With men," said Alonzo, "I am. With ladies I am not so much so. I think a good woman ought to be told——"

"But you are interested," she interrupted, "in defeating that bill?"

"Yes, ma'am," he returned. "It is an in-iquitous measure."

"Why?"

"Mrs. Protheroe!" he exclaimed, taken aback. "I thought all the ladies were against it. My own mother wrote to me from Stackpole that she'd rather see me in my grave than votin' for such a bill, and I'd rather see myself there!"

"But are you sure that you understand it?"

"I only know it desecrates the Sabbath. That's enough for me!"

She leaned toward him and his breath came quickly.

"No. You're wrong," she said, and rested the tips of her fingers upon his sleeve.

"I don't understand why—why you say that," he faltered. "It sounds kind of—surprising to me—"

"Listen," she said. Perhaps Mr. Truslow told you that I am studying such things. I do not want to be an idle woman; I want to be of use to the world, even if it must be only in small ways."

"I think that is a noble ambition!" he exclaimed. "I think all good women ought—"

"Wait," she interrupted gently. "Now, that bill is a worthy one, though it astonishes you to hear me say so. Perhaps you don't understand the conditions. Sunday is the laboring man's only day of recreation—and what recreation is he offered?"

"He ought to go to church," said Alonzo promptly.

"But the fact is that he doesn't—not often—not at all in the afternoon. Wouldn't it be well to give him some wholesome way of employing his Sunday afternoons? This bill provides for just that, and it keeps him away from drinking, too, for it forbids the sale of liquor on the grounds."

"Yes, I know," said Alonzo plaintively. "But it ain't *right!* I was raised to respect the Sabbath and——"

"Ah, that's what you should do! You think *I* could believe in anything that wouldn't make it better and more sacred?"

"Oh, no, ma'am!" he cried reproachfully. "It's only that I don't see——"

"I am telling you." She lifted her veil and let him have the full dazzle of her beauty. "Do you know that many thousands of laboring people spend their Sundays drinking and carousing about the low country road-houses because the game is played at such places on Sunday? They go there because they never get a chance to see it played in the city. And don't you understand that there would be no Sunday liquor trade, no workingmen poisoning themselves every seventh day in the low groggeries, as hundreds of them do now, if they had something to see that would interest them?—something as wholesome and fine as this sport would be, under the conditions of this bill; something to keep them in the open air, something to bring a little gayety into their dull lives!" Her voice had grown louder and it shook a little, with a rising emotion, though its sweetness was only the more poignant. "Oh, my dear Senator, she cried, "don't you see how wrong you are? Don't you want to *help* these poor people?"

Her fingers, which had tightened upon his sleeve, relaxed and she leaned back, pulling the veil down over her face as if wishing to conceal from him that her lips trembled slightly; then resting her arm upon the leather cushions, she turned her head away from him, staring fixedly into the gaunt beech woods lining the country road along which they were now coursing. For a time she heard nothing from him, and the only sound was the monotonous chug of the machine.

"I suppose you think it rather shocking to hear a woman talking practically of such commonplace things," she said at last, in a cold voice, just loud enough to be heard.

"No, ma'am," he said huskily.

"Then what *do* you think?" she cried, turning toward him again with a quick, imperious gesture.

"I think I'd better go back to Stackpole," he answered very slowly, "and resign my job. I don't see as I've got any business in the Legislature."

"I don't understand you."

He shook his head mournfully. "It's a simple enough matter. I've studied out a good many bills and talked 'em over and I've picked up some influence and——"

"I know you have," she interrupted eagerly. "Mr. Truslow says that the members of your drains-and-dikes committee follow your vote on every bill."

"Yes, ma'am," said Alonzo Rawson meekly, "but I expect they oughtn't to. I've had a lesson this afternoon."

"You mean to say——"

"I mean that I didn't know what I was doing about that baseball bill. I was just pig-headedly goin' ahead against it, not knowing nothing about the conditions, and it took a lady to show me what they were. I would have done a wrong thing if you hadn't stopped me."

"You mean," she cried, her splendid eyes widening with excitement and delight; "you mean that you—that you——,"

"I mean that I will vote for the bill." He struck his clinched fist upon his knee. "I come to the Legislature to do *right!*"

"You will, ah, you *will* do right in this?" Mrs. Protheroe thrust up her veil again and her face was flushed and radiant with triumph. "And you'll work, and you'll make a speech for the bill?"

At this the righteous exaltation began rather abruptly to simmer down in the soul of Alonzo Rawson. He saw the consequences of too violently reversing, and knew how difficult they might be to face.

"Well, not—not exactly," he said weakly. "I

expect our best plan would be for me to lay kind of low and not say any more about the bill at all. Of course, I'll quit workin' against it; and on the roll-call I'll edge close up to the clerk and say 'Aye' so that only him'll hear me. That's done every day—and I—well, I don't just exactly like to come out too publicly for it, after my speech and all I've done against it."

She looked at him sharply for a short second, and then offered him her hand and said: "Let's shake hands *now* on the vote. Think what a triumph it is *for* me to know that I helped to show you the right."

"Yes, ma'am," he answered confusedly, too much occupied with shaking her hand to know what he said. She spoke one word in an under-tone to the driver and the machine took the very shortest way back to the city.

After this excursion several days passed before Mrs. Protheroe came to the State-house again. Rawson was bending over the desk of Senator Josephus Battle, the white-bearded leader of the opposition to the "Sunday Baseball Bill," and was explaining to him the intricacies of a certain drainage measure, when Battle, whose attention had wandered, plucked his sleeve and whispered:

"If you want to see a mighty pretty woman that's doin' no good here, look behind you, over there in the chair by the big fireplace at the back of the room."

Alonzo looked.

MRS. PROTHEROE

It was she whose counterpart had been in his dream's eye every moment of the dragging days which had been vacant of her living presence. A number of his colleagues were hanging over her almost idiotically; her face was gay and her voice came to his ears, as he turned, with the accent of her cadenced laughter running through her talk like a chime of tiny bells flitting through a strain of music.

"This is the third time she's been here," said Battle, rubbing his beard the wrong way. "She's lobbyin' for that infernal Sabbath-Desecration bill, but we'll beat her, my son."

"Have you made her acquaintance, Senator?" asked Alonzo stiffly.

"No, sir, and I don't want to. But I knew her father—the slickest old beat and the smoothest talker that ever waltzed up the pike. She married rich; her husband left her a lot of real estate around here, but she spends most of her time away. Whatever struck her to come down and lobby for that bill I don't know—yet—but I will! Truslow's helping her to help himself; he's got stock in the company that runs the baseball team, but what she's up to—well, I'll bet there's a nigger in the woodpile *somewhere!*"

"I expect there's a lot of talk like that!" said Alonzo, red with anger, and taking up his papers abruptly.

"Yes, *sir!*" said Battle emphatically, utterly misunderstanding the other's tone and manner.

"Don't you worry, my son. We'll kill that venomous bill right here in this chamber! We'll kill it so dead that it won't make one flop after the axe hits it. You and me and some others'll tend to *that!* Let her work that pretty face and those eyes of hers all she wants to! I'm keepin' a little lookout, too—and I'll—"

He broke off, for the angry and perturbed Alonzo had left him and gone to his own desk. Battle, slightly surprised, rubbed his beard the wrong way and sauntered out to the lobby to muse over a cigar. Alonzo, loathing Battle with a great loathing, formed bitter phrases concerning that vicious-minded old gentleman, while for a moment he affected to be setting his desk in order. Then he walked slowly up the aisle, conscious of a roaring in his ears (though not aware how red they were) as he approached the semicircle about her.

He paused within three feet of her in a sudden panic of timidity, and then, to his consternation, she looked him squarely in the face, over the shoulders of two of the group, and the only sign of recognition that she exhibited was a slight frown of unmistakable repulsion, which appeared between her handsome eyebrows.

It was very swift; only Alonzo saw it; the others had no eyes for anything but her, and were not aware of his presence behind them, for she did not even pause in what she was saying. Alonzo walked slowly away with the wormwood in his heart. He had not grown up among the young people of Stackpole without similar experiences, but it had been his youthful boast that no girl had ever "stopped speaking" to him without reason, or "cut a dance" with him and afterward found opportunity to repeat the indignity.

"What have I *done* to *her?*" was perhaps the hottest cry of his bruised soul, for the mystery was as great as the sting of it.

It was no balm upon that sting to see her pass him at the top of the outer steps, half an hour later, on the arm of that one of his colleagues who had been called the "best-dressed man in the Legislature." She swept by him without a sign, laughing that same laugh at some sally of her escort, and they got into the black automobile together and were whirled away and out of sight by the impassive bundle of furs who manipulated the wheel.

For the rest of that afternoon and the whole of that night no man, woman, or child heard the voice of Alonzo Rawson, for he spoke to none. He came not to the evening meal, nor was he seen by any who had his acquaintance. He entered his room at about midnight, and Trumbull was awakened by his neighbor's overturning a chair. No match was struck, however, and Trumbull was relieved to think that the Senator from Stackpole intended going directly to bed without troubling to light the gas, and that his prayers would soon be over. Such was not the case, for no other sound came from the room, nor were Alonzo's prayers uttered that night, though the unhappy statesman in the next apartment could not get to sleep for several hours on account of his nervous expectancy of them.

After this, as the day approached upon which hung the fate of the bill which Mr. Josephus Battle was fighting, Mrs. Protheroe came to the Senate Chamber nearly every morning and afternoon. Not once did she appear to be conscious of Alonzo Rawson's presence, nor once did he allow his eyes to delay upon her, though it can not be truthfully said that he did not always know when she came, when she left, and with whom she stood or sat or talked. He evaded all mention or discussion of the bill or of Mrs. Protheroe; avoided Truslow (who, strangely enough, was avoiding *him*) and, spending upon drains and dikes all the energy that he could manage to concentrate, burned the midnight oil and rubbed salt into his wounds to such marked effect that by the evening of the Governor's Reception—upon the morning following which the mooted bill was to come up—he offered an impression so haggard and worn than an actor might have studied him for a make-up as a young statesman going into a decline.

Nevertheless he dressed with great care and bitterness, and paced the fragrant blossom of a geranium—taken from a plant belonging to his landlady—in the lapel of his long coat before he set out.

And yet, when he came down the Governor's broad stairs, and wandered through the big rooms, with the glare of lights above him and the shouting of the guests ringing in his ears, a sense of emptiness beset him; the crowded place seemed vacant and without meaning. Even the noise sounded hollow and remote—and why had he bothered about the geranium? He hated her and would never look at her again—but why was she not there?

By and by, he found himself standing against a wall, where he had been pushed by the press of people.

He was wondering drearily what he was to do with a clean plate and a napkin which a courteous negro had handed him, half an hour earlier, when he felt a quick jerk at his sleeve. It was Truslow, who had worked his way along the wall, and who now, standing on tiptoe, spoke rapidly but cautiously, close to his ear.

"Senator, be quick," he said sharply, at the same time alert to see that they were unobserved. "Mrs. Protheroe wants to speak to you at once. You'll find her near the big palms under the stairway in the hall."

He was gone—he had wormed his way half across the room—before the other, in his simple amazement, could answer. When Alonzo at last found a word, it was only a monosyllable, which, with his accompanying action, left a matron of years, who was at that moment being pressed fondly to his side, in a state of mind almost as dumfounded as his own. *"Here!"* was all he said as he pressed the plate and napkin into her hand and departed forcibly for the hall, leaving a spectacular wreckage of trains behind him.

The upward flight of the stairway left a space underneath, upon which, as it was screened (save for a narrow entrance) by a thicket of palms, the crowd had not encroached. Here were placed a divan and a couple of chairs; there was shade from the glare of gas, and the light was dim and cool. Mrs. Protheroe had risen from the divan when Alonzo entered this grotto, and stood waiting for him.

He stopped in the green entrance-way with a quick exclamation.

She did not seem the same woman who had put such slights upon him, this tall, white vision of silk, with the summery scarf falling from her shoulders. His great wrath melted at the sight of her; the pain of his racked pride, which had been so hot in his breast, gave way to a species of fear. She seemed not a human being, but a white spirit of beauty and goodness who stood before him, extending two fine arms to him in long, white gloves.

She left him to his trance for a moment, then seized both his hands in hers and cried to him in her rapturous, low voice: "Ah, Senator, you have come! I *knew* you understood!"

"Yes ma'am," he whispered chokily.

She drew him to one of the chairs and sank gracefully down upon the divan near him.

"Mr. Truslow was so afraid you wouldn't," she went on rapidly, "but I was sure. You see I didn't want anybody to suspect that I had any influence with you. I didn't want them to know, even, that I'd talked to you. It all came to me after the first day that we met. You see I've believed in you, in your power and in your reserve, from the first. I want all that you do to seem to come from yourself and not from me or any one else. Oh, I *believe* in great, strong men who stand upon their own feet and conquer the world for themselves! That's *your* way, Senator Rawson. So, you see, as they think I'm lobbying for the bill, I wanted them to believe that your speech for it to-morrow comes from your own great, strong mind and heart and your sense of right, and not from any suggestion of mine."

"My speech!" he stammered.

"Oh, I know," she cried; "I know you think I don't believe much in speeches, and I don't ordinarily, but a few simple, straightforward and vigorous words from you, to-morrow, may carry the bill through. You've made such *progress*, you've been so *reserved*, that you'll carry great weight—and there are three votes of the drains-and-dikes that are against us now, but will follow yours absolutely. Do you think I would have '*cut*' *you* if it hadn't been *best?*"

"But I—"

"Oh, I know you didn't actually promise me to speak, that day. But I knew you would when the time came! I knew that a man of power goes over *all* obstacles, once his sense of *right* is aroused! I *knew*—I never doubted it, that once *you* felt a thing to be right you would strike for it, with all your great strength—at all costs—at all—"

"I can't—I—I—can't!" he whispered nervously. "Don't you see—don't you see—I—"

She leaned toward him, lifting her face close to his. She was so near him that the faint odor of her hair came to him again, and once more the unfortunate Senator from Stackpole risked a meeting of his eyes with hers, and saw the light shining far down in their depths.

At this moment the shadow of a portly man who was stroking his beard the wrong way projected itself upon them from the narrow, green entrance to the grotto. Neither of them perceived it.

Senator Josephus Battle passed on, but when Alonzo Rawson emerged, a few moments later, he was pledged to utter a few simple, straightforward, and vigorous words in favor of the bill. And—let the shame fall upon the head of the scribe who tells it—he had kissed Mrs. Protheroe!

MRS. PROTHEROE

The fight upon the "Sunday Baseball Bill" the next morning was the warmest of that part of the session, though for a while the reporters were disappointed. They were waiting for Senator Battle, who was famous among them for the vituperative vigor of his attacks and for the kind of personalities which made valuable copy. And yet, until the debate was almost over, he contented himself with going quietly up and down the aisles, whispering to the occupants of the desks, and writing and sending a multitude of notes to his colleagues. Meanwhile, the orators upon both sides harangued their fellows, the lobby, the unpolitical audience, and the patient presiding officer to no effect, so far as votes went. The general impression was that it would be close.

Alonzo Rawson sat bent over his desk, his eyes fixed with gentle steadiness upon Mrs. Protheroe, who occupied the chair wherein he had first seen her. A senator of the opposition was finishing his denunciation, when she turned and nodded almost imperceptibly to the young man.

He gave her one last look of pathetic tenderness and rose.

"The Senator from Stackpole!"

"I want," Alonzo began, in his big voice—"I want to say a few simple, straightforward but vigorous words about this bill. You may remember I spoke against it on its second reading—"

"You did *that!*" shouted Senator Battle suddenly.

"I want to say now," the Senator from Stackpole continued, "that at that time I hadn't studied the conditions of the case, nor the facts, but since then a great light has broke in upon me—"

"I should say it had! I saw it break!" was Senator Battle's second violent interruption.

When order was restored, Alonzo, who had become very pale, summoned his voice again. "I think we'd ought to take into consideration that Sunday is the working-man's only day of recreation and not drive him into low groggeries, but give him a chance in the open air to indulge his love of wholesome sport—"

"Such as the ancient Romans enjoyed!" interposed Battle vindictively.

"No, sir!" Alonzo wheeled upon him, stung to the quick. "Such a sport as free-born Americans and *only* free-born Americans can play in this wide world—the American game of baseball, in which no other nation of the *Earth* is our equal!"

This was a point scored and the cheering lasted two minutes. Then the orator resumed:

"I say: 'Give the working-man a chance!' Is his life a happy one? You know it ain't! Give him his one day. *Don't* spoil it for him with your laws—he's only got one! I'm not goin' to take up any more of your time, but if there's anybody

260

here who thinks my well-considered opinion worth following I say: *'Vote for this bill.'* It is right and virtuous and ennobling, and it ought to be passed! I say: *'Vote for it.'*"

The reporters decided that the Senator from Stackpole had "wakened things up." The gavel rapped a long time before the chamber quieted down, and when it did, Josephus Battle was on his feet and had obtained the recognition of the chair.

"I wish to say, right here," he began, with a rasping leisureliness, "that I hope no member of this honored body will take my remarks as personal or unparliamentary—*but*"—he raised a big forefinger and shook it with menace at the presiding officer at the same time suddenly lifting his voice to an unprintable shriek—"I say to *you, sir,* that the song of the siren has been *heard* in the land, and the call of Delilah has been answered! When the Senator from Stackpole rose in his chamber, less than three weeks ago, and denounced this iniquitous measure, I heard him with pleasure—we *all* heard him with pleasure— *and* respect! In spite of his youth and the poor quality of his expression, *we* listened to him. *We* knew he was sincere! What has caused the change in him? What *has*, I ask? I shall not tell you, upon this floor, but I've taken mighty good care to let most of you know, during the morning, either by word of mouth or by *note* of hand! Especially those of you of the drains-and-dikes and others who might follow this young Samson, whose locks have been shore! *I've told* you all about that, and more—*I've* told you the *inside* history of some *facts* about the bill that I will not make public, because I am too confident of our strength to defeat this devilish measure, and **prefer** to let our vote speak our opinion of it! Let me not detain you longer. *I thank you!*"

Long before he had finished, the Senator from Stackpole was being held down in his chair by Truslow and several senators whose seats were adjacent; and the vote was taken amid an uproar of shouting and confusion. When the clerk managed to proclaim the result over all other noises, the bill was shown to be defeated and "killed," by a majority of five votes.

A few minutes later, Alonzo Rawson, his neck-wear disordered and his face white with rage, stumbled out of the great doors upon the trail of Battle, who had quietly hurried away to his hotel for lunch as soon as he had voted.

The black automobile was vanishing round a corner. Truslow stood upon the edge of the pavement staring after it ruefully:

"Where is Mrs. Protheroe?" gasped the Senator from Stackpole.

"She's gone," said the other.

"Gone where?"

"Gone back to Paris. She sails day after to-morrow. She just had time enough to catch her train for New York after waiting to hear how the vote went. She told me to tell you good-by, and that she was sorry. Don't stare at me, Rawson! I guess we're in the same boat!— Where are you going?" he finished abruptly.

Alonzo swung by him and started across the street. "To find Battle?" the hoarse answer came back.

The conquering Josephus was leaning meditatively upon the counter of the cigar-stand of his hotel when Alonzo found him. He took one look at the latter's face and backed to the wall, tightening his grasp upon the heavy-headed ebony cane it was his habit to carry, a habit upon which he now congratulated himself.

But his precautions were needless. Alonzo stopped out of reaching distance.

"You tell me," he said in a breaking voice; you tell me what you meant about Delilah and sirens and Samsons and inside facts! You tell me!"

"You wild ass of the prairies," said Battle, "I saw you last night behind them pa'ms! But don't you think I told it—or ever will! I just passed the word around that she'd argued you into her way of thinkin', same as she had a good many others. And as for the rest of it, I found out where the nigger in the woodpile was, and I handed that out, too. Don't you take it hard, my son, but I told you her husband left her a good deal of land around here. She owns the ground that they use for the baseball park, and her lease would be worth considerable more if they could have got the right to play on Sunday!"

Senator Trumbull sat up straight, in bed, that night, and, for the first time during his martyrdom, listened with no impatience to the prayer which fell upon his ears.

"O Lord Almighty," through the flimsy partition came the voice of Alonzo Rawson, quaveringly, but with growing strength: "Aid Thou me to see my way more clear! I find it hard to tell right from wrong, and I find myself beset with tangled wires. O God, I feel that I am ignorant, and fall into many devices. These are strange paths wherein Thou hast set my feet, but I feel that through Thy help, and through great anguish, I am learning!"

MR. DOOLEY ON THE PURSUIT OF RICHES

BY F. P. DUNNE

MR. DOOLEY ON THE PURSUIT OF RICHES

BY F. P. DUNNE

"DEAR me, I wish I had money," said Mr. Hennessy.

"So do I," said Mr. Dooley. "I need it."

"Ye wudden't get it fr'm me," said Mr. Hennessy.

"If I didn't," said Mr. Dooley, "'twud be because I was poor or tired. But what d'ye want money f'r? Supposin' I lost me head an' handed over all me accumylated wealth? What wud ye do with that gr-reat fortune? Befure ye had spint half iv it, ye'd be so sick ye'd come to me an' hand me back th' remainin' eighteen dollars.

"A man has more fun wishin' f'r th' things he hasn't got thin injyin' th' things he has got. Life, Hinnissy, is like a Pullman dinin' car: a fine bill iv fare, but nawthin' to eat. Ye go in fresh an' hungry, tuck ye'er napkin in ye'er collar, an' square away at th' list iv groceries that th' black man hands ye. What'll ye have first? Ye think ye'd like to be famous an' ye ordher a dish iv fame an' bid th' waither make it good an' hot. He's gone an age, an' whin he comes back ye'er appytite is departed. Ye taste th' ordher an' says ye: "Why, it's cold an' full iv broken glass,' 'That's th' way we always sarve Fame on this car,' says th' coon. 'Don't ye think ye'd like money f'r th' sicond coorse? Misther Rocky-fellar over there has had forty-two helpin's,' says he. 'It don't seem to agree with him,' says ye, 'but ye may bring me some,' ye say. Away he goes an' stays till ye're bald an' ye'er teeth fall out, an' ye set dhrummin' on th' table an' lookin' out at th' scenery. By an' by he comes back with ye'er ordher, but jus' as he's goin' to hand it to ye, Rockyfellar grabs th' plate. 'What kind iv a car is this?' says ye. 'Don't I get anything to eat? Can't ye give me a little happiness?' 'I wudden't ricommend th' happi-ness,' says th' waither. 'It's canned an' it kilt th' las' man that thried it.' 'Well, gracious,' says ye, 'I've got to have something. Give me a little good health an' I'll thry to make a meal out iv that.' 'Sorry, sir,' says th' black man, 'but we're all out iv good health. Besides,' he says, takin' ye gintly by th' ar-rm, 'we're goin' into th' deepo an' ye'll have to get out,' he says.

"An' there ye ar-re. Ye'll niver get money on-less ye fix th' waither an' grab th' dishes away fr'm th' other passengers. An' ye won't do that. So ye'll niver be rich. No poor man iver will be. Wan iv th' sthrangest things about life is that th' poor who need th' money th' most ar-re th' very wans that niver have it. A poor man is a

THE PURSUIT OF RICHES

poor man an' a rich man is a rich man. Ye're ayether born poor or rich. It don't make anny diff'rence whether or not ye have money to begin with. If ye're born to be rich, ye'll be rich, an' if ye're born to be poor, ye'll be poor. Th' buttons on ye'er vest tell th' story. Rich man, poor man, beggar man, rich man, or wurruds to that effect. I always find that I have ayether two buttons or six.

"A poor man is a man that rayfuses to cash in. Ye don't get annything f'r nawthin', an' to gather in a millyon iv thim beautiful lithographs iv Salmon P. Chase, ye have to go down ivry day with something undher ye-er ar-rm to th' great pawnshop. Whin Hogan wants four dollars, he takes th' clock down to Moses. Whin Rocky-fellar wants tin millyon, he puts up his peace iv mind or his health or something akelly valyable. If Hogan wud hock his priceless habit iv sleepin' late in th' mornin', he wud be able to tell th' time iv day whin he got up without goin' to th' corner dhrug store.

"Look at McMullin. He's rowlin' in it. It bulges his pocket an' inflates his convarsation. Whin he looks at me, I always feel that he's won-dhrin' how much I'd bring at a forced sale. Well, McMullin an' I had th' same start, about forty yards behind scratch an' Vanderbilt to beat. They always put th' best man in anny race be-hind th' line. Before McMullin gets through he'll pass Vanderbilt, carry away th' tape on his shouldhers, an' run two or three times around th' thrack. But me an' him started th' same way. Th' on'y diff'rence was that he wud cash in an' I wudden't. Th' on'y thing I iver inpicted to get money on was me dhream iv avarice. I always had that. I cud dhream iv money as hard as anny man ye iver see an' can still. But I niver thought iv wurrukin' f'r it. I've always looked on it as dishon'rable to wurruk f'r money. I wurruk f'r exercise an' I get what th' lawyers call an honor-aryium be dilutin' th' spirits. Th' on'y way I iver expict to make a cint is to have it left to me be a rich relation, an' I'm th' pluthycrat iv me fam'ly, or to stub me toe on a gambler's roll or stop a runaway horse f'r Pierpont Morgan. An' th' horse mustn't be runnin' too fast. He must be jus' goin' to stop, on'y Morgan don't know it, havin' fainted. Whin he comes to, he finds me at th' bridle, modestly waitin' f'r him to weep on me bosom. But as f'r scramblin' down town arly in th' mornin' an' buyin' chattel morgedges, I niver thought iv it. I get up at siven o'clock. I wudden't get up at a quarther to siven f'r all th' money I dhream about. I have a lot iv things ar-round here I cud cash in if I cared f'r money. I have th' priceless gift iv laziness. It's made me what I am, an' that's th' very first thing ivry rich man cashes in. Th' millyonaires ye r-read about thryin' to give th' rest iv th' wurruld a good time be runnin' over thim in autymobills all started with a large stock iv indolence which they cashed in. Now, whin they cud enjoy it, they can't buy it back. Thin I have me good health. Ye can always get money on that. An' I have me frinds; I rayfuse to cash thim in. I don't know that I cud get much on thim, but if I wanted to be a millyonaire, I'd tuck you an' Hogan an' Donahue undher me ar-rm an' carry ye down to Mose.

"McMullin did cash. He had no more laziness thin me, but he cashed it in befure he was twinty-wan. He cashed in his good health, a large stock iv fam'ly ties, th' affiction if his wife, th' comforts iv home, an' wan frind afther another. Wanst in a while, late in life, he'd thry to redeem a pledge, but he niver cud. They wasn't annything in th' wurruld that McMullin wudden't change f'r th' roly-boly. He cashed in his vote, his pathreetism, his rellijon, his rilitives, an' fin'lly his hair. Ye heerd about him, didn't ye? He's lost ivry hair on his head. They ain't a spear iv vigitation left on him. He's as arid as th' desert iv Sahara. His head looks like an iceberg in th' moonlight. He was in here th' other day, bewailin' his fate. 'It's a gr-reat misfortune, says he. 'What did ye get f'r it?' says I. 'That's th' throuble,' says he. 'Well, don't complain,' says I. 'Think what ye save in barber's bills,' I says, an' he wint away lookin' much cheered up.

"No, Hinnissy, you an' I, me frind, was not cut out be Provydence to be millyionaires. If ye had nawthin' but money, ye'd have nawthin' but money. Ye can't ate it, sleep it, dhrink it, or carry it away with ye. Ye've got a lot iv things that McMullin hasn't got. Annybody that goes down to Mose's won't see ye'er peace iv mind hangin' in th' window as an unredeemed pledge. An' annyhow, if ye're really in search iv a fortune, perhaps I cud help ye. Wud a dollar an' a half be anny use to ye?"

"Life is full iv disappointments," said Mr. Hennessy.

"It is," said Mr. Dooley, "if ye feel that way. It's thrue that a good many have thried it an' none have come back f'r a post-gradjate coorse. But still it ain't so bad as a career f'r a young man. Ye niver get what ye ordher, but it's pretty good if ye'er appytite ain't keen an' ye care f'r th' scenery."

THE CHARGE

BY W. DOUGLAS NEWTON

THE CHARGE

BY W. DOUGLAS NEWTON

THE guns, cleverly masked behind the battle scene like the ministrants of stage thunder, began to pulse up and up with the enormous clamor of concentrated fire. The earth began to tremble beneath this excess of sound; the keen, high raging of the rifle fire became marked against the mighty noise of the artillery with a sound no more than the whimper of a fretful baby. The guns were crushing out all opposition in the market-place of clangor.

The firing-line behind the thousand tiny mounds it had dug to protect itself, stiffened when the first Homeric burst of the guns swamped over the battle-field. A perceptible ripple of preparation swept over the line, an intuitive easing of harness and tautening of straps. Hats were pulled down firm on the brows, rifles were held forward and examined with eyes of ruthless analysis. Clips were whipped from pouches and thumbed home crisply into magazines. At one impulse eyes swiveled round and fixed themselves on a little group of officers sitting under cover of a wall. One of the officers had a whistle lifted ready for instant action. An

275

orderly was crouching close to the ground with the disk-head of a field telephone to his ear. The officers, particularly the officer with the poised whistle, watched the orderly, their bodies set in the graven lines of infinite attention.

The officers knew what the men in the firing-line had sensed. This gigantic outburst of massed artillery was the prelude to their advance. When the lashing shrapnel had prepared the way to the Commanding Officer's satisfaction, a message would come to them over the four miles of the telephone wire. Then they would do their best to rush the enemy's trenched position.

Second-Lieutenant Hugo Bellair of Company B lay on his stomach a little to the rear of the men in his section. He was watching the officer with the whistle with an intentness so fierce that it was painful. When that whistle sounded the entire regiment would start up and they would charge, and it would be his first charge.

He had lived for and feared this moment for the last ten years. All the glory and all the terror of it that had fought in his heart for those years would now be put to the test. He himself would be put to the test. Would he come out well, or would fear unnerve him into mean and ignoble disgrace? He was an imaginative boy; he saw every bullet that was fired at the regiment, every shell that split the air with a loud crash overhead—and he felt the pain of every

THE CHARGE

wound they made. He saw himself unstrung by his fear of pain, and turning tail and scuttling away to safety before the eyes of all the army. He feared that act above all other things.

As he waited he could hear the voices of the men before him, standing out with the curious definition of small sounds against a background of huge noise. The men were feeling the tension, fretting at the suspense. He heard the voice of a man standing near him muttering over and over again:

"Oh, get on. Oh, do get on. For th' Lord's sake get on with it." He mentally agreed with the tense and irritable eagerness of the private. But as he agreed the orderly at the telephone jerked upright. The officers round him stirred spasmodically. The officer holding the whistle jumped about and faced the man in the firing-line. His hand lifted to his lips. . . . .

Lieutenant Bellair came to his knee at once. As he arose something flicked like a fly against his neck, and in an unexpected way, his vision became blurred with the intensity of his emotion. In a flash, however, his senses cleared. He felt himself running forward with his men in the opening movements of the charge.

At once, as he ran, he knew that his fears had been baseless. He was not going to turn tail at all. He was going to do immense things. He was going to carry the charge right home on his own

277

shoulders. He was going to win the battle for his country.

He ran on nursing his men in the short section rushes with a skill that was genius. He seemed to be able to gage the psychological moment for whipping them up and on, and the moment to halt them and fling them prone so that little or no hurt came their way. He dropped them at cover by instinct, and he got them over dead ground in a way quite uncanny. This new, fine sense of generalship was indeed intoxicating. It gave him the strong clear emotions of a batsman well set. He could do nothing wrong. He laughed aloud at his fears. He saw himself covered with glory now, and throughout the campaign.

Even the plain that had looked so cramped before their charge began, appeared illimitable now they were on their feet. On the other hand, though the high scarp of downs had backed miles away from them, they also loomed higher and more menacing. Their sides sleek here, dotted with tufts of gorse like the hide of a mangy poodle there, seemed to have become impregnably steep. The thin, trailing fume of picric that had burned weakly upward from the slopes and crest, had now thickened ominously and hung in the sky in a slate-black pall of death and slaughter. The whole face of the hill seemed to lift itself in thunder and hurl its avalanche of death down upon them. The charging line however lunged on with the headlong impulse of men who knew their lives were charmed.

The first field was a paddock as green as aqua-marine, and soft from recent rain; they were over that quickly. A hedge came up before them and they crushed through it, hammered across a white-hot tape of road, then up a steep bank onto a field arid and slippery with stubble. The full-throated gale of the firing hit them here. The first men up the bank hung in the fierce wind of it and were then blown clean away. For a moment there was a minor chaos. The shrapnel felt for them, found them. A squall of shells leaped into the air above their heads, smashed the sky to fragments with their harsh shattering crashes, and drove down an infernal rain of iron death. The men ran about like insects under the canopy of the shrapnel's soft white and magenta-colored smoke, like insects they sought blindly for and never found, places to hide from this aerial de-stroyer.

Bellair forgot all about the shrapnel and spurred on his men. The clarity of his mind was extraordinary. He whipped them with his tongue, soothed them with his voice in an admir-able instinctive manner. He pulled them into order and then hurled them across the stubble field. With a sort of divine *flair* he had found a ditch under a hedge-set mound. In the lee of the mound he ran his men toward the enemy. And not his own men only. He discovered that his captain and the senior lieutenant had been killed, and he was in sole charge of the entire company.

The stubble field was full of the whirling mist of battle, and countless men moving like wraiths in this mist. Thanks to the mound, his own men were not suffering much, but across the field through the mist he saw men diving earthward in the final and nerveless way of death, and men spinning and falling under the thresh of the bullets. The air above this field seemed packed with puff-balls of shrapnel, as though some monstrous crop with invisible stems were blossoming there. Now and then the surface of the field would gush earth and flame and thick greasy smoke in one vast hiccup, as a high power shell landed and burst. Always overhead, even beating at the hedge above Bellair with flail-like fingers of steel, passed the whirring hiss of ceaseless rifle bullets. The uproar was indescribable; the charging men were living in the core of a giant, palpitating hell of sound.

The ditch came to an end with stunning abruptness. With stunning abruptness the great hill towered right over their heads in a way that made them feel that it was about to fall down on top of them and crush them flat. There was a short sloping piece of brown turned earth between them and the foot of the hill, a thick belt of bush and trees, then out of the bush rose the hillside as steep as the roof of a house.

THE CHARGE

The entire surface of the hill was quick and humming with battle. Its olive surface was slashed right up to the crest with the acid light of rifle fire, and draped with the veiling crêpe of picric fume. Trenches masked with turfs to render them indistinguishable from the slope, ran, with no more dignity than bunkers, in odd terraces up to the summit. On platforms screened and defended with tree branches and thick gorse, were many viperish little machine guns spitting and jetting like steam exhaust-pipes. Where the hill yielded itself in more easy and supple lines field guns were placed behind felled trees whose branches stuck out in the face of the enemy. These guns could rake the attack with a harrowing enfilading fire. At one place where a gap came down almost to the plain, the sturdy star-angle of a field redan showed; the slope facing it was webbed with wire entangle-ments, and supporting trenches had been scarred on various sections of the hillside.

Directly his men halted at the end of the ditch, Bellair's eyes found this place. The instinct that had carried him so splendidly forward fastened upon it at once, and he saw at once a weakness. His men had dropped to earth immediately, where there was a tiny cliff of earth affording cover. They should have gone on, but Bellair held them while they recovered wind enough to take them over the final lap of the charge.

The rest of the regiment heaved across the turned land and fell thundering on the thick bush in a great wave crested with the spume of bayonets. The bush which had been lying passive all through the advance, started to life with an appalling clap. Even before it spoke Bellair's instinct told him that it was packed with the enemy's infantry. As the two bodies of men came together in a great worrying tangle of battling, the sound they made was like that of two immense dogs fighting to kill. The smoke of the battle began to whirl in great spirals, catching at the leaves with trailing fingers as it rose. Since the armies had intermingled the firing of the artillery tailed off to nothing, but the shrill and hateful screaming of the rifles rose and rose until it reached an insane point of shrewish fury. Stabbing into this sound beat the febrile hammering of the spiteful automatic guns. The one pound shells detonated in the heart of the fight with the sound of giant crackers and their bursting charges strung the gray blanket of the smoke with pretty flower-like flames. The flames from the rifles slit and stabbed the smoke like knives.

Bellair looked at the mad incoherence of the battling and knew instantly that it could end but one way. Section after section went charging into the fight, but by a mere frontal attack, men of flesh and blood could not break through the strong line of works hidden by the bushes and trees. Bellair knew that the fight could not be won at that point. Again he looked up at the redan and the gap it guarded. Yes, if he took his company up at that in a certain way there need be no disastrous frontal attack.

The battle under the trees wore itself down to a sullen and heavy crackling of rifles. The attacking force began to struggle limply out of the smoke in ones and twos, and then in little groups. But they were good soldiers. Though death slashed through the little squads with a regularity that was monotonous to behold, the men failed to show excitement or hurry. They were veterans retiring in their own way and at their own pace. When they had fallen back a score of yards they faced about with the calmness of men on a parade ground. With icy deliberation they fired a shouting and defiant volley at their enemies in the bush. As they loosed, their supports came swarming up, and caught in the swing of this surge of men, they, nothing loath, went back at a rush into the inferno under the trees.

Bellair had already passed the word to his sergeants, and when the fight had raged a few seconds, he had his men on their feet. Without a moment's hesitation he flung them in a superb and sweeping gesture of attack at the redan.

His company springing across the brown turned earth came into the fight with all the dramatic qualities of surprise. The defenders concentrating all their energies on the main attack missed the initial movement of their rush. For eternities of seconds the handful of men in the company raced forward through what seemed to them the thick and heavy silence before a cyclone. Death must come blasting in fury onto them at any moment, they knew. Running with all the speed they could, they yet waited with scarcely beating hearts the squall of death. They could see the entire surface of the hill with the startling clarity of things perceived in a mirror. They could see the mechanic-like zeal of the machine gunners as they flicked shell after shell into the wings of the fight about the bushes, they could see little rills of men being hurried toward this main fight, they could see even the artillerymen in the redan craning forward, looking down toward the bushes and wondering when they would get their chance. They saw it all with a vivid flash. Then the picture blurred with hurry: they, themselves, were seen.

The men in the redan became volatile with an abrupt nervousness, they turned about wildly like men cringing before an unexpected blow, darting nervous glances allwhither to discover from what angle the attack would strike at them. They saw the headlong company and began fussing with a frantic effort to meet and stop it with gun-fire. Men hurled themselves at the guns behind the abatis, tried to lift them by sheer muscular effort to meet the charge. Riflemen came flinging into line, the place seemed to take fire and blaze away in a mad effort to sweep the company off the face of the earth at once.

But the defenders were too late. Bellair's infallible instinct had served him well. It had found for him a line of attack that not only took the redan at on unprotected spot, but also carried his men onto it in such a way that no decimating fire could stop them. Before the guns could be swung round, before the infantry in the redan and in the supporting trenches could bring to bear on the attackers a steady man-stopping fire, the company was on the redan and in it. The feeble few infantry left in the bush-trenches by the resistance of the main attack fired one nerveless volley, and Bellair's men were on them, tossing them aside, punching through them. Their defense went out as a snuffed candle goes out and the company was going up the hill with unthwartable élan.

The fret of a ragged rifle fire caught a fringe of his men and sent them flopping down the hill, but it mattered not at all. The company was through that zone immediately, across a flattish slope and into the unprotected rear of the redan. Men scrambled from the guns and thrust themselves at them. Bellair's men blazed one volley and then the angry bayonets flashed in the sun and drove deep and home. The muck of men fought and scrambled amid the guns. A large officer gorgeted with the scarlet of the staff, swung down on the lieutenant; Bellair parried his thrust with an unthinking ease; circled with his sword and took the man in the throat. A sergeant sprang to a gun, and began wrenching free its breech-piece; Bellair's revolver hand came up in a crisp jerk and the sergeant jumped and came down smash on the gun. A gunner tried to shoot, Bellair got in under the rifle and hammered the man insensible with his sword hilt. Then it was all over. The gunners and infantry were scuttling from the redan. The men in the supporting trenches were breaking away and running. They knew well enough that with the capture of that gap their flank was turned, that the battle was lost for them. The general in command of the attackers knew it, too. Like lightning he snatched at the chance Bellair had given him, and right on the heels of the victorious company there came lunging regiment after regiment of attacking infantry. They came rolling through the gap in irresistible swarms, smashing the back of the defense with the awful pressure of their thrust.

Bellair saw them pass. As they went by they looked up at him and cheered. The air was full of cheering; as he heard, the lieutenant became intoxicated with the glory of it and of the deed that he had done. He that had been filled with the terror of his own cowardice had achieved this wonder, had proved himself in this marvelous and splendid way. He began to grow weak with joy, his vision blurred with the immense reaction of

emotion. . . . The whole world seemed to fade
—to grow black. Was he really falling——

The officer who had the whistle in his hand had
almost lifted it to his lips. The men behind the
mounds braced themselves for an instant's up-
rising. The man who had wanted to "get on with
it" stopped grumbling.

" 'Allo," he jerked, "th' little lootenant 'as got
it in th' neck."

"Hey?" said the man beside him.

"Right in th' neck," said the first man. "Blown
'arf of it away. Look 'e's down!"

"Oo?" asked the man beside him.

"Lootenant Bellair, look!"

"Shut yer face," snapped the sergeant close
by. "We're off. Now boys, leg it proper."

The whistle had reached the lips of the officer.
Its thin keen sound cut into the giant uproar of
the concentrated guns like a thread of silver.
Just as Lieutenant Hugo Bellair of Company B
dived forward onto his face, the regiment rose
up and like a crowd bursting over a race-course,
went forward at a rush.

The charge had only just begun.

BONDAGE

BY LEILA BURTON WELLS

BONDAGE

BY LEILA BURTON WELLS

MRS. RANDALL quietly and without excitement of any kind folded the letter she had been reading and slipped it into its waiting envelope, holding the flap down with careful patience, for she told herself that if she could cover up that one sentence she could think; and it was necessary for her to think, and think quickly—*very* quickly, for now the words she had been trying to hide seemed to be oozing through the paper, deriding her effort to efface with a material act a mental impression. They were standing out as plainly as if a supernatural hand had traced them there: "You will have to tell your husband. . . ."

She arose and, going to the waste-basket, tore the envelope with its hidden letter three times straight across, watching the white strips flutter from her hands. Then, with the instinctive fear of detection that inevitably follows a secretive act, she glanced hastily over her shoulder.

No one had entered. She turned back to the basket and, seeing on one of the torn fragments, "You will have to tell . . ." she knelt down and, picking out each separate strip, tore it into

291

smaller pieces—wondering, as she watched her slender fingers, at their passionless deliberation. She might have been destroying a dinner invitation, for all the emotion they evidenced. She felt a sudden hatred for her body, that quiet body that she had trained to present always such a smiling and placid front.

She got to her feet and, going over to a small art-mirror that hung between the two windows, studied her reflected image with unpitying criticism. The atmosphere of stillness that hung about her seemed to penetrate even to the woman in the glass. The lace was not moving over her bosom; her hands, as she raised them to put back a stray lock, moved like drugged butterflies—the very folds of her dress hung peacefully, seeming to whisper against the floor as she stepped. Yes, she had conquered her body—but had she ever conquered her mind? Was her mind still? Or was it, at this crucial moment, like an untuned instrument, hideous with unuttered discords?

How easy for one who had not walked hand in hand with a glorified love to say, "Tell your husband." How easy for a woman like her adopted mother, who had lived an ordinary life with an ordinary man; who had worked and hoped and striven, and got up and gone to bed, with the dull, drab thing she called life, to say, "Tell your husband." A wan smile of self-pity touched her lips. The tearing of that letter had been, after all, but the death-stroke of a strong swimmer who makes a final if quite useless effort to stem the tide of an ocean. It was an incompetent little act, for she would have to tell him, or let him hear through the crueler voice of publicity.

With a sudden impulse she noticed, as she turned from the glass, the tragic and beautiful blackness of her hair where it dipped into little glossy pools as the waves sank downward; the tiny mole that rested under her eye with indicative coquetry; the white skin running into the white dress so softly that there seemed no dividing-line between flesh and cloth; the fine, true lines of her neck and head and bosom and hips— lines drawn so surely that it seemed an artist must have etched them in dry-point. She noted all these things, and for the first time with a calculating eye. Up to this exact moment she had never used any of the cheaper arts to hold her husband's love—their intercourse had been builded far above that, on the supersensible bulwarks of spiritual communion. Now she knew that she was cravenly wondering if her beauty would not offer her an undeserved protection.

But even as she realized that the impulse was finding formative being in her mind, she turned from it with loathing, and, going over to the huge center-lamp that had shed its kind light down on her shoulders for so many happy evenings, she pulled the silken cord and let the rosy light, like a released firefly, burst into the little room.

This was a room to which the world had been

very kind. It was loving and lovable, as if nothing harsh had ever happened in it. With a contraction of the heart she noted each perfect article which bore, like a bill of sale, its invisible story of love and privation. How they had worked and stinted to buy that luxuriously long sofa, that stretched its length so comfortably before the fireplace! How often they had walked past that very lamp when it had reposed in haughty isolation in the window of a Fifth Avenue shop; and how often they had placed it mentally, before they had ever dreamed of placing it actually, on the book-laden library-table that fitted its side into the back of the sofa with such carefully careful ease. And that smoking-set—how she had cleaned laces and gloves, and washed waists and handkerchief, and saved and calculated, to secure that coveted treasure for him; and how interminably he had worn a thin and shiny summer overcoat to surprise her with those old bookcases, at whose shrine she had worshiped for so many patient months. No, it seemed quite, quite impossible that any cruel thing should happen here.

The little clock on the mantel-shelf was striking five . . . and then she heard the servant go to the front door of the apartment. Instantly there was a sudden tensing of her mind, as if every loose ribbon of thought were gathered toward a common center. It was at this hour always that the evening paper was brought in.

She heard the heavy door open and shut—and then a silence. The steps were retreating toward the kitchen. She called:

"Ellen."

"Yes, ma'am."

"Didn't the evening paper come?"

The maid stepped to the door of the dining-room. "No, ma'am."

"I particularly wanted it." She noted, as she spoke, with a subconscious and separate sense from the one that was writhing and fencing with her life tragedy, the young, unlined face under the white cap, and wondered, with an absurd mental irrelevancy, if Ellen had ever been unhappy; her face looked so very smooth and slick and soft.

"Perhaps Mr. Randall will bring one home."

The girl's voice was indifferent.

"Oh, no!" Her mind quickly leaped to the defensive. "He *never* buys the paper—he always reads it here." And then, with lightning rapidity, she calculated the unforeseen probability of his buying an early edition on his way from the office—even while she was directing the girl to "look again in a few minutes."

"Strange the paper should be late to-night," she marveled.

"Oh, it often is, ma'am."

"*Is* it?"

"Oh, often—they leave it at the other apartment."

She watched the girl go away, and then she passed over to the table and picked up a book and began turning over the pages. It was a sardonic commentary on life that she should stand turning over the leaves of a book in the warm security of her own home, and yet know that here, where she had reigned a sovereign, she would be nailed upon the cross; here she would be stripped of all things, destitute as a beggar, going down before the relentless cruelty of life. Before the breaking of another day her life would be the target for the unpitying eyes of publicity—and not her life alone, but, through her, her husband's, her children's. And the knowledge that was paralyzing her was not that *she* could not avert disaster, but that no earthly hand could do it. When she told her husband, he must stand, even as she was, foolishly idle.

She heard his key turning in the lock, and, gently laying down her book, went forward to meet him—went forward as she had gone so many happy times, with the old winging steps of welcome, for this was one of their happy hours. Outwardly nothing was changed. She had the same outstretched hands, the same smile, was folded in the same strong arms! It seemed at the moment both cruel and kind that everything should be so utterly usual. She felt as if, through that white, still body of hers, he must feel a different mind, as if he *must* have some sense of apprehension—of fear. But no—he was even laughing as he pulled off his snow-covered coat, *laughing...*.

She started to pass through the door, but he pulled her back into his arms and, bending her head away, pressed his lips to the soft flesh under her throat, his happy eyes seeking hers in the dusk.

At that moment she wished, for his sake, that she might even confess to a desecrated body—take the shame wholly to herself; that she might say, "I love another man; let me go——" It would be easier.

Unconsciously her hands tightened proprietorially on his coat, but he was already passing into the other room, looking around with contented eyes, as he asked:

"Where are the children?"

She found herself answering the customary question without any apparent effort: "It is Ellen's evening out, you know. They are having supper early."

"I had forgotten." He put his hand in his pocket and pulled out some bulky packages, flinging them on the center-table as he passed. "I got these for them as I came along, from a man in the street—almost frozen, poor beggar. They'll amuse them—especially the dancing lady." He opened the door of the bedroom. "I'm going to change my coat before dinner." He flung the words over his shoulder as he disappeared.

She stood by the center-table unwrapping the bulging bundles, the lamp-light falling across her waist so that her slim whiteness seemed to be cut in two by its dividing glow. She loosened the string, took off the paper, and looked down—just a cheap, befurred monkey chasing itself up a string, and a ballet-girl with a key in her back so she could dance—and dance she must when the key was turned, even if her little wooden heart was breaking! Not much difference between a human being and a mechanical toy, she thought. Was not she herself hopelessly dancing because the key of life had been turned by an invisible hand?

"Aren't they dandy?"

Her husband had come to the door and was watching her. "It's a circus to see the lady tango." He turned toward the hall.

Her mind instantly flew to intercept him. "Where are you going?"

"Just to get the evening paper."

"It didn't come." She wondered that her voice could be so still.

"That doesn't matter." He was feeling in his pocket. "I bought an extra. I only had time to glance at the headlines. I want—"

But she interrupted him with a little cry. He turned quickly toward her. She was holding out the toy in her hands. "I can't wind it up," she complained, "and I want to see the lady dance."

"Hold on—" She quickly picked up the paper

298

as he flung it down, and at the same moment resigned the toy to his hands. "You are winding
it the wrong way."

She came close to his shoulder, holding the
paper behind her. "I haven't spoiled it, have I?"
Where should she put the paper? How should
she keep him from reading it?

He was bending his dark head over the childish
bauble, the eternal boy struggling through thirty
years of manhood.

"You shouldn't have touched it until I showed
you." He knelt on the floor and began winding
the key.

She dropped the paper over the back of the
sofa, and pulled a pillow over it, with a little
indrawn breath of relief, for she heard the voices
of the children.

Then, as one who watches from a great spiritual distance, she saw herself going through the
simple routine of home life—saw herself kneeling with him on the carpet, watching the tiny
painted toy prancing around to a musical tune;
heard the rapturous shouts of the children;
watched them romping with their father. Usu-
ally she asked him not to play quite so noisily, but
to-night she said no word—for was it not the last
time that she would see those chubby arms
clasped around his neck, those yellow heads so
close to his dark head?

Because the maid was going out he helped her
put the baby to bed, and she noted, as he bent

over the crib, how stern his face was, now that the lines of laughter were smoothed out of it, how deep the lines between the eyes, how determined the jaw.

Then she sat opposite him at the round, candle-lighted table, and listened while he detailed some humorous happening at the office, and as she listened a sudden fear of the impenetrability of the flesh assailed her. How dense was that fleshly substance when she could sit opposite him for six years in the closest possible union, and yet be thinking secret, separate thoughts! Her body, her love, her allegiance she had abandoned to him utterly, but she had withheld her thoughts. She had been afraid to give her thoughts, for even as mankind looks with a certain shame on a naked body, so it shrinks from looking on a naked thought; and with a little thrill of bewildered fear she realized that a thought could *never* be exposed. He could take from her her hope, her happiness, her honor, her life—but her withheld thoughts could not be wrested from her. With the hangman's noose about her neck she would still be a free thinker. Even the law could not electrocute, guillotine, or hang her thoughts. She would go down into darkness, if she so willed, defiantly thinking, thinking, thinking.

And as she looked across the table at her husband's face she could have wept had not tears been so utterly impotent—wept at the facility with which she, who would have laid her body down and had it mangled to spare him a pang, had crucified him with her hidden thoughts.

"It seems to me you are looking very pretty to-night," he observed, watching her idly through the rings of tobacco smoke floating ceilingward—watching happily that secret, separate thinker that was his wife. "Is that a new dress?"

"This!" The feminine instinct was so strong that for the first time she presented to him a fully focused mind. "This!" touching it with disdainful fingers. "Why, it is a million years old."

She arose from the table as she spoke, and he, flinging down his napkin, followed her.

"Well, its antediluvian tatters are very becoming—or is it because you have so much color to-night?" He caught her by the arms and turned her toward the small art-mirror. "Look! You remind me of the princess in the story-book who was 'as white as snow, and as black as ebony, and as red as blood—'"

She looked up in face, recoiling from the words in horror. Should she tell him *now*? Now, while his eyes were kind; now while he was smiling at her, now while he was within reach of her arms? But even as she grappled with hesitation the maid brought in coffee.

He went over to the fireplace and held out his hands to the blaze, and she turned mechanically to the little silver tray. She wondered whether, on the Day of Judgment, if some one should bring in coffee, she would rise with the same reluctant ease and pour it out?

"You needn't wait for the tray, Ellen," she heard herself saying in her even, tranquil voice. "I will carry the things into the pantry."

And then she heard the girl cross to the dining-room—heard her close one intervening door after another—and she knew she was alone with her husband, quite alone. She no longer had any excuse for waiting.

She heard the snow-laden wind beat against the window-pane, heard the crackling fire-sparks as they were hurled up through the chimney into the frozen world outside; and she carried the little Dresden cup over to his side, as she had carried it so many times before, with the same soft, sure steps.

He had taken some letters from his pocket and was sorting them out and placing them in careful, separate packages.

"Evidence in the Woodhall divorce case," he explained, laconically, as she stood there silently waiting; and then, as she put the cup down on the arm of the sofa, he turned back to his work with the absolute preoccupation of the trained lawyer.

She stood there silently, her hand resting on the arm of the sofa. How should she tell him? How could she *begin*? How penetrate the impregnable armor of his unconsciousness? There must be some way to prepare—some introductory word—some little simple thing to say, that would uncover—that would show! She looked down at the letters in his hand, with an almost inane detachment from the subject-matter, though she knew the case well. She asked:

"Do they— Will they—*exonerate* her—in any way?" She was putting the words together blindly, her mind aflame with her own cruel cause.

"Exonerate her!" He snapped the band about the letters with contemptuous finality. "You *couldn't* exonerate a woman with *that* blood." He threw the letters on the table and reached for a cigarette. "It's the old story—a rotten woman —and the devil to pay!"

Then she saw that he had taken a cue from the hand of accidental circumstance and given it to her. She turned away her face and closed her eyes.

"Are you absolutely *sure* that she was a bad woman?" she asked.

He shrugged his shoulders. "It depends upon what you call bad. If a bad woman is one who is foredoomed to contaminate everything she touches, she was a bad woman."

"Foredoomed—"

"Well, the kindest thing he could have done, for his children's sake and his own, was—to have put her out of the way—"

"Killed her, you mean?"

He nodded.

There was a little shocked silence, while she heard the wind beat against the window-pane, heard her own breathing.

Then she said: "Is that what *you* would have done—? Things are—sometimes—a little different—when they touch us personally. Would you—would *you* have killed her?"

He shrugged his shoulders with a man's lack of interest in improbabilities. "I? Oh, I would never have to make that decision."

Then she knew that her hour had come, and she crossed over to the little stool by the fire-place, where she could sit facing him. "I know a case," she began, stoically.

"The exception to the rule?" His voice was derisive. He bent to strike another match.

"I don't know whether *you* will think it the exception to the rule, but—it is an indicative case, for the girl made what you would call a bad beginning. You see, her father shot her mother in a fit of insane rage, caused by a belief in her infidelity—shot her mother through the back, when she was bending over, putting some clothes away in a chest in the attic, and then went and gave himself up to the authorities. . . . When the neighbors found them the woman was quite dead and the little two-year-old girl was playing in her mother's blood—dabbling it over her white dress — making finger-prints on the sunlit floor—"

"Horrible!"

"Yes, but you see she didn't know—she was quite unconscious. She would have been glad, if she had had a choice, to begin life some other way—but you see she wasn't given one. . . ."

"Well?" His lazily contented voice seemed to reach her from a great distance.

She started.

"Was the father tried?"

"Oh, yes—he was tried." She steadied her voice. "He was tried for murder in the first degree. The defense pleaded—insanity!" She tightened her hands in her lap at that word.

"But he was found guilty and sentenced to be—hanged. . . . A childless lady traveling in the state with an invalid husband, adopted the child and took her away. There were no relatives."

"And the father was executed?"

She lifted her stoical eyes. "Oh, no. You see, that would not have been so far-reaching in its results. Oh, no, he was not executed. Friends made a strong appeal for pardon, and the governor reprieved him for a year—,"

"And then?"

"Kept reprieving him year after year until he went out of office." She was speaking automatically, as a child speaks who is repeating a lesson. "The succeeding governor followed the same precedent during his term of office. So did his successor——"

"Extraordinary!"

She drew a pained breath. "Yes—it was extraordinary—but you see that is why it is true. The strange things are always true. . . . But the tragic part was the child. She grew up knowing nothing of her parentage. You see, five years after the—the—murder, the lady returned home, widowed—with a little girl, whom she *said* was her own. It looked very safe and simple, and the girl grew up as any girl might, surrounded by love and indulgence; and the years passed—and lovers came. . . ."

"I see!" Her husband's eyes were contemplative.

"Yes—it all worked inevitably toward the end. Lovers came—but there was something different in her lovers from those of other girls. They stayed for a little while, and then they just went away. You see the lady had to tell them the truth—"

"Of course."

"—and they were not willing to take the risk. But the girl couldn't understand. She used to look in the mirror and wonder if she were hateful, or unlovable, or queer. She couldn't understand; and for the first time she was unhappy. And then the man she loved came into her life—"

"Yes—" He was leaning forward, interested at last.

"He did not go away!"

"Ah!"

"The mother did not tell him. . . . You see,

the girl was what you might call temperamental, and her love for this man filled her life as water fills a bowl. She was happy. She used to write the word 'wife' on a little piece of paper and kneel before it as a saint kneels before a shrine. . . . Then, the night before she was married, the woman who had made herself her mother told her all. She wanted to shift the burden of decision. She was afraid. And so into the startled innocence of that girl's mind she poured the whole story—the whole cruel inheritance that was hers she laid upon the girl's shoulders, and told her she could choose! She could tell the man she was to marry and he would go away as the others had gone away; or she could close her lips. She closed her lips."

"She *married* him?"

"Yes. You see she, too, was afraid. She thought she would lose his love. She was so young. She couldn't take it all in at once. She only knew she *wanted* him—that he was hers. She was just a girl. What did heredity and the curse of blood and jealousy and murder mean to her? She was only conscious of love."

"Common honesty might have meant something to her."

"Yes. But you see she didn't quite realize then what she was doing. Her adopted mother had made her think she was secure—that nothing, no exposure or disgrace, would ever come. That her father was obliterated, and that even when he was hanged there would be no exposure for her, because so few knew the truth of her birth. And the girl was intoxicated with love, just as a man is intoxicated with wine. . . ."

"And the man?"

"He was happy, too. . . . It seems strange, but he was. You see, he loved her. He took her away to a strange city, and they had one little room in a boarding-house, for they were very poor. But poverty didn't matter to them at all, they were so happy. They used to make a joke of it, and laugh at the tired faces of the rich people they saw riding by in carriages, and then— her baby was laid in her arms."

He nodded comprehendingly.

"And she began to think! Up to that time she hadn't *thought*, you see. . . . She used to lie with the little soft head pressed against her breast, and go over all the terrible inheritance the world has said a mother such as she must give her children. And then the arraigning realization came to her, that this was *his* child, too, and that he had had the right to select the mother to his child—and that she had taken it away from him."

"Rather late in the day to come to that con- clusion!"

"Yes, that was what she told herself, that it was too late—*all* too late! The child was born. He could divorce *her*—but the child was born, and she was its mother! . . . And all she had to give it was a heritage of hatred and jealousy and

murder, and—insanity; and she was afraid! Oh,
so bitterly afraid . . . afraid with a terrible,
blind, helpless fear. . . .

"Then one day in a sentence in a book she came
across the word 'overcome.' It seemed to stand
out like the point of a needle pricking through
cloth. It let in an overwhelming light. The
Bible had said—and men after it—that the sins
of the fathers should be visited on the children;
but had any one ever said the children should not
overcome those visitations?"

Her husband was smiling ironically. "The
same old story," he commented, throwing his
cigarette stump into the fire and clasping his
hands thoughtfully over his head.

"No; not *quite* the same old story. You see,
she thought she could overcome her inheritance.
It seemed unjust to her that she should be condemned—and her innocent child after her—because of something *intangible.* . . . She began to
watch herself—to undo the curses of her parentage one by one, first in herself, then in her children—for another child was born to her. She
had always been impatient, impetuous, and passionate. She became very still and gentle and
patient. . . . She never allowed herself to be
irritable over trifles as other people were. She
dared not. She had been jealous, exacting. She
taught herself to be generous and indulgent.
It wasn't easy—it was hard. It took years of
labor, but she was willing to labor—she was pay-

ing him back in happiness for the theft of his name. . . .

"And after a while people came to her for peace. She was so still they said her hands and voice eased pain. She seemed to be able to make people *happy*. They—they called her a very good woman. That child who had begun life playing in her mother's blood had become, because of that very inheritance, what we call a good woman."

Her husband shook his head, unconvinced.

"Where did you hear this story?" he demanded.

"It doesn't matter." She pushed his question away. "Nothing matters except that that woman *was* conquering . . . coming out, as it seemed, into smooth waters. He had succeeded in his profession; they had lovely things around them; their children were a joy and a blessing. She felt safe, even though that man, her father, was lying in prison. She felt safe. And then one day she picked up a paper and *saw*— one day she picked up a paper and saw that, after reprieving him for twenty-four years —they had just forgotten him. The sheriff and all the officials had just forgotten him."

"Forgotten him?"

"Forgotten the day of execution. He was not reprieved, and when they took the case to court they found that he was neither dead nor alive. The day of execution had passed. He was hanged under the law, but alive. . . ."

"By Jove!" He arose to his feet.

"Yes—you see how far-reaching it was! They had no right to even keep him in prison. He was old and incompetent. His care devolved on the state. . . . And then the papers took it up because of the sensational aspect of the case, and began looking for the child!"

"Who told you this story?" Her husband had come toward her. He was frowning, but she sat there by the fireplace, still and stolid like a prisoner at the bar.

"You see," she said, looking up at him and ignoring his question, "she was trapped. She needn't have struggled, she needn't have worked, she needn't have *lied.* It was all coming out. Her father was old and incompetent and they were looking for her—they were looking for her. Don't you see? They were going to pry into her beautiful home and drag her out. . . ."

"How did you know this story? Answer me!" He was bending over her, his face startled into apprehension.

Then she lifted her eyes. "I know it—because——"

"Well?" He reached down and laid his hand heavily on her shoulder, and she found her voice.

"I am the woman," she said. And then she thought she screamed it out, over and over again, "I am the woman!" But her habit of physical repression must have prevented her from making a sound, for she saw no understanding in his face.

Then, she heard herself repeating the words
over again, very carefully, watching his face as a
mother watches the face of a sick child. "I am
the woman! I haven't any mother at all. . . .
My mother was murdered. . . . My father killed
her. . . . He is free and they are looking for me.
. . . He is free and they are looking for me! We
thought it was hidden, but you see it all came out
—it came out."

Then she knew that he understood. And she
looked at him as one looks who, through some
accident, has destroyed a rare and precious treasure. She felt as a surgeon must feel who has cut
into flesh without being able to give an anesthetic.

She heard him asking incredulous, dazed questions; heard herself making answers. Over and
over she heard him ask and heard herself answer.
And then at last she saw him go over to the sofa.
He sat stock-still, his hands falling between his
knees. And she watched him. She had no words
—she just sat and watched him suffer.

After a while he asked, stolidly, "Why have
you told me *now*?"

It was characteristic of the closeness of their
intercourse that the tragedy of it all, for him as
for her, lay not in the hideous facts of the revela-
tion she had made, but in their mental aloofness
—that he was groping in a strange mind when
he was speaking to her now; that they had lived
side by side, breath against breath, heart beating
against heart—and thought apart! The passion

that was rising in him toward its climax was not that birth had unfitted her to be his wife, but that spiritually she had never been wholly his.

But she was beginning all over again, explaining and re-explaining. "Don't you understand? Don't you *see*? It is all going to be in the papers. It *is* in the papers. I couldn't let you see it there. . . . She wrote me to tell you. Oh, *try* to understand what it means—exposure, disgrace; you and the children pointed at—pitied. And no one can do anything. He is there waiting for me —my father! Don't you understand? *He* is alive and free! Don't you understand I had to tell you? He is alive and free and they are looking for me!"

Then he stared in her face—stared long, as one stares who is trying to focus thought. Then he spoke.

"He is *dead*," he said.

She looked at him with uncomprehending eyes.

"I didn't understand at first what you were saying, it all came so fast. The man is dead, if you are talking about that case in Kentucky. It's in the evening paper. I read it in the car coming up. I couldn't take in what you were saying at first, but—there'll be no exposure; it's a small notice."

"Dead!" She felt for the word as a blind person feels for some guiding object.

"He died on the way to the almshouse."

She saw him looking around for something and

she pointed to the sofa, and watched him, fascinated, while he found the paper he had brought; fascinated, but without any realization of the ultimate meaning of what he was doing.

He brought the paper over and laid it in her lap, pointing with his finger.

"There it is: 'On His Way to the Almshouse.' . . . They don't mention—you. They don't have to find the child—now. Your father is dead!"

Then she looked down and saw some letters that all seemed to run into one word. She didn't know how long she sat there trying to put them together. But at last she found, with a great effort, that she could make out a sentence. She read it over and over. She felt she must read it many, many times to understand. "Having no relatives, he is to be buried at the expense of the state." Having no relatives. . . . There was something else farther down that seemed to mean something, too. "He missed the almshouse only to find his last resting-place in the—potter's field." . . . And farther down still: "This man, who was neither dead nor alive, will be remembered as the one who murdered—" And at last: "The child has never been located."

The paper slipped from her hands to the floor. She raised her dazed eyes to her husband's face.

"If the paper had come early I would have seen it first." Her voice was stunned.

"Yes."

"And you would never have known?"

"No."

"But I was—just *afraid*, and so—I told?"

"Yes."

"There wasn't any reason for it?"

"No."

"It's odd, isn't it?"

Then she sat quite still. There would be no exposure. His name was safe—his children's future would be untarnished; but everything was over for her. He *knew*, and he need not have known. Her own fear had destroyed her, and all the time there had been nothing to be afraid of. He would never trust her again. He would *fear*, too, now that there was nothing to fear—now that at last he knew the whole naked reaches of her thought. She could have laughed at the relentless tragedy of it all. She looked at the clock on the mantel-shelf and saw that it pointed to half-past eight. Ten minutes ago he had not known!

He was standing by the mantel, looking down into the fire, his face set, his jaws locked. It seemed as if she was looking at some quiet stranger. She would never know his thoughts, now. He was afraid of her—afraid of his wife! Afraid of the inheritance she would give his children.

The silence was becoming crueler than any words could have been. She had looked at him, but he seemed unconscious alike of her gaze or her presence.

"Won't — you say — *something* — to me — please?"

Then the man turned. "Stand up," he said. She stood up.

"Come here."

She went over to him, dragging her white draperies, but with her head no longer held high. It had fallen to her bosom.

He put his hands on either side of her face and lifted it to his. Then she saw with frightened pain in her eyes that he looked quite old. The youth had been wiped away from his face.

Tears began to run down her cheeks, from her open eyes, that were fixed on his. They ran down her cheeks until they fell on the white stuff of her gown.

The man groaned. "You poor woman!" he said. "You—*poor* woman. . . ."

Then suddenly she saw far beyond his eyes into his mind. She trembled. His eyes were prophetic.

"You couldn't use it *alone*; but there is a remedy."

"A remedy." She stared at him uncomprehendingly.

"Don't you understand . . . ?"

She smiled. "You think—if you put *me* out of the way—it would—help?"

"That isn't the end of fear. I know it now. It is the *beginning*." He groaned as one groans who is passing through some great spiritual travail, and as he groaned it was given to him to *see.*

This woman whom he called his wife was but the type of countless other women, buried in the centuries, whose problem was netted to hers even as link is clasped in link in a metal purse. And even as those women had crept to a man's side with their primal inheritance, too weak to undo it quite alone, even so she was standing at his side now, holding up mutely the manacles of her fear for him to break off her wrists. Those men before him had not broken the chains of bondage with their strength—they had taken the yoke from the weaker woman and passed it down from generation to generation. Even as the first man had eaten the first fear, in the Garden, so had they continued eating of it, because they had not been able to make perfect that one word she had cried aloud.

Then this individual man, who was facing the age-long problem, dropped his hands from the woman's face and turned away, too.

She stood there straight and tall where he had left her, neither putting out hand nor raising voice. "You are going. . . . ?"

Then he turned back to her, and his face wore the half-shamed, half-wondering expression of one who has touched with fleshly hands an incredible and incommunicable emotion.

"I am going," he said, "to catch the nine-fifty from the Grand Central. . . ." As she swayed, he caught her; and, faint with a sublime and in-experienced sense of nearness, she felt him bend her head back in the old way, and opening her eyes she looked straight into his eyes. They were quite fearless and ineffably tender. "I am going to catch the nine-fifty from the Grand Central," he repeated, slowly. "I am going to Kentucky, to bring *our* father's body—*home!*"

THE CELEBRATED JUMPING
FROG OF CALAVERAS COUNTY

BY MARK TWAIN

THE CELEBRATED JUMPING FROG OF CALAVERAS COUNTY

BY MARK TWAIN

IN compliance with the request of a friend of mine, who wrote me from the East, I called on good-natured, garrulous old Simon Wheeler, and inquired after my friend's friend, *Leonidas W.* Smiley, as requested to do, and I hereunto append the result. I have a lurking suspicion that *Leonidas W.* Smiley is a myth; that my friend never knew such a personage; and that he only conjectured that, if I asked old Wheeler about him it would remind him of his infamous *Jim* Smiley, and he would go to work and bore me nearly to death with some infernal reminiscence of him as long and tedious as it should be useless for me. If that was the design, it certainly succeeded.

I found Simon Wheeler dozing comfortably by the bar-room stove of the old, dilapidated tavern in the ancient mining camp of Angel's, and I noticed that he was fat and bald-headed, and had an expression of winning gentleness and simplicity upon his tranquil countenance. He roused up and gave me good-day. I told him a friend of mine had commissioned me to make some inquiries about a cherished companion of his boyhood named *Leonidas W. Smiley—Rev. Leonidas W. Smiley—a* young minister of the Gospel, who he had heard was at one time a resident of Angel's Camp. I added that if Mr. Wheeler could tell me any thing about this Rev. Leonidas W. Smiley, I would feel under many obligations to him.

Simon Wheeler backed me into a corner and blockaded me there with his chair, and then sat me down and reeled off the monotonous narrative which follows this paragraph. He never frowned, he never smiled, he never changed his voice from the gentle-flowing key to which he turned the initial sentence, he never betrayed the slightest suspicion of enthusiasm; but all through the interminable narrative there ran a vein of impressive earnestness and sincerity, which showed me plainly that, so far from his imagining that there was anything ridiculous or funny about his story, he regarded it as a really important matter, and admired its two heroes as men of transcendent genius in *finesse.* To me the spectacle of a man drifting serenely along through such a queer yarn without ever smiling was exquisitely absurd. As I said before, I asked him to tell me what he knew of Rev. Leonidas W. Smiley, and he replied as follows. I let him go on in his own way, and never interrupted him once:

There was a feller here once by the name of *Jim* Smiley, in the winter of '49—or may be it

THE JUMPING FROG

was the spring of '50—I don't recollect exactly, somehow, though what makes me think it was one or the other is because I remember the big flume wasn't finished when he first came to camp; but any way he was the curiosest man about, always betting on anything that turned up you ever see, if he could get any body to bet on the other side; and if he couldn't, he'd change sides. Any way that suited the other man would suit him—any way just so's he got a bet, *he* was satisfied. But still he was lucky, uncommon lucky; he most always come out winner. He was always ready and laying for a chance; there couldn't be no solitary thing mentioned but that feller'd offer to bet on it, and take any side you please, as I was just telling you. If there was a horse-race, you'd find him flush, or you'd find him busted at the end of it; if there was a dog-fight, he'd bet on it; if there was a cat-fight, he'd bet on it; if there was a chicken-fight, he'd bet on it; why, if there was two birds sitting on a fence, he would bet you which one would fly first; or if there was a camp-meeting, he would be there reg-lar, to bet on Parson Walker, which he judged to be the best exhorter about here, and so he was, too, and a good man. If he even seen a straddle-bug start to go anywheres, he would bet you how long it would take him to get wherever he was going to, and if you took him up, he would foller that straddle-bug to Mexico but what he would find out where he was bound for and how long he was on the road. Lots of the boys here has seen that Smiley, and can tell you about him. Why, it never made no difference to *him*—he would bet on *any* thing—the dangdest feller. Parson Walker's wife laid very sick once, for a good while, and it seemed as if they warn't going to save her; but one morning he come in, and Smiley asked how she was, and he said she was considerable better—thank the Lord for His inf'nit mercy—and coming on so smart that, with the blessing of Prov'dence, she'd get well yet; and Smiley, before he thought, says, "Well, I'll risk two-and-a-half that she don't anyway."

This-yer Smiley had a mare—the boys called her the fifteen-minute nag, but that was only in fun, you know, because, of course, she was faster than that—and he used to win money on that horse, for all she was so slow and always had the asthma, or the distemper, or the consumption, or something of that kind. They used to give her two or three hundred yards' start, and then pass her under way; but always at the fag-end of the race she'd get excited and desperate-like, and come cavorting and straddling up, and scattering her legs around limber, sometimes in the air, and sometimes out to one side amongst the fences, and kicking up m-o-r-e dust, and raising m-o-r-e racket with her coughing and sneezing and blowing her nose—and always fetch up at the stand just about a neck ahead, as near as you could cipher it down.

And he had a little small bull pup, that to look at him you'd think he wan't worth a cent, but to set around and look onery, and lay for a chance to steal something. But as soon as the money was up on him, he was a different dog; his under-jaw'd begin to stick out like the fo'castle of a steamboat, and his teeth would uncover, and shine savage like the furnaces. And a dog might tackle him, and bully-rag him, and bite him, and throw him over his shoulder two or three times, and Andrew Jackson—which was the name of the pup—Andrew Jackson would never let on but what *he* was satisfied, and hadn't expected nothing else—and the bets being doubled and doubled on the other side all the time, till the money was all up; and then all of a sudden he would grab that other dog jest by the j'int of his hind leg and freeze to it—not chaw, you understand, but only jest grip and hang on till they throwed up the sponge, if it was a year. Smiley always come out winner on that pup, till he harnessed a dog once that didn't have no hind legs, because they'd been sawed's off by a circular saw, and when the thing had gone along far enough, and the money was all up, and he come to make a snatch for his pet holt, he saw in a minute how he'd been imposed on, and how the other dog had him in the door, so to speak and he 'peared surprised, and then he'd looked sorter discouraged-like, and didn't try no more to win the fight, and so he got shucked out bad. He give Smiley a look, as much as to say his heart was broke, and it was *his* fault, for putting up a dog that hadn't no hind legs for him to take holt of, which was his main dependence in a fight, and then he limped off apiece and laid down and died. It was a good pup, was that Andrew Jackson, and would have made a name for hisself if he'd lived, for the stuff was in him, and he had genius —I know it, because he hadn't had no opportunities to speak of, and it don't stand to reason that a dog could make such a fight as he could under them circumstances, if he hadn't no talent. It always makes me feel sorry when I think of that last fight of his'n, and the way it turned out.

Well, this-year Smiley had rat-tarriers, and chicken cocks, and tom-cats, and all them kind of things, till you couldn't rest, and you couldn't fetch nothing for him to bet on but he'd match you. He ketched a frog one day, and took him home, and said he cal-klated to edercate him; and so he never done nothing for three months but set in his back yard and learn that frog to jump. And you bet you he *did* learn him, too. He'd give him a little punch behind, and the next minute you'd see that frog whirling in the air like a doughnut—see him turn one somerset, or may be a couple, if he got a good start, and come down flat-footed and all right, like a cat. He got him up so in the matter of catching flies, and kept him in practice so constant, that he'd nail a fly every time as far as he could see him. Smiley said all a frog wanted was education, and he could do most anything—and I believe him. Why, I've seen him set Dan'l Webster down here on this floor—Dan'l Webster was the name of the frog—and sing out, "Flies, Dan'l, flies!" and quicker'n you could wink, he'd spring straight up, and snake a fly off'n the counter there, and flop down on the floor again as solid as a gob of mud, and fall to scratching the side of his head with his hind foot as indifferent as if he hadn't no idea he'd been doin' any more'n any frog might do. You never see a frog so modest and straight for-ard as he was, for all he was so gifted. And when it come to fair and square jumping on a dead level, he could get over more ground at one straddle than any animal of his breed you ever see. Jumping on a dead level was his strong suit, you understand; and when it come to that, Smiley would ante up money on him as long as he had a red. Smiley was monstrous proud of his frog, and well he might be, for fellers that had travelled and been everywheres, all said he laid over any frog that ever *they* see.

Well, Smiley kept the beast in a little lattice box, and he used to fetch him down town sometimes and lay for a bet. One day a feller—a stranger in the camp, he was—come across him with his box, and says:

"What might it be that you've got in the box?"

And Smiley says, sorter indifferent like, "It might be a parrot, or it might be a canary, may-be, but it ain't—it's only just a frog."

And the feller took it, and looked at it careful, and turned it round this way and that, and says, "H'm, so 'tis. Well, what's *he* good for?"

"Well," Smiley says, easy and careless, "he's good enough for *one* thing, I should judge—he can out-jump any frog in Calaveras county."

The feller took the box again, and took another long, particular look, and give it back to Smiley, and says, very deliberate, "Well, I don't see no p'ints about that frog that's any better'n any other frog."

"May be you don't," Smiley says. "May be you understand frogs, and may be you don't understand 'em; may be you've had experience, and may be you ain't, only a amatur, as it were. Any ways, I've got *my* opinion, and I'll risk forty dollars that he can outjump any frog in Calaveras county."

And the feller studied a minute, and then says, kinder sad like,

"Well, I'm only a stranger here, and I ain't got no frog; but if I had a frog, I'd bet you."

And then Smiley says, "That's all right—that's all right—if you'll hold my box a minute, I'll go and get you a frog." And so the feller took the box, and put up his forty dollars along with Smiley's and set down to wait.

So he set there a good while thinking and thinking to hisself, and then he got the frog out and prized his mouth open and took a tea-spoon and filled him full of quail shot—filled him pretty near up to his chin—and set him on the floor. Smiley he went to the swamp and slopped around in the mud for a long time, and finally he ketched a frog, and fetched him in, and give him to this feller, and says:

"Now, if you're ready, set him alongside of Dan'l, with his fore-paws just even with Dan'l, and I'll give the word." Then he says, "One—two—three—jump!" and him and the feller touched up the frogs from behind, and the new frog hopped off, but Dan'l give a heave, and hysted up his shoulders—so—like a Frenchman, but it wan't no use—he couldn't budge; he was planted as solid as an anvil, and he couldn't no more stir than if he was anchored out. Smiley was a good deal surprised, and he was disgusted too, but he didn't have no idea what the matter was, of course.

The feller took the money and started away; and when he was going out at the door, he sorter jerked his thumb over his shoulders—this way—at Dan'l and says again, very deliberate, "Well, I don't see no p'ints about that frog that's any better'n any other frog."

Smiley he stood scratching his head and looking down at Dan'l a long time, and at last he says, "I do wonder what in the nation that frog throw'd off for—I wonder if there ain't something the matter with him—he 'pears to look mightly baggy, somehow." And he ketched Dan'l by the nap of the neck, and lifted him up and says,

"Why, blame my cats, if he don't weigh five pound!" and turned him upside down, and he belched out a double handful of shot. And then he see how it was, and he was the maddest man —he set the frog down and took out after that feller, but he never ketched him. And—

(Here Simon Wheeler heard his name called from the front yard, and got up to see what was wanted.) And turning to me as he moved away, he said: "Just set where you are, stranger, and rest easy—I ain't going to be gone a second."

But, by your leave, I did not think that a continuation of the history of the enterprising vagabond *Jim* Smiley would be likely to afford me much information concerning the *Rev. Leonidas W.* Smiley, and so I started away.

At the door I met the sociable Wheeler returning, and he buttonholed me and recommenced:

"Well, this-yer Smiley had a yaller one-eyed cow that didn't have no tail, only just a short stump like a bannanner, and—"

"Oh, hang Smiley and his afflicted cow!" I muttered good-naturedly, and bidding the old gentleman good-day, I departed.

ROSEMARY FOR REMEMBRANCE

BY HENRY HARLAND

ROSEMARY FOR REMEMBRANCE

BY HENRY HARLAND

I

I WONDER why I dreamed last night of Zabetta. It is years since she made her brief little transit through my life, and passed out of it utterly. It is years since the very recollection of her—which for years, like an accusing spirit, had haunted me too often—like a spirit was laid. It is long enough, in all conscience, since I have even thought of her, casually, for an instant. And then, last night, after a perfectly usual London day and evening, I went to bed and dreamed of her vividly. What had happened to bring her to my mind? Or is it simply that the god of dreams is a capricious god?

The influence of my dream, at any rate—the bitter-sweet savor of it—has pursued me through my waking hours. All day long to-day Zabetta has been my phantom guest. She has walked with me in the streets; she has waited at my elbow while I wrote or talked or read. Now, at tea-time, she is present with me by my study fireside,

By permission of the publisher. From "Comedies and Errors," copyright, 1898, by John Lane.

in the twilight. Her voice sounds faintly, plaintively, in my ears; her eyes gaze at me sadly from a pale, reproachful face. . . . She bids me to the theatre of memory, where my youth is rehearsed before me in mimic show. There was one—no, there were two little scenes in which Zabetta played the part of leading lady.

II

I do not care to specify the year in which it happened; it happened a terrible number of years ago; it happened when I was twenty. I had passed the winter in Naples—oh, it had been a golden winter!—and now April had come, and my last Neapolitan day. To-morrow I was to take ship for Marseilles, on the way to join my mother in Paris.

It was in the afternoon; and I was climbing one of those crooked staircase alleys that scale the hillsides behind the town, the salita—is there, in Naples, a Salita Santa Margherita? I had lunched (for the last time!) at the Café d'Europe, and had then set forth upon a last haphazard ramble through the streets. It was tremulous spring weather, with blue skies, soft breezes, and a tender sun; the sort of weather that kindles perilous ardors even in the blood of middle age, and turns the blood of youth to wildfire.

Women sat combing their hair, and singing, and gossiping, before the doorways of their pink and yellow houses; children sprawled, and laughed, and quarreled in the dirt. Pifferari, in sheepskins and sandals, followed by prowling, gaunt-limbed dogs, droned monotonous nasal melodies from their bagpipes. Priests picked their way gingerly over the muddy cobblestones, sleek, black-a-vised priests, with exaggerated hats, like Don Basilio's in the "Barbière." Now and then one passed a fat brown monk; or a soldier; or a white-robed penitent, whose eyes glimmered uncannily from the peep-holes of the hood that hid his face; or a comely contadina, in her smart costume, with a pomegranate blossom flaming behind her ear, and red lips that curved defiantly as she met the covetous glances wildfire-and-twenty no doubt bestowed upon her—whereat, perhaps, wildfire-and-twenty halted and hesitated for an instant, debating whether to accept the challenge and turn and follow her. A flock of milk-purveying goats jangled their bells a few yards below me. Hawkers screamed their merchandise, fish, and vegetables, and early fruit—apricots, figs, green almonds. Brown-skinned, bare-legged boys shouted at long-suffering donkeys, and whacked their flanks with sticks. And everybody, more or less, importuned you for coppers. *"Mossou, mossou! Un piccolo soldo, per l'amor di Dio!"* The air was vibrant with southern human noises and dense with southern human smells—among which, here and there, wandered strangely a lost waft of perfume from some neighboring garden, a scent of jasmine or of orange flowers.

And then, suddenly, the salita took a turn, and broadened into a small piazza. At one hand there was a sheer terrace, dropping to tiled roofs twenty feet below; and hence one got a splendid view, over the town, of the blue bay, with its shipping, and of Capri, all rose and purple in the distance, and of Vesuvius with its silver wreath of smoke. At the other hand loomed a vast, discolored, pink-stuccoed palace, with grated windows, and a porte-cochère black as the mouth of a cavern; and the upper stories of the palace were in ruins, and out of one corner of their crumbling walls a palm-tree grew. The third side of the piazza was inevitably occupied by a church, a little pearl-gray rococo edifice, with a bell, no deeper toned than a common dinner-bell, which was now frantically ringing. About the doors of the church countless written notices were pasted, advertising indulgences; beggars clung to the steps, like monster snails; and the greasy leathern portière was constantly being drawn aside to let some one enter or come out.

III

It was here that I met Zabetta.

The heavy portière swung open, and a young girl stepped from the darkness behind it into the sunshine.

336

ROSEMARY FOR REMEMBRANCE

I saw a soft face, with brown eyes; a plain black frock, with a little green nosegay stuck in its belt; and a small round scarlet hat.

A hideous old beggar woman stretched a claw toward this apparition, mumbling something. The apparition smiled, and sought in its pocket, and made the beggar woman the richer by a soldo.

I was twenty, and the April wind was magical. I thought I had never seen so beautiful a smile, a smile so radiant, so tender.

I watched the young girl as she tripped down the church steps, and crossed the piazza, coming toward me. Her smile lingered, fading slowly, slowly, from her face.

As she neared me, her eyes met mine. For a second we looked straight into each other's eyes. . . .

Oh, there was nothing bold, nothing sophisticated or immodest, in the momentary gaze she gave me. It was a natural, spontaneous gaze of perfectly frank, of perfectly innocent and impulsive interest, in exchange for mine of open admiration. But it touched the wildfire in my veins, and made it leap tumultuously.

IV

Happiness often passes close to us without our suspecting it, the proverb says.

The young girl moved on; and I stood still,

feeling dimly that something precious had passed close to me. I had not turned back to follow any of the brazenly provocative contadine. But now I could not help it. Something precious had passed within arm's reach of me. I must not let it go, without at least a semblance of pursuing it. If I waited there passive till she was out of sight, my regrets would be imbittered by the recollection that I had not even tried.

I followed her eagerly, but vaguely, in a tremor of unformulated hopes and fears. I had no definite intentions, no designs. Presently, doubtless, she would come to her journey's end—she would disappear in a house or shop—and I should have my labor for my pains. Nevertheless, I followed. What would you? She was young, she was pretty, she was neatly dressed. She had big bright brown eyes, and a slender waist and a little round scarlet hat set jauntily upon a mass of waving soft brown hair. And she walked gracefully, with delicious undulations, as if to music, lifting her skirts up from the pavement, and so discoloring the daintiest of feet, in trim buttoned boots of glazed leather, with high Italian heels. And her smile was lovely—and I was twenty.—and it was April. I must not let her escape me, without at least a semblance of pursuit.

She led me down the salita that I had just ascended.

She could scarcely know that she was being

followed, for she had not once glanced behind her.

V

At first I followed meekly, unperceived, and contented to remain so.

But little by little a desire for more aggressive measures grew within me. I said, "Why not—instead of following meekly—why not overtake and outdistance her, then turn round, and come face to face with her again? And if again her eyes should meet mine as frankly as they met them in the piazza. . . ."

The mere imagination of their doing so made my heart stop beating.

I quickened my pace. I drew nearer and nearer to her. I came abreast of her—oh, how the wildfire trembled! I pressed on for a bit, and then, true to my resolution, turned back.

Her eyes did meet mine again quite frankly. What was more, they brightened with a little light of surprise, I might almost have fancied a little light of pleasure.

If the mere imagination of the thing had made my heart stop beating, the thing itself set it to pounding, racing, uncontrollably, so that I felt all but suffocated and had to catch my breath.

She knew now that the young man she had passed in the piazza had followed her of set purpose; and she was surprised, but, seemingly, not displeased. They were wonderfully gentle, wonderfully winning eyes, those eyes she raised so frankly to my desirous ones; and innocent, innocent, with all the unsuspecting innocence of childhood. In years she might be seventeen, older perhaps; but there was a child's fearless unconsciousness of evil in her wide brown eyes. She had not yet been taught (or, anyhow, she clearly didn't believe) that it was dangerous and unbecoming to exchange glances with a stranger in the streets.

She was as good as smiling on me. Might I dare the utmost? Might I venture to speak to her? . . . My heart was throbbing too violently. I could not have found an articulate human word, nor a shred of voice, nor a pennyweight of self-assurance, in my body.

So, thrilling with excitement, quailing in panic, I passed her again.

I passed her, and kept on up the narrow alley for half a dozen steps, when again I turned.

She was standing where I had left her, looking after me. There was the expression of unabashed disappointment in her dark eyes now, which, in a minute, melted to an expression of appeal.

"Oh, aren't you going to speak to me, after all?" they pleaded.

Wooed by those soft monitors, I plucked up a sort of desperate courage. Hot coals burned in my cheeks, something fluttered terribly in my breast; I was literally quaking in every limb.

My spirit was exultant, but my flesh was faint. Her eyes drew me, drew me. . . . I fancy myself awkwardly raising my hat; I hear myself accomplish a half-smothered salutation.

"*Buon' giorno, Signorina.*"

Her face lighted up with that celestial smile of hers, and in a voice that was like ivory and white velvet, she returned, "*Buon' giorno, Signorino.*"

VI

And then I don't know how long we stood together in silence.

This would never do, I recognized. I must not stand before her in silence, like a guilty schoolboy. I must feign composure. I must carry off the situation lightly like a man of the world, a man of experience. I groped anxiously in the confusion of my wits for something that might pass for an apposite remark. "What— what fine weather," I gasped. "*Che bel tempo!*"

"*Oh, molto bello,*" she responded. It was like a cadenza on a flute.

"You—you are going into the town?" I questioned.

"Yes," said she.

"May I—may I have the pleasure——" I faltered.

"But yes," she consented, with an inflection

that wondered. "What else have you spoken to me for?"

And we set off down the salita, side by side.

VII

She had exquisite little white ears, with little coral earrings, like drops of blood; and a perfect rosebud mouth, a mouth that matched her eyes for innocence and sweetness. Her scarlet hat burned in the sun, and her brown hair shook gently under it. She had plump little soft white hands.

Presently, when I had begun to feel more at my ease, I hazarded a question. "You are a republican, Signorina?"

"No," she assured me, with a puzzled elevation of the brows.

"Ah, well, then you are a cardinal," I concluded.

She gave a silvery trill of laughter, and asked, "Why must I be either a republican or a cardinal?"

"You wear a scarlet hat—a *bonnet rouge*," I explained.

At which she laughed again, crisply, merrily.

"You are French," she said.

"Oh, am I?"

"Aren't you?"

"As you wish, Signorina; but I had never thought so."

And still again she laughed.

"You have come from church," said I.

"Già," she assented; "from confession."

"Really? And did you have a great many wickednesses to confess?"

"Oh, yes; many, many," she answered, simply.

"And now have you got a heavy penance to perform?"

"No; only twenty *aves*. And I must turn my tongue seven times in my mouth before I speak, whenever I am angry."

"Ah, then you are given to being angry? You have a bad temper?"

"Oh, dreadful, dreadful," she cried, nodding her head.

It was my turn to laugh now. "Then I must be careful not to vex you."

"Yes. But I will turn my tongue seven times before I speak, if you do," she promised.

"Are you going far?" I asked.

"I am going nowhere. I am taking a walk."

"Shall we go to the Villa Nazionale, and watch the driving?"

"Or to the Toledo, and look at the shop windows?"

"We can do both. We will begin at the Toledo, and end in the Villa."

"*Bene*," she acquiesced.

After a little silence, "I am so glad I met you," I informed her, looking into her eyes.

Her eyes softened adorably. "I am so glad too," she said.

"You are lovely, you are sweet," I vowed, with enthusiasm.

"Oh, no!" she protested. "I am as God made me."

"You are lovely, you are sweet. I thought—when I first saw you, above there, in the piazza.—when you came out of church, and gave the soldo to the old beggar woman—I thought you had the loveliest smile I had ever seen."

A beautiful blush suffused her face, and her eyes swam in a mist of pleasure. "*E vero?*" she questioned.

"*Oh, vero, vero.* That is why I followed you. You don't mind my having followed you?"

"Oh, no; I am glad."

After another interval of silence, "You are not Neapolitan?" I said. "You don't speak like a Neapolitan."

"No; I am Florentine. We live in Naples for my father's health. He is not strong. He can not endure the cold winters of the north."

I murmured something sympathetic; and she went on, "My father is a violinist. To-day he has gone to Capri, to play at a festival. He will not be back until to-morrow. So I was very lonesome."

"You have no mother?"

"My mother is dead," she said, crossing herself. In a moment she added, with a touch of pride,

ROSEMARY FOR REMEMBRANCE

"During the season my father plays in the orchestra of the San Carlo."

"I am sure I know what your name is," said I.

"Oh? How can you know? What is it?"

"I think your name is Rosabella."

"Ah, then you are wrong. My name is Elisabetta. But in Naples everybody says Zabetta. And yours?"

"Guess."

"Oh, I can not guess. Not—not Federico?"

"Do I look as if my name were Federico?"

She surveyed me gravely for a minute, then shook her head pensively. "No; I do not think your name is Federico."

And therewith I told her my name, and made her repeat it till she could pronounce it without a struggle. It sounded very pretty, coming from her pretty lips, quite southern and romantic, with its r's tremendously enriched.

"Anyhow, I know your age," said I.

"What is it?"

"You are seventeen."

"No—ever so much older."

"Eighteen then."

"I shall be nineteen in July."

VIII

Before the brilliant shop windows of the Toledo we dallied for an hour or more, Zabetta's eyes sparkling with delight as they rested on the

345

bright-hued silks, the tortoise-shell and coral, the gold and silver filagree work, that were there displayed. But when she admired some one particular object above another, and I besought her to let me buy it for her, she refused austerely. "But no, no, no! It is impossible." Then we went on to the Villa, and strolled by the sea-wall, between the blue-green water and the multi-colored procession of people in carriages. And by and by Zabetta confessed that she was tired, and proposed that we should sit down on one of the benches.

"A café would be better fun," submitted her companion. And we placed ourselves at one of the out-of-door tables of the café in the garden, where, after some urging, I prevailed upon Zabetta to drink a cup of chocolate. Meanwhile, with the ready confidence of youth, we had each been desultorily autobiographical; and if our actual acquaintance was only the affair of an afternoon, I doubt if in a year we could have felt that we knew each other better.

"I must go home," Zabetta said at last.

"Oh, not yet, not yet," cried I.

"It will be dinner-time. I must go home to dinner."

"But your father is at Capri. You will have to dine alone."

"Yes."

"Then don't. Come with me instead, and dine at a restaurant."

ROSEMARY FOR REMEMBRANCE

Her eyes glowed wistfully for an instant; but she replied, "Oh, no; I can not."

"Yes, you can. Come."

"Oh, no; impossible."

"Why?"

"Oh, because."

"Because what?"

"There is my cat. She will have nothing to eat."

"Your cook will give her something."

"My cook!" laughed Zabetta. "My cook is here before you."

"Well, you must be a kind mistress. You must give your cook an evening out."

"But my poor cat?"

"Your cat can catch a mouse."

"There are no mice in our house. She has frightened them all away."

"Then she can wait. A little fast will be good for her soul."

Zabetta laughed, and I said, "*Andiamo!*"

At the restaurant we climbed to the first floor, and they gave us a table near the window, whence we could look out over the villa to the sea beyond. The sun was sinking, and the sky was gay with rainbow tints, like mother-of-pearl.

Zabetta's face shone joyfully. "This is only the second time in my life that I have dined in a restaurant," she told me. "And the other time was very long ago, when I was quite young. And it wasn't nearly so grand a restaurant as this, either."

"And now what would you like to eat?" I asked, picking up the bill of fare.

"May I look?" said she.

I handed her the document, and she studied it at length. I think, indeed, she read it through. In the end she appeared rather bewildered.

"Oh, there is so much. I don't know. Will you choose, please?"

I made a shift at choosing, and the sympathetic waiter flourished kitchenward with my commands.

"What is that little green nosegay you wear in your belt, Zabetta?" I inquired.

"Oh, this—it is a rosemary. Smell it," she said, breaking off a sprig and offering it to me.

"Rosemary, that's for remembrance," quoted I.

"What does that mean? What language is that?" she asked.

I tried to translate it to her. And then I taught her to say it in English. "Rrosemérri—tsat is forr rrememberrance."

"Will you write it down for me?" she requested. "It is pretty."

And I wrote it for her on the back of one of my cards.

IX

After dinner we crossed the garden again, and again stood by the sea-wall. Over us the soft spring night was like a dark sapphire. Points of red, green, and yellow fire burned from ships

ROSEMARY FOR REMEMBRANCE

in the bay, and seemed of the same campany as the stars above them. A rosy aureole in the sky, to the eastward, marked the smouldering crater of Vesuvius. Away in the Chiaja a man was singing comic songs to an accompaniment of mandolins and guitars; comic songs that sounded pathetic, as they reached us in the distance.

I asked Zabetta how she wished to finish the evening.

"I don't care," said she.

"Would you like to go to the play?"

"If you wish."

"What do *you* wish?"

"I think I should like to stay here a little longer. It is pleasant."

We leaned on the parapet, close to each other. Her face was very pale in the starlight; her eyes were infinitely deep, and dark, and tender. One of her little hands lay on the stone wall, like a white flower. I took it. It was warm and soft. She did not attempt to withdraw it. I bent over it and kissed it. I kissed it many times. Then I kissed her lips. "Zabetta, I love you, I love you," I murmured fervently. Don't imagine that I didn't mean it. It was April, and I was twenty. "I love you, Zabetta. Dearest little Zabetta! I love you so."

"*E vero?*" she questioned, scarcely above her breath.

"Oh, *sì; é vero, vero, vero,*" I asseverated. "And you?"

"Yes, I love you," she whispered. And then I could say no more. The ecstasy that filled my heart was too poignant. We stood there speechless, hand in hand, and breathed the air of heaven.

By and by Zabetta drew her bunch of rosemary from her belt, and divided it into two parts. One part she gave to me, the other she kept. "Rosemary—it is for constancy," she said. I pressed the cool herb to my face for a moment, inhaling its bitter-sweet fragrance; then I fastened it in my buttonhole. On my watch-chain I wore—what everybody in Naples used to wear —a little coral hand, a little clinched coral hand, holding a little golden dagger. I detached it now, and made Zabetta take it. "Coral—that is also for constancy," I reminded her; "and besides, it protects one from the Evil Eye."

X

At last Zabetta asked me what time it was; and when she learned that it was half-past nine, she insisted that she really must go home. "They shut the outer door of the house we live in at ten o'clock, and I have no key."

"You can ring up the porter."

"Oh, there is no porter."

"But if we had gone to the theatre?"

"I should have had to leave you in the middle of the play."

"Ah, well," I consented; and we left the Villa and took a cab.

"Are you happy, Zabetta?" I asked her, as the cab rattled us toward our parting.

"Oh, so happy, so happy! I have never been so happy before."

"Dearest Zabetta!"

"You will love me always?"

"Always, always."

"We will see each other every day. We will see other to-morrow?"

"Oh, to-morrow!" I groaned suddenly, the actualities of life rushing all at once upon my mind.

"What is it? What of to-morrow?"

"Oh, to-morrow, to-morrow!"

"What? What?" Her voice was breathless with suspense, with alarm.

"Oh, I had forgotten. You will think I am a beast."

"What is it? For heaven's sake, tell me."

"You will think I am a beast. You will think I have deceived you. To-morrow—I can not help it—I am not my own master—I am summoned by my parents—to-morrow I am going away—I am leaving Naples."

"You are leaving Naples?"

"I am going to Paris."

"To Paris?"

"Yes."

There was a breathing-space of silence. Then,

"*Oh, Dio!*" sobbed Zabetta; and she began to cry as if her heart would break.

I seized her hands; I drew her to me. I tried to comfort her. But she only cried and cried and cried.

"Zabetta . . . Zabetta . . . Don't cry. . . . Forgive me. . . . Oh, don't cry like that."

"*Oh, Dio! Oh, caro Dio!*" she sobbed.

"Zabetta—listen to me," I began. "I have something to say to you. . . ."

"*Cosa?*" she asked faintly.

"Zabetta—do you really love me?"

"*Oh, tanto, tanto!*"

"Then listen, Zabetta. If you really love me —come with me."

"Come with you. How?"

"Come with me to Paris."

"To Paris?"

"Yes, to-morrow."

There was another instant of silence, and then again Zabetta began to cry.

"Will you? Will you? Will you come with me to Paris?" I implored her.

"Oh, I would, I would. But I can't. I can't."

"Why not?"

"Oh, I can't."

"Why? Why can't you?"

"Oh, my father—I can not leave my father."

"Your father? But—if you love me——"

"He is old. He is ill. He has no one but me. I can not leave him."

"Zabetta!"

"No, no. I can not leave him. *Oh, Dio mio?*"

"But Zabetta——"

"No. It would be a sin. Oh, the worst of sins. He is old and ill. I can not leave him. Don't ask me. It would be dreadful."

"But then? Then what? What shall we do?"

"Oh, I don't know. I wish I were dead."

The cab came to a standstill, and Zabetta said, "Here we are." I helped her to descend. We were before a dark porte-cochère, in some dark back street, high up the hillside.

"*Addio,*" said Zabetta, holding out her hand.

"You won't come with me?"

"I can't. I can't. *Addio.*"

"Oh, Zabetta! Do you— Oh, say, say that you forgive me."

"Yes. *Addio.*"

"And, Zabetta, you—you have my address. It is on the card I gave you. If you ever need anything—if you are ever in trouble of any kind —remember you have my address—you will write to me."

"Yes. *Addio.*"

"*Addio.*"

She stood for a second, looking up at me from great brimming eyes, and then she turned away

353

and vanished in the darkness of the porte-cochère. I got into the cab, and was driven to my hotel.

And here, one might have supposed was an end of the episode; but no.

XI

I went to Paris, I went to New York, I returned to Paris, I came on to London; and in this journeying more than a year was lost. In the beginning I had suffered as much as you could wish me in the way of contrition, in the way of regret too. I blamed myself and pitied myself with almost equal fervor. I had trifled with a gentle human heart; I had been compelled to let a priceless human treasure slip from my possession. But—I was twenty. And there were other girls in the world. And a year is a long time, when we are twenty. Little by little the image of Zabetta faded, faded, faded. By the year's end, I am afraid it had become very pale indeed. . . .

It was late June, and I was in London, when the post brought me a letter. The letter bore an Italian stamp, and had originally been directed to my old address in Paris. Thence (as the numerous redirections on the big square foreign envelope attested) it had been forwarded to New York; thence back again to Paris; and thence finally to London.

The letter was written in the neatest of tiny

copperplate; and this is a translation of what it said:

"DEAR FRIEND—My poor father died last month in the German Hospital, after an illness of twenty-one days. Pray for his soul. "I am now alone and free, and if you still wish it, can come to you. It was impossible for me to come when you asked me; but you have not ceased to be my constant thought. I keep your coral hand.—Your ever faithful. ZABETTA COLLALUCE."

Inclosed in the letter there was a sprig of some dried, bitter-sweet smelling herb; and, in pencil, below the signature—laboriously traced, as I could guess, from what I had written for her on my visiting-card—the English phrase: "Rosemary—that's for remembrance."

The letter was dated early in May, which made it six weeks old.

What could I do? What answer could I send? Of course, you know what I did do. I procrastinated and vacillated, and ended by sending no answer at all. I could not write and say, "Yes, come to me." But how could I write and say, "No, do not come"? Besides, would she not have given up hoping for an answer by this time? It was six weeks since she had written. I tried to think that the worst was over.

But my remorse took a new and a longer and a stronger lease of life. A vision of Zabetta, pale, with anxious eyes, standing at her window, waiting, waiting for a word that never came—for months I could not chase it from my conscience; it was years before it altogether ceased its accusing visits.

XII

And then, last night, after a perfectly usual London day and evening, I went to bed and dreamed of her vividly; and all day long to-day the fragrance of my dream has clung about me—a bitter-sweet fragrance, like that of rosemary itself. Where is Zabetta now? What is her life? How have the years treated her?... In my dream she was still eighteen. In reality—it is melancholy to think how far from eighteen she has had leisure, since that April afternoon, to drift.

Youth faces forward, impatient of the present, panting to anticipate the future. But we who have crossed a certain sad meridian, we turn our gaze backward, and tell the relentless gods what we would sacrifice to recover a little of the past, one of those shining days when to us also it was given to sojourn among the Fortunate Islands. *Ah, si jeunesse savait!* . . .

SUCH AS WALK IN DARKNESS

BY SAMUEL HOPKINS ADAMS

SUCH AS WALK IN DARKNESS

BY SAMUEL HOPKINS ADAMS

IN ALL the trade of the city you might not find such another quaint business firm as Solomon John and Billy Wigg. The senior partner was a gentle old giant; the junior a brisk and shaggy little dog. It was Solomon John's business to stand on a roaring corner and sell papers; it was Billy Wigg's business to take care of him while he did it, for he was blind. It was our business—Dr. Harvey's and mine—to pay for our papers and pass on, but we seldom strictly minded it. Instead, we would stop to talk to Solomon John, to the detriment of trade, and to be patronized by Billy Wigg, who was much puffed up with self-importance, conceiving himself to be principal owner of the earth and sole proprietor of Solomon John. In the half of which he was correct.

I was very fond of Billy Wigg, despite his airs of superiority. Harvey preferred old Solomon; but this was a semi-professional interest, for my medical friend had contracted the pamphlet habit, which he indulged before scientific bodies

Reprinted by permission from "McClure's Magazine" for August, 1902.

made up of gentlemen with weak eyes who knew more about ophthalmology than can be found in many fat tomes. Solomon John was a remarkable case of something quite unpronounceable, and Harvey used to gaze into his eyes with rapt intensity, while Billy Wigg fidgeted and struggled against the temptation to gnaw such portions of him as were within reach; for Billy Wigg didn't understand, and what he didn't understand he disapproved of on principle. In the light of subsequent events I believe Billy's uneasiness to have been an instance of animal prevision.

To see Billy Wigg conduct his master across that mill-race of traffic that swirled between curb and curb, as he did every morning in time for business, was an artistic pleasure. Something more than a mere pilot was the dog; rather the rudder to whose accurate direction old Solomon responded with precise and prompt fidelity. A tug of the trouser leg from behind would bring the ancient newsboy to a halt. A gentle jerk forward would start him again, and in obedience to a steady pull to one side or the other he would trustingly suffer himself to be conducted around a checked wagon or a halted cable car. All the time Billy Wigg would keep up a running conversation made up of admonition, warning, and encouragement.

"Come on, now"—in a series of sharp yaps as they started from the curb. "Push right ahead.

360

Hold hard. That's all right; it's by. Hurry now. Hurry, I said. *Will* you do as I tell you?" Then, to a too pressing cabby, in an angry bark, "What's the matter with you, anyway? Trying to run folks down? Hey? Well" —apologetically, in response to a jerk on his string—"these fool drivers do stir me up. Wait a bit. Now for it. And here we are."

How many thousand times dog and man had made the trip in safety before the dire day of the accident not even Solomon John can reckon. Harvey and I had started downtown early, while our pair of paper-vending friends chanced to be a little late. As we reached the corner they were already half-way across the street, and Billy Wigg, with all the strength of terror, was striving to haul Solomon John backward.

"What's the matter with Billy?" said Harvey.

A second later the question was answered, as there plunged into view from behind a car the galloping horse of a derelict delivery wagon.

"Good heavens! Look at the old man," I cried, and in the same breath, "Look at the dog," gasped Harvey.

With one mighty jerk Billy Wigg had torn the leash from his master's hand. Bereft of his sole guidance in the thunder and rush of traffic, the blind man stretched out piteous hands, warding the death he could not see.

"Billy," he quavered, "where are you, Billy? Come back to me, Billy-dog."

For once Billy Wigg was deaf to his master's voice. He was obeying a more imperious call, that unfathomed nobility of dog-nature that responds so swiftly to the summons. He was casting his own life in the balance to save another's. Straight at the horse's throat he launched himself, a forlorn hope. It was a very big horse, and Billy was a very little dog. The up-stroke of the knee caught him full; he was flung, whirling, fell almost under the wheels of a cab, rolled into the gutter, and lay there quiet. The horse had swerved a little, not quite enough. There was a scream, and the blind man went down from the glancing impact of the shoulder. Harvey and I were beside him almost as soon as the crosswalk policeman. The three of us carried him to the sidewalk.

"No need to call an ambulance, officer," said Harvey. "I'm a physician and the man is a friend of mine."

"Bedad, thin, the dawg is a frind of mine," said the big fellow. "Couldn't ye take him along too, sir?"

"Well—rather," said Harvey heartily. "Where is he?" He turned to look for the dog.

Billy Wigg came crawling toward us. Never tell me that dogs have no souls. The eyes in Billy's shaggy little face yearned with a more than human passion of anxiety and love, as, gasping with pain—for he had been cruelly shaken—he dragged himself to his partner's face. At the touch of the warm, eager tongue, Solomon John's eyes opened. He stretched out his hand and buried it in the heavy fur.

"Hello, Billy," he said weakly. "I was afraid you were hurt. Are you all right, old boy?"

And Billy, burrowing a wet nose in Solomon John's neck, wept for joy with loud whines.

Some rapid and expert wire-pulling on the part of Harvey landed our pair of friends in a private hospital, where Solomon John proved a most grateful and gentle patient, and Billy Wigg a most tumultuous one until arrangement was made for the firm to occupy one and the same cot. Then he became tractable, even enduring the indignity of a flannel jacket and splints with a sort of humorous tolerance. Every day Harvey came and gazed soulfully into Solomon John's glazed eyes—which is a curious form of treatment for broken collar-bone, not sanctioned by any of the authorities who have written on the subject. It soon became evident that Harvey didn't care anything about the rib; he had other designs. On a day he came to the point.

"Solomon John, would you like to have your sight back?"

The blind man sat up in his cot and pressed his hands to his head.

"Do you mean it, sir?" he gasped. "You—you wouldn't go to fool an old man."

"Will you let me operate on you to-morrow?"

"Anything you think best, sir. I don't quite

seem to take it all in yet, sir—not the whole sense of it. But if it does come out right," added Solomon John in the simplicity of his soul, "won't Billy Wigg be surprised and tickled!"

Billy Wigg raged mightily and rent the garments of his best friends, because he was shut out during the operation. When he was admitted after it was over he howled tumultuously, because Solomon John was racked with ether sickness, which he mistook for the throes of approaching dissolution. Followed then weeks during which Solomon John wore a white bandage, in place of the old green eye-shade, and at frequent intervals sang a solemn but joyous chant which Billy Wigg accompanied with impatient yelps, because he couldn't make out what it meant.

> "We're going to have our sight again,
> Billy Wigg, Billy Wigg;
> We're going to see the world again,
> Billy, my dog."

It was a long, nerve-trying wait, but the day finally came when the white bandages were removed. After the first gasp of rapture, Solomon John looked about him eagerly.

"Let me see my dog," he said. "Billy, is this you?" as the junior partner looked with anxious and puzzled eyes into his face. "Well, you're certainly a mighty handsome doggy, old boy." (Billy Wigg was homelier than a stack of hay in January, but the eyes that looked on him were as those of a mother when she first sees her babe.)

364

SUCH AS WALK IN DARKNESS

Unhappiness was the portion of Billy in the days that followed. A partner who wandered about unchaperoned and eluded obstacles without relying on his sense of touch was quite beyond his comprehension. So he sulked consistently until the time came for leaving the hospital. Then he chirked up a bit, thinking, presumably, that Solomon John would resume his old habit of blind reliance upon him when once the doors had closed behind them. Poor Billy!

It was three weeks after the operation that they left, Solomon John being discharged as cured. Harvey exulted. He said it was a great operation and proved things. I thought, myself, it was a mean trick on Billy Wigg. My unprofessional diagnosis was that he was on the road to becoming a chronic melancholiac.

The partners called on Harvey soon after the departure from the hospital. They were a study in psychological antithesis; Solomon John bubbling over with boyish happiness, Billy Wigg aged with the weight of woe he was carrying. The old man was touchingly grateful, but his ally surreptitiously essayed to bite a piece out of Harvey's leg when his back was turned. He nursed an unavenged wrong.

Months passed before we saw the pair again. We returned from our European vacation confident of finding them on the same old corner, and sure enough, there they were. But as we approached Harvey seized me by the arm.

"Good heavens! Bob! Look at the old man!"

"What's wrong with him?" said I. "He looks just the same as he used to."

"Just the same as he used to," echoed Harvey bitterly. "Eye-shade and all. All my work gone for nothing. Poor old boy!"

"Billy Wigg's all right, anyway," said I.

"Think so?" said Harvey. "It strikes me that it isn't exactly welcome that he's trying to express." Then, in a louder voice to Solomon John, "How did it happen, old Sol?"

At the sound of his voice Solomon John whirled about and started to thrust up his shade, as if involuntarily. Then he held out tremulous hands, crying:

"What! Is that you, Dr. Harvey? God bless you, sir! And is Mr. Roberts with you? Well, well, but this does me good. You're a sight for sore eyes!"

"Not for yours, Solomon John."

"And why not, then? Whist! I forgot," he broke off scaredly, jerking his head toward Billy Wigg, who held us all under jealous scrutiny. "Wait a breath."

Thrusting his hand into his pocket, he whipped it out suddenly. A flight of coins scattered and twinkled and rolled diversely on the sidewalk. "Dear, dear!" cried the old man cunningly. "The old fool that I am! I'll never be rich this way. Pick them up, Billy-boy."

Billy hated it, for picking small coins from a

smooth pavement with lip and tooth is no easy job; hated worse leaving his partner to two such unscrupulous characters as he well knew us to be. But he knew his business, and set about it with all his energies.

"Whisper now," said the senior partner as Billy swore under his breath at a slithery and elusive dime. "I've as fine a pair of eyes as you'd want for star-gazing at noonday."

"Then what on earth—"

"She-h-h! Soft and easy! The beast's cocking his little ear this way. Sure 'twas all on his account, sirs."

"On Billy's account?" we both exclaimed in a breath.

"You didn't think I'd be faking it?" he asked reproachfully.

We didn't; and we said so. But we required further enlightenment.

"All on account of Billy Wigg there, sirs. The eyesight was a million blessings to me, but 'twas death to poor Billy. Not a pleasure in life would he take after we left the hospital. When I'd walk free and easy along the streets that looked so pretty to my old eyes, the dog'd be crazy with fear that some harm would come to me through him not leading me. At the last he just laid down and set out to die. He'd not sleep, he'd not eat; and the eyes of him when he'd look at me were fit to make a man weep. I sent for a dog doctor—you being away, sir," put in

Solomon John in polite parenthesis to my friend. 'He says,' "The dog's dying of a broken heart. I've seen it before,' he says. 'What'll I do?' says I. 'He'll not be content till you are as you were before,' says the dog doctor. It was a minute before I sensed what he meant. Then my heart got thick and sick inside me. 'Is that what you mean?' 'You old fool,' says the dog doctor, 'can't you do a bit of play-acting? You've had enough practice in the part,'" he says.

"'Over I went and got my stick and put on the old shade that I hadn't ever thought to use again, thanks to you, sir, and tap-tapped across the floor to Billy Wigg. 'Come on, Billy,' says I; 'I want you to take me out for a walk.' Billy jumped up with a kind of choky bark, and I hugged Billy and Billy hugged me, and—we've been doing business on the corner ever since."

There was a long pause. Harvey's expression was queer. I felt a little queer myself. It was a queer story, you know. Finally I asked the old man if business was good.

"Nicely, sir, thank you," said Solomon John; "but I want to ask you, Is it a dishonesty, think you, for me to be wearing my shade like a blind man, and me able to see a flea on the end of Billy Wigg's tail the length of the block away? The Lord's been mighty good to me, sir—you and the Lord—giving me back my sight," said Solomon John simply, turning to Harvey, "and I

SUCH AS WALK IN DARKNESS

wouldn't want to do anything that wasn't just square."

"I wouldn't let it weigh on my mind," said Harvey.

"I'd been thinking of a bit of a sign," proceeded Solomon John. "A friend of mine printed it out for me, but the idea's my own." After some fumbling under his coat he produced a placard artfully designed in large and flourishy letters. This was the order of it:

```
I Am NOT Blind
     but
  The Dog
Thinks I Am.
```

Billy Wigg seemed pleased because Harvey kicked me. No doubt he would have been equally pleased if I had kicked Harvey. But it happened to be I who laughed. Harvey covered it up by soberly telling Solomon John that the sign was sure to be a grand success.

It was a grand success; quite stupendous, in fact. Old Sol did a business on the strength of it that would have made his eyes pop out if he hadn't kept them tight shut out of respect to Billy's prejudices. Reporters found his simplicity and naïve honesty a mine of "good stuff," and the picture of the firm was in all the papers. Billy Wigg began to suffer from swelled head; became haughty, not to say snobbish. But the fierce light of publicity wore upon the simple soul of Solomon John. He discarded the extraordinary placard, and was glad when he faded away from fame. Billy wasn't. He liked notoriety as well as authority.

Billy continued to exercise his authority. But even so meek a soul as that of Solomon John has limits of endurance beyond which it is not well to press. Only the other day it was that the old man said to Harvey, while Billy Wigg was otherwise engaged:

"It's as bad as being a henpecked husband, sir. Last night, as I was quietly stepping out the window to take a mug of ale with some friends, Billy wakes up, and the fuss he makes rouses the neighborhood. Sure, he wouldn't hark to my going at all. You can see his teeth marks on my shin this minute, sir. Could you give me something harmless to put in his food that'd make him sleep the sounder?"

Harvey said he'd think about it. He wasn't obliged to. Less than a week later he got a note in the mail:

"DEAR SIR—I could not stand it any longer. I have Absconded to Buffalo to Take a Rest. Please be Good to Billy Wigg. I inclose his Board and Lodging any place you Put him. He is a good Dog, but too Bossy. I am Going to See Things till my Eyes get Tired. I will come Back in Future.

"Yrs respectfully,
"SOLOMON J. BOLES.

"P. S.—I know you will Treat Billy Good."

The inclosure was a twenty-dollar bill. It was the price of freedom, and cheap at the price.

HIS FIRST PENITENT

BY JAMES OLIVER CURWOOD

HIS FIRST PENITENT

BY JAMES OLIVER CURWOOD

IN a white wilderness of moaning storm, in a wilderness of miles and miles of black pine-trees, the Transcontinental Flier lay buried in the snow.

In the first darkness of the wild December night, engine and tender had rushed on ahead to division headquarters, to let the line know that the flier had given up the fight, and needed assistance. They had been gone two hours, and whiter and whiter grew the brilliantly lighted coaches in the drifts and winnows of the whistling storm. From the black edges of the forest, prowling eyes might have looked upon scores of human faces staring anxiously out into the blackness from the windows of the coaches.

In those coaches it was growing steadily colder. Men were putting on their overcoats, and women smuggled deeper in their furs. Over it all, the tops of the black pine-trees moaned and whistled in sounds that seemed filled both with menace and with savage laughter.

In the smoking-compartment of the Pullman sat five men, gathered in a group. Of these, one was Forsythe, the timber agent; two were traveling men; the fourth a passenger homeward bound from a holiday visit; and the fifth was Father Charles.

All were smoking, and had been smoking for an hour, even to Father Charles, who lighted his third cigar as one of the traveling men finished the story he had been telling. They had passed away the tedious wait with tales of personal adventure and curious happenings. Each had furnished his share of entertainment, with the exception of Father Charles.

The priest's pale, serious face lit up in surprise or laughter with the others, but his lips had not broken into a story of their own. He was a little man, dressed in somber black, and there was that about him which told his companions that within his tight-drawn coat of shiny black there were hidden tales which would have gone well with the savage beat of the storm against the lighted windows and the moaning tumult of the pine-trees.

Suddenly Forsythe shivered at a fiercer blast than the others, and said:

"Father, have you a text that would fit this night—and the situation?"

Slowly Father Charles blew out a spiral of smoke from between his lips, and then he drew himself erect and leaned a little forward, with the cigar between his slender white fingers.

"I had a text for this night," he said, "but I have none now, gentlemen. I was to have married a couple a hundred miles down the line. The guests have assembled. They are ready, but I am not there. The wedding will not be to-night, and so my text is gone. But there comes another to my mind which fits this situation—and a thousand others—'He who sits in the heavens shall look down and decide.' To-night I was to have married these young people. Three hours ago I never dreamed of doubting that I should be on hand at the appointed hour. But I shall not marry them. Fate has enjoined a hand. The Supreme Arbiter says 'No,' and what may not be the consequences?"

"They will probably be married to-morrow," said one of the traveling men. "There will be a few hours' delay—nothing more."

"Perhaps," replied Father Charles, as quietly as before. "And—perhaps not. Who can say what this little incident may not mean in the lives of that young man and that young woman—and, it may be, in my own? Three or four hours lost in a storm—what may they not mean to more than one human heart on this train? The Supreme Arbiter plays His hand, if you wish to call it that, with reason and intent. To some one, somewhere, the most insignificant occurrence may mean life or death. And to-night—this—means something."

A sudden blast drove the night screeching over their heads, and the wailing of the pines was almost human voices. Forsythe sucked a cigar that had gone out.

"Long ago," said Father Charles, "I knew a young man and a young woman who were to be married. The man went West to win a fortune. Thus fate separated them, and in the lapse of a year such terrible misfortune came to the girl's parents that she was forced into a marriage with wealth—a barter of her white body for an old man's gold. When the young man returned from the West he found his sweetheart married, and hell upon earth was their lot. But hope lingers in young hearts. He waited four years; and then, discouraged, he married another woman. Gentlemen, *three days* after the wedding his old sweetheart's husband died, and she was released from bondage. Was not that the hand of the Supreme Arbiter? If he had waited but three days more, the old happiness might have lived.

"But wait! One month after that day the young man was arrested, taken to a Western State, tried for murder, and hanged. Do you see the point? In three days more the girl who had sold herself into slavery for the salvation of those she loved would have been released from her bondage only to marry a murderer!"

II

There was a silence, in which all five listened to that wild moaning of the storm. There seemed to be something in it now—something more than the inarticulate sound of wind and trees.

Forsythe scratched a match and relighted his cigar.

"I never thought of such things in just that light," he said.

"Listen to the wind," said the little priest. "Hear the pine-trees shriek out there! It recalls to me a night of years and years ago—a night like this, when the storm moaned and twisted about my little cabin, and when the Supreme Arbiter sent me my first penitent. Gentlemen, it is something which will bring you nearer to an understanding of the voice and the hand of God. It is a sermon on the mighty significance of little things, this story of my first penitent. If you wish, I will tell it to you."

"Go on," said Forsythe.

The traveling men drew nearer.

"It was a night like this," repeated Father Charles, "and it was in a great wilderness like this, only miles and miles away. I had been sent to establish a mission; and in my cabin, that wild night, alone and with the storm shrieking about me, I was busy at work sketching out my plans. After a time I grew nervous. I did not smoke then, and so I had nothing to comfort me but my thoughts; and, in spite of my efforts to make them otherwise, they were cheerless enough. The forest grew to my door. In the fiercer blasts I could hear the lashing of the pine-tops over my head, and now and then an arm of one of the moaning trees would reach down and sweep across my cabin roof with a sound that made me shudder and fear. This wilderness fear is an oppressive and terrible thing when you are alone at night, and the world is twisting and tearing itself outside. I have heard the pine-trees shriek like dying women, I have heard them wailing like lost children, I have heard them sobbing and moaning like human souls writhing in agony—"

Father Charles paused, to peer through the window out into the black night, where the pine-trees were sobbing and moaning now. When he turned, Forsythe, the timber agent, whose life was a wilderness life, nodded understandingly.

"And when they cry like that," went on Father Charles, "a living voice would be lost among them as the splash of a pebble is lost in a roaring sea. A hundred times that night I fancied that I heard human voices; and a dozen times I went to my door, drew back the bolt, and listened, with the snow and the wind beating about my ears.

"As I sat shuddering before my fire, there came a thought to me of a story which I had long ago read about the sea—a story of impossible achievement and of impossible heroism. As vividly as if I had read it only the day before, I recalled the description of a wild and stormy night when the heroine placed a lighted lamp in the window of her sea-bound cottage, to guide her lover home in safety. Gentlemen, the reading of that book in my boyhood days was but a trivial thing. I had read a thousand others, and of them all it was possibly the least significant; but the Supreme Arbiter had not forgotten.

"The memory of that book brought me to my feet, and I placed a lighted lamp close up against my cabin window. Fifteen minutes later I heard a strange sound at the door, and when I opened it there fell in upon the floor at my feet a young and beautiful woman. And after her, dragging himself over the threshold on his hands and knees, there came a man.

"I closed the door, after the man had crawled in and fallen face downward upon the floor, and turned my attention first to the woman. She was covered with snow. Her long, beautiful hair was loose and disheveled, and had blown about her like a veil. Her big, dark eyes looked at me pleadingly, and in them there was a terror such as I had never beheld in human eyes before. I bent over her, intending to carry her to my cot; but in another moment she had thrown herself upon the prostrate form of the man, with her arms about his head, and there burst from her lips the first sounds that she had uttered. They were not much more intelligible than the wailing grief of the pine-trees out in the night, but they told me plainly enough that the man on the floor was dearer to her than life.

"I knelt beside him, and found that he was breathing in a quick, panting sort of way, and that his wide-open eyes were looking at the woman. Then I noticed for the first time that his face was cut and bruised, and his lips were swollen. His coat was loose at the throat, and I could see livid marks on his neck.

"'I'm all right,' he whispered, struggling for breath, and turning his eyes to me. 'We should have died—in a few minutes more—if it hadn't been for the light in your window!'

"The young woman bent down and kissed him, and then she allowed me to help her to my cot. When I had attended to the young man, and he had regained strength enough to stand upon his feet, she was asleep. The man went to her, and dropped upon his knees beside the cot. Tenderly he drew back the heavy masses of hair from about her face and shoulders. For several minutes he remained with his face pressed close against hers; then he rose, and faced me. The woman—his wife—knew nothing of what passed between us during the next half-hour. During that half-hour, gentlemen, I received my first confession. The young man was of my faith. He was my first penitent."

It was growing colder in the coach, and Father Charles stopped to draw his thin black coat closer about him. Forsythe relighted his cigar for the third time. The transient passenger gave a sudden start as a gust of wind beat against the window like a threatening hand.

"A rough stool was my confessional, gentlemen," resumed Father Charles. "He told me the

HIS FIRST PENITENT

story, kneeling at my feet—a story that will live with me as long as I live, always reminding me that the little things of life may be the greatest things, that by sending a storm to hold up a coach the Supreme Arbiter may change the map of a world. It is not a long story. It is not even an unusual story.

"He had come into the North about a year before, and had built for himself and his wife a little home at a pleasant river spot ten miles from my cabin. Their love was of the kind we do not often see, and they were as happy as the birds that lived about them in the wilderness. They had taken a timber claim. A few months more, and a new life was to come into their little home; and the knowledge of this made the girl an angel of beauty and joy. Their nearest neighbor was another man, several miles distant. The two men became friends, and the other came over to see them frequently. It was the old, old story. The neighbor fell in love with the young settler's wife.

"As you shall see, this other man was a beast. On the day preceding that night of terrible storm, the woman's husband set out for the settlement to bring back supplies. Hardly had he gone, when the beast came to the cabin. He found himself alone with the woman.

"A mile from his cabin, the husband stopped to light his pipe. See, gentlemen, how the Supreme Arbiter played His hand. The man attempted to unscrew the stem, and the stem broke. In the wilderness you must smoke. Smoke is your company. It is voice and companionship to you. There were other pipes at the settlement, ten miles away; but there was also another pipe at the cabin, one mile away. So the husband turned back. He came up quietly to his door, thinking that he would surprise his wife. He heard voices—a man's voice, a woman's cries. He opened the door, and in the excitement of what was happening within neither the man nor the woman saw or heard him. They were struggling. The woman was in the man's arms, her hair torn down, her small hands beating him in the face, her breath coming in low, terrified cries. Even as the husband stood there for the fraction of a second, taking in the terrible scene, the other man caught the woman's face to him, and kissed her. And then—it happened. It was a terrible fight; and when it was over the beast lay on the floor, bleeding and dead. Gentlemen, the Supreme Arbiter broke a *pipe-stem*, and sent the husband back in time!"

III

No one spoke as Father Charles drew his coat still closer about him. Above the tumult of the storm another sound came to them—the distant, piercing shriek of a whistle.

"The husband dug a grave through the snow

the frozen earth," concluded Father ———; "and late that afternoon they packed up a bundle and set out together for the settlement. The storm overtook them. They had dropped for the last time into the snow, about to die in each other's arms, when I put my light in the window. That is all; except that I knew them for several years afterward, and that the old happiness returned to them—and more, for the child was born, a miniature of its mother. Then they moved to another part of the wilderness, and I to still another. So you see, gentlemen, what a snow-bound train may mean, for if an old sea tale, a broken pipe-stem——"

The door at the end of the smoking-room opened suddenly. Through it there came a cold blast of the storm, a cloud of snow, and a man. He was bundled in a great bearskin coat, and as he shook out its folds his strong, ruddy face smiled cheerfully at those whom he had interrupted.

Then, suddenly, there came a change in his face. The merriment went from it. He stared at Father Charles.

The priest was rising, his face more tense and whiter still, his hands reaching out to the stranger.

In another moment the stranger had leaped to him—not to shake his hands, but to clasp the priest in his great arms, shaking him, and crying out a strange joy, while for the first time that

night the pale face of Father Charles
up with a red and joyous glow.

After several minutes the newcomer releas
Father Charles, and turned to the others with
great, hearty laugh.

"Gentlemen," he said, "you must pardon me
for interrupting you like this. You will understand when I tell you that Father Charles is an
old friend of mine, the dearest friend I have on
earth, and that I haven't seen him for years. I
was his first penitent!"

H

and in
Charl
u